WITH OR WITHOUT

SM ERICKSON

For everyone who didn't hit a home run the first time at bat.
Keep swinging for the fence. I am.

ONE

No one ever accused me of being cautious. After all, I'd finished building my illegal computer months ago, and I was still figuring out how to get anything worthwhile on it. This despite the fact that if my contraband were found, I'd be locked away for the rest of my days at a minimum. Not that there were many left. At eighteen, I was only weeks away from my date. One of the few to die so young. A Rarity, as it were.

Maybe that's why I couldn't be bothered to care anymore. What did I have to lose? We were immortal—until we weren't.

Possibly not the best philosophy to have when I worked at the garbage incineration plant. Admittedly, I made some poor choices that day, but that wasn't the point. The point was I happened to glance over at a moment that can only be described as fate, and laid eyes on the most beautiful diamond in the rough making its slow crawl toward the incinerator.

It was a chip. A tiny silver bit of power that would be the key to unlocking my Frankensteined creation and helping me push deeper into things the Withouts had. Luxuries. Entertainment. Answers.

The questions were what kept me up at night. I knew the answers to the easy ones. Withs like me and my best friend Jace had dangerous, unsavory jobs because we couldn't die until that hateful number on the inside of our arms. Withouts had cushy jobs, big houses, and lavish vacations all the time, because they could die at any moment. The fear drove their every decision.

But as I watched that silver chip crawl closer and closer to its doom, I realized I had to stop it. I didn't want answers to the easy questions. I wanted answers to the tough ones. Why did we put up with this? Why did we just accept our lots in life as Withs? Why didn't we strive for the cushy jobs? Not a single With had ever been president or in any kind of leadership position, yet decisions were made for us constantly. It felt like what niceties we had left were being taken away on a daily basis. Why? Every time I asked, I got longer hours at work to help me "learn gratitude for what I had." So far, I'd learned how to spot computer parts with surprising accuracy, but gratitude remained just out of reach. But that chip wouldn't.

I sprang into action, launching myself onto the conveyor belt and hopping over the discarded metal bits being carried to their doom.

"Rarity!" My name was screamed across the room loudly enough it overpowered the roar of the incinerator. Jace ran toward me with a bit of panic on his face, but I ignored him.

He ran alongside the belt, trying to catch up to me, but there were machines and obstacles in his way. I crawled through a tunnel, but he was still one step behind me. I was nearly in arm's reach of my prize, though.

Unfortunately for me, we'd both reached the end of the line. The belt dumped into a huge funnel. All belts led to this spot. At the bottom, the furnace burned everything to ash, which was then spewed across our lovely neighborhood to give it a gorgeous sooty glow. Truth be told, I hadn't intended to end up in the funnel. I thought I could get the blasted thing before that point.

But oh well, I'd get out somehow. Luckily for me, I was heavier than the chip and fell faster than it did toward the center. I grabbed it as I slid down. Then my brain kicked into problem-solving mode. I scrambled to grab something on the sides of the huge funnel, but it was smooth, built intentionally to prevent escape.

I was soaked in sweat, and the heat started to make me uncomfortable when I realized this may not have been my most brilliant idea. Mistake number three sixty-five— looking down into the maw of the incinerator. The glow coming from the hole was far too close for my comfort and anything but welcoming. Frankly, it seemed like I was sliding straight into the jaws of hell... and it wasn't going to be a handsome fallen angel waiting to greet me like the ones in the romance books my mom read.

But before I met my maker, the glow stopped. The noise stopped, leaving my ears ringing. The motion stopped. An alarm sounded. If possible, my heart rate climbed to a seriously unhealthy speed. After all, I wasn't a hummingbird. This wasn't good. I glanced down at the gateway to hell, willing it to come back on. But it stayed dark. The heat I'd been feeling through my over-worn shoes dissipated almost immediately, along with my hopes and dreams for the next few weeks.

Jace peeked his head over the edge of the funnel. "Rarity, are you okay?"

"Fine and dandy. Yourself?"

Shaking his head, he threw me a rope. Well, actually, after it whacked me in the shoulder, I saw it was the fire hose. One tied to the wall for emergencies. Well, if that wasn't just a skid mark on what was shaping up to be a crap-tastic day, I didn't know what was. He'd broken the glass on a precaution we were basically told never to use **and** stopped the incinerator, something we were told should *never* happen under any circumstance. Great. Crap creek was flowing hard, and my paddle was in that incinerator.

"What did you do?" I asked as he rather unceremoni-ously hauled me over the edge, settling me in a super unglamorous heap at his feet.

"Saved your life is what I did," Jace said, glowering. The least he could've done was offered me a hand up.

"Hey, we're immortal right?"

He flashed the inside of his arm, revealing his own date, which was only two and a half weeks away. "Until we're not."

The supervisor appeared as if from nowhere, startling me. I hated it when they did that. My parents were supervi-sors in other parts of the plant, and they would never tell me how they did it. They both claimed they never did, but I didn't believe them. It was some talent the higher-ups had, to suddenly appear angry and ready to lay down the hammer in an instant.

"Rarity Delman, come with me." When I stood, that feeling of dread settled over me as I clutched the chip in my hand. I wouldn't give it up. Whatever they did to me, it wouldn't be for nothing, I promised myself. Sullenly, I followed behind the man who'd never quite taken a shining to my apparently off-putting sense of humor. At least, that was what he'd called it.

"Jace, you too." Frowning, he fell in line next to me as we marched to our doom.

People stared as we walked, but they averted their gazes when I made eye contact. No one wanted to associate with the one doing the walk of shame. Couldn't say I blamed them.

As the machines kicked back to life, the sounds of crunching, sorting, and clunking were muffled when our supervisor closed his office door.

He didn't speak to us as he rounded his wooden desk. There wasn't anywhere for us to sit, so we just waited as he sat and looked out at the sorting floor from the wall-to-wall window.

"What. Happened," he asked it like two separate sentences.

Before I could condemn myself by vomiting the truth all over his desk, Jace sprang into action. "I dropped my grandfather's watch into the sorter. It means a lot to me. Rarity went in after it."

He thumbed the old watch on his arm, and I watched the supervisor for a reaction.

I guessed the crease that was forming between his eyebrows deep enough to swallow a man whole wasn't a good sign.

"You are less than two days from your departure to the island, Jace." He turned his cavernous scowl my direction, and I shifted. "You're not far behind him. You know we don't stop the incinerator for any reason. It takes hours to reset it."

"Which makes no sense to me. It seems like with some more efficient programming—"

He held a hand up, cutting me off. "Yes. I've heard your efficiency song and dance before, Rarity. You're not a programmer. You're a With." He took a deep breath in, then let it out so hard I swore the pieces of black hair that had fallen out of my ponytail blew back from his sheer exasperation.

"I just thought a person falling into the intake spout was a good reason to shut her down," Jace said quietly, keeping his eyes down on his hands, which were still fiddling with the watch.

The supervisor's mouth formed a thin line, making the stubble just below his bottom lip stand out straight. "I've half a mind to dock your credits for the week." He must've seen the expression on my stricken face. My parents and I barely made enough for the three of us to get by. There'd be adjustments to make when I was gone. No need for those to come prematurely. He sighed again, as if our existence was the scourge of his life. "I suppose your impending deaths are punishment enough. But so help me, you *both* need to stay out of trouble, or there'll be no credits until you make your merry way to the island." He pointed at Jace. "*You* only have one full workday left." He pointed at me. "And you only have six. So keep your acts together."

"Yes, sir," we said in unison. "Thank you, sir."

That night, we walked home ahead of my parents. My house resembled the others on the rural street. A cookie-cutter home, it had been called in the time before. Now, these neighborhoods were used for Withs while the Without lived in fancy condos or on the ocean. Wherever they wanted.

But I didn't mind. Not about my home, at least. It was perfect for us. It was the only green one on the street. Although Jace argued it was from algae growing on the outside, I wasn't convinced. All the homes had taken on a bit of a grey hint to them as the decades went by, but ours still held on to some of its color. The windows barely opened, and the carpet had been torn up before we ever lived in it, revealing rough, unfinished wood flooring. But it was ours. Furnishings that had seen their prime before I was born only made it feel lived in and warm. My room was no exception to that.

A single oak tree dominated the front yard, offering shade from the evening sun. When we walked up the front stoop, the front door creaked its welcome. We went straight to my room, where my own Frankenstein waited. "You won that watch in a card game against Lenny and the boys last month," I said. I headed to my desk, which was made from milk crates and a couple pieces of plywood salvaged from the incinerator, and installed the hard won chip.

When I glanced out the single window in my room, I saw my folks walking hand in hand down the sidewalk toward our house. They always took their time coming home. It was their time.

He shrugged. "Yeah, well. The boss doesn't know that."

"Apparently not. You'd better hope Lenny doesn't talk."

He looked up from his drawing. He had a black streak of charcoal across the left side of his face, but I wasn't sure if it was left over from work or from the drawing he was working on. One bonus from working at the incinerator plant was as much charcoal as he could get his hands on.

"Or what? What exactly will they do to me with one workday left, Rarity?"

One workday left. The sentence hung in the air between us. We'd been friends our whole lives, grew up right across the street from each other. He'd spent every waking moment at my house, since my parents were light-years cooler than his. He'd even started spending nights over here, sleeping on the couch downstairs. We never asked why, but

Dad always left a pillow and blanket down there for him just in case. And he'd taken to using it more and more lately.

One workday until he left me. One workday until he went to the island to live out any fantasy he might have, and then...he'd expire.

I stared at the numbers on my own arm. Just over two weeks to go. Like I was a gallon of milk about to expire. When I reached the two-week mark, I'd join Jace at the island. For a brief moment, we could have our paradise together. And then...

It felt like a rhino scuffing its foot in the dust—getting ready to charge. It wasn't a problem for today, but it loomed over us. Ready to bowl me over.

Until then...I'd work on my Frankenstein. And Jace? Well, he'd work on whatever he wanted.

"What do you think?" he asked as I screwed the back onto my machine.

"I think this just might work."

"Not about that. About this." He held up a striking charcoal landscape. Stone buildings towered over a cliff, where waves crashed below. A path wound back and forth into the foreground. Trees and bushes lined either side, making it appear as if it were calling me toward it.

"Where is that?" I reached for the picture, but he pulled back.

"You'll smudge it," he said.

"No, I most certainly will not," I protested. "Anyway, you didn't answer me."

He turned the picture toward himself, and I crawled onto my bed beside him to study it. He'd drawn individual stones in the path as it got closer, along with wispy clouds in the sky. It was perfect. Idyllic. And it made me wonder if he'd been born a Without, where he'd be. Certainly not sitting on my threadbare bed drawing with charcoal we took from the pile at work.

I'd been blissfully hopeful when we were in school. When I was fourteen, one teacher even encouraged me. Helped me draw up plans for Frank. She said maybe I could work in programming at the incinerator. But that ended rather unceremoniously three years ago when they shipped us off to the plant. Jace, the four other kids in our class, and me. They said we had to start at the bottom. People didn't just become programmers. Or whatever. Problem was, Jace and I didn't have time to work our way up. We'd never be anything more than trash sorters.

Withouts were the ones with the fancy jobs. The entertainers. The artists. The CEOs. Anything glamorous and without risk, they got to do because they hadn't been born with the day they'd die on the inside of their arm. They could die at any moment. And with that fact came more privileges than seemed fair.

It was why I'd had to build my Frankenstein in secret. I wasn't allowed to be a computer engineer like I'd wanted to be. That job was for Withouts. And Jace couldn't be an artist, like he was clearly born to be, because of the damning black numbers on the insides of our arms.

"It's the island. Or at least, how I imagine it'll be," he finally answered.

"But don't you think there'll be a beach there?"

"Oh, so now you're an expert Miss My Date is Five Days After Yours?"

"Well, just because you're going the day after tomorrow doesn't make you an expert either," I countered rather lamely.

He brushed at one of the clouds with the side of his hand, blurring it and making it appear even softer. "No. But by the time you get there, I will be. I'll show you all around that place."

I smiled, but I didn't feel it. "I'd rather spend the next fifty years here with you, than nine days on that island together."

"All right, Debbie Downer." He put his finger under my chin, forcing it up. "Listen. We can't stop the march of time. So let's just enjoy the days for what they are, okay?"

"When did you become a motivational poster?" I asked, nudging him away. He snorted, and I felt better after dodging the serious moment. I didn't like to be serious. I liked to laugh. Our world could be a bit bleak if we let it. Laughing reminded us where the sun was, and that it was good to turn toward it every once in awhile.

He ignored me and nodded toward Frank, which was what I'd started calling the computer. "You get her running better?"

"Not sure. You distracted me."

"Happy to do that any time," he said with a sly grin.

I got down off my bed to plug in my Frank. She fired up beautifully, faster than ever. My problem had always been connecting her to a network. We weren't allowed things the Withouts had. Computers, Internet, they were luxuries we didn't need. Every time I asked about it, I was told to be grateful for the food in my stomach and the roof over my head. Even though the food was barely enough to live on and our roof leaked. But I knew better than to point those things out. Sassing my mom never played out well for me, surprisingly as that may be.

I hoped the new chip would open some doors for me. Or give me the power to do it myself. Frank opened to the main screen, offering options I'd never seen before. Networks that hadn't been there when I'd turned Frank on yesterday. I was just about to investigate when Mom knocked on my door.

"Dinner. Come on, you two." She said nothing about Frank, but I didn't miss the way her eyes lingered on my creation. My parents didn't support my desires to be more than a With, but they also didn't stifle me. Not like Jace's parents did him. Though he never told me what their beef was, I assumed it was his artistic nature that didn't quite fit into the mold of landfill incinerator worker.

When dinner was over, my mom went to the fridge and brought out a beautiful single-tiered frosted cake. It was even chocolate. I almost cried at the sight of it, but all the liquid in my body went straight to my mouth. The thought of eating even one bite of it made my throat clench.

"Surprise," she said as she brought it to the table. Excitedly, Jace swung wide eyes to me.

"Dang, Mrs. D. Where'd you get the credits for that?" he asked.

I kicked him under the table, and he recoiled.

"We just thought it would be a nice send-off for you both. I know you'll get whatever you want on the island, but we wanted to do this for you," she said, getting a bit misty-eyed.

I'd never had cake before. Sugar was such a premium ingredient. It cost too many credits for something we didn't need. Chocolate, too. No. Credits were saved for staples. New-to-us clothes. Toilet paper. Things like that.

Right after I started working, I saved all my credits for over a year and bought Mom a whole chocolate bar. Not one of those little ones, either, but full-sized. Nine pieces total. She cried happy tears. It was awesome. Dad only got her a used cardigan. I definitely won that year.

"If you can't play with the big boys, take your ball and go," I'd told him. Laughingly, he'd shoved me aside.

This cake had both. Sugar *and* chocolate. I didn't want to think about what such an indulgence cost. As I tasted the smooth sweetness, I no longer cared about anything. The cost. The reason we were having it. Nothing. All I cared about was the cake and the flavor exploding on my taste buds. I tried to say thank you, but my mouth was full, so I gave up and had another bite for good measure.

"I'm glad you like it," Mom said as she lifted a more reasonably sized piece on her fork. Dad's was already gone. Jace and I both had seconds, leaving just enough for Mom and Dad to eat later.

It was a sacrifice I could never repay. And for that, I was grateful.

THAT NIGHT, Jace didn't go home. As I was going upstairs and he was settling on the couch, I turned. "Don't you want to spend some time with your folks...before?" I couldn't bring myself to finish the sentiment.

"No. I asked them to pick me up here."

Them. I knew who he meant. The people from the island who'd collect him.

"You don't want to say goodbye?" I asked from the foot of the staircase.

He didn't turn. "Nothing much to say—not really. They're not keen on me at the moment."

I started to ask why, but he stopped me. "It doesn't matter. I'll spend my last moments with the family I chose."

I nodded and went up to bed, catching a glimpse of Jace's rhino just over his shoulder. The dust rose all around us. Soon we'd be trampled, whether we said goodbye or not.

TWO

Goodbye was a terrible word. Almost as bad as death. I much prefer hello.

Jace's goodbye was odd. Like trying to say goodbye to a severed limb. The rest of my body functioned, but every time I reached for something with my missing arm, I was reminded it wasn't there. It felt like it should be, but it wasn't. And it drove me crazy. Like an itch I couldn't scratch.

I threw myself into work during the days. And when I got home, I spent as much time with Frank as my parents would let me.

Jace left me a hand-drawn portrait of us, his arm slung heavily around my shoulder, smiles on our faces. I taped it to my wall just behind the monitor so I could see him whenever I wanted. I planned to leave it behind for Mom and Dad when *they* came for me.

On the third day alone, I hacked into a news station feed. One specifically for the Withouts. We didn't get news updates, unless it was really bad. Only some kind of nuclear fallout or something would be worthy enough to inform us. It had never happened, so we didn't get updates.

The feed was a bit like an old-fashioned ticker tape running across the bottom of my screen. Coding with head-lines jammed in the middle of it took me a moment to deci-pher. **Scientists say life beyond dates within arm's reach. More test subjects needed.**

"What on earth?" I said aloud as I tried to click on it, but my connection terminated. Someone had found me.

I sat back in my chair, trying to puzzle it out. Maybe they were making a movie? Some show they needed to promote. It couldn't mean what it sounded like. That life was the past. Something the Withouts made movies about. Movies Withs would never get to see, but I wasn't bitter.

Logically, that had to be the answer. But somehow, I couldn't stop thinking about it. Elimination of Withs and Withouts? Was that even possible?

"Mom, what do you know about...immortality?" I asked over breakfast the day before they'd come for me. It was a stretch, but I couldn't think of any other way to phrase it.

"What?" she asked as she stood at the sink. She washed dishes in cold, dirty water that should've been rinsed down last night, but wasn't because we needed to conserve.

"What do you know about immortality?" I pressed.

"Well..." She put the threadbare rag in the sink and turned to me, wiping her hands on her patched-up apron. Her familiar blue eyes searched mine for the source of my question. "I guess I don't know much of anything about the subject. Why?"

"I saw something last night that made me wonder..."

When I didn't pick up the thought, she prompted me. "Wonder what?"

"If it were real. Something scientifically achievable."

Snorting, she returned to her task. "You feel pretty invincible after making Frank, don't you?"

Normally, I would've said yes. Frank made me feel empowered. The skill came naturally. Like another language I just...knew. But today, I saw my rhino out the window behind my mom.

I swallowed hard. "I guess," I said quietly.

Mom must have sensed my misgivings. She followed my gaze out the window, but, of course, her rhino was decades away, so she didn't see anything. Or maybe she did. Maybe she saw her baby's rhino and wanted to stand in the way of it. Wanted to flail her arms to get its attention off her one and only. But there was nothing she could do. Because she was sentenced to be the mother of a With whose expiration date came before hers.

It wasn't unheard of, but it wasn't common either. Jace and I were the only two kids in our zone with such early dates. The next person would be in their thirties, which was still considered young. It was one of those phenomena people heard about and thanked their lucky stars when it didn't happen to their kids. Yet, here we sat. They'd come for me tomorrow, and there wasn't a thing any of us could do about it.

She didn't look back at me, but she did let out a shuddering breath.

Putting the last bit of toast in my mouth, I grabbed the meager lunch she'd packed for me. "If it's all the same to you, I'm going to head over now. Maybe they'll let me leave early today." I didn't add why. It wasn't necessary.

With a nod, she leaned over to accept my kiss. She hugged me so tightly I wasn't sure she'd ever let me go. But she did. Somehow, she did, and I wasn't sure I even wanted her to.

"I'll see you at lunch."

"Sounds great." I threw a wave over my shoulder and headed out, trying to run from the confrontation. Emotion. All of it. I had no idea how to deal with it. Running from it felt like the best option at the moment. I was still trying to figure out how to function without Jace. How could I say a proper goodbye to my parents?

All day long, I thought about Jace and what he'd said to me when he left. "Stay out of trouble. I know it'll be hard to do without me here to rescue you."

I'd smacked him on the arm, and he'd enveloped me in a smothering hug. "I could say the same to you," I said when he finally let me go. "You're the one heading to Hedonism Island." They didn't actually call it that, but I'd taken to the name. After all, it was a place for the Withs to live out their fantasies. *No* didn't exist on the island. *Ask and ye shall receive* was the mantra of the Utopia. It was our just desserts after working the crap jobs and living in subpar conditions for our entire lives. Or so we were told.

He'd laughed, then quickly hugged me again. Like if he held on, he may never let go. And I didn't want him to.

He'd gotten into the car, and he waved before he shut the door. I'd watched him go, then glanced at the house across the street, thinking I saw movement in the front window, but I wasn't sure. His parents hadn't come out. They hadn't said goodbye. He'd last seen them days ago. But somehow, I couldn't feel sorry for them. They'd thrown away their chance with him, and I'd scooped it up like the treasure it was.

As I'd watched the car disappear around the corner, I hadn't cried. I'd waited until it was completely out of sight. I hadn't wanted him to see.

My parents had gotten me inside and to bed, and I'd cried most of the night. By morning, I'd known I had to function. Missing work wasn't something Withs could do. For everything we didn't have, medicine was something we couldn't go without. The healing technologies that had come out of the With Revolution were astounding. They could cure almost anything the Withs had, keeping them alive until the precise moment stamped on the inside of their arm.

Death was the only thing eluding them, much to the Withouts chagrin. But the thought brought me back to that headline. How much longer did death elude them?

That last morning, I knew I'd never live to see them figure it out.

I zipped my suitcase, ready to go. In reality, the only reason I wanted to go was because Jace was already there. Most people had to go to the island alone. Not that I would ever wish an early date on my best friend, but I thought our dates had brought us closer together. His was only five days before mine. I tried not to think about the last five days I'd be on the island without any friends. Would there be kids my age there? Or would it be like a retirement community full of white-haired people playing shuffleboard and canasta? Was it wrong to hope someone else's family was suffering the same fate as me, just so I wouldn't have to be alone?

I pushed the thoughts from my mind, trying desperately not to spiral, and brought my suitcase into the living room where my parents sat. Mom wrung her hands while Dad had his arm around her. When I set my suitcase down, her whole demeanor changed. She smiled broadly at me. Even though it was obviously fake, she put her heart and soul into it.

"What are you hoping to see and do?" she asked as she stood and came over to me, taking my hands in hers.

"I don't know. Everyone says it's amazing, but I've never talked to anyone who has actually been there."

"I mean, I'd rather not talk to a dead person," Dad quipped.

"Robert," Mom scolded.

I snorted. "He has a point." The island was created for Withs to spend their last two weeks just like the Withouts. No responsibilities, endless resources, whatever I wanted, when I wanted it.

The possibilities were so endless. I was feeling a bit overwhelmed. There was a lot of pressure to live the rest of my life to the fullest. After years of standing on the incineration line, what did I want to do with my free time?

"Mom, what will you do when you get to the island?"

Sighing, she gazed up at the ceiling a bit wistfully. "I think I'd put my toes in the ocean. Dig them into the sand and let the water rush over my ankles."

"Maybe do a little skinny-dipping," Dad said as he hooked his arm around Mom's waist.

"Oh, gross. Okay, Dad, way to ruin the moment," I said as I squeezed my eyes shut, trying to erase the image he'd given me.

"I would just want to be with your mother," he said, turning uncharacteristically sentimental. His date was first. Hers was almost a decade later. They'd never see the island together, but it wasn't something they talked about, at least not to me. It was unchartered territory, and I wasn't sure I liked where it was heading.

"You're lucky to have Jace waiting for you. He'll show you around, take you to all the good places. Just promise you'll stay out of trouble," Dad said.

"Please, Daddy. It's the island. There isn't any trouble." Which was true in a sense. All bets were off, except violence, of course. But if someone needed to hit something, there was a place for that. Or so I read in the pamphlet they sent my way two days ago. Of course, Jace had shown me his, so I was familiar with it already, but I'd still poured over it. The paper was so shiny and new, and crisp color images besides. Even the packaging of our so-called food didn't look that nice.

The pamphlet had boasted everything from boxing rings—*no, thank you*—to beaches—*yes, please*—and everything in between. It would've been exciting if I weren't about to embark on a death march.

Mom's chin quivered, and I tilted my chin up. I wouldn't cry. Not here. I'd be strong, so they could be strong. I refused to be one of those kids who were torn from their parent's arms kicking and wailing. Everyone talked about little Bobby Wheelan, the poor boy. But I always thought about his parents. How they couldn't go to him. Comfort him. How their last memory was him screaming bloody murder about being parted from them. According to the story, he'd only been eight, so his reluctance was understandable.

The more I thought about little Bobby Wheelan, poor boy, the more I wondered if it were even a true story. I had no idea where I'd first heard about him. It was just one of those things everyone knew. Admittedly, the kids in early school told me the story a lot, since I was one of the first to go. By a lot. Save for Jace. Maybe that was what drove Jace and me together. We didn't have this odd fascination with each other. We could be normal. We didn't look at each other sympathetically like the other kids seemed to. Well, none of it mattered now. They were all working at the incinerator while I was facing down my rhino.

And I'd do it with a smile on my face and a song in my heart if it killed me. Which I knew it wouldn't, because I still had two weeks go to. No matter what, I'd willingly go out to the car. No Little Billy Wheelan here, poor boy. I'd give my parents peace as I hugged them before walking away on my own. At least, that was my plan.

Our life wasn't perfect, but whose was? All I knew was I didn't want to leave it behind.

"I'm sorry," I blurted as I threw my arms around them both, dissolving into a weepy mess. So much for Plan A.

"Oh, my baby," Mom said as she put her hand on the back of my head. Even Dad held me tightly, the man who always told me there wasn't time to cry. *Tuck in your bottom lip and turn your face to the sun* was his philosophy.

"We sure will miss you," he said. His voice wavered. Needless to say, the sound did nothing to stem my flood of tears.

A knock at the door made me clutch them even harder, but Dad patted my back. "Come on now..." He cleared his throat. "They're here for you. It'll be fun. You'll see."

I peered over at Mom, who also had tears swimming in her eyes. People said I looked like her with our olive skin and piercing blue eyes. With Dad's dark hair, I wasn't terrible to look at.

She pulled me close, then planted a long kiss on my forehead. Our last one. "Go. Have an adventure. Live." It was an order, not a request, so I nodded.

"I love you."

"We love you, too," Dad said as Mom held a hand to her mouth.

They followed me to the door, Dad carrying my suitcase. We didn't say anything else to each other as I walked to the fancy convertible. I couldn't help but smile when I saw my request had been fulfilled.

"See, Dad? If you don't ask, the answer is always no." He hadn't thought they'd honor such a stupid request. But I'd never ridden in a convertible. In fact, I'd never ridden in a car before. We lived so close to the city we didn't need one. No one did. Nor could anyone on my street afford one. But I wanted to feel the wind in my hair. Maybe it was a stupid request, but it had been fulfilled.

Jace's car had been a black box of a thing with windows almost as dark as the paint. But he'd said he hadn't cared. I did.

My dad smiled. "I'll keep that in mind in twenty-seven years." When he winked, I ran back to them as the driver waited, holding the door open. I threw myself into their open arms one last time, and they clung to me just as hard as I did to them.

We didn't speak. There were no words left. The driver was patient and didn't rush us. He didn't even clear his throat. He just stood there, holding the car door open while we shared one last moment together.

Finally, long before I was ready, Dad gave me a gentle push. When he nodded toward the car, I walked backward toward it, keeping my eyes on them.

"Don't do anything I wouldn't do," Dad said with a forced smile.

"I won't," I said. I blew them a kiss before getting in my seat, then turned to see them one last time. At least they had each other. For almost the next three decades at least. They clung together so tightly I knew they'd hold each other up. They'd be okay.

As the car drove off, I watched them get smaller and

smaller until he turned a corner. Just like that, they were gone.

I swallowed the urge to scream at the driver. To tell him to go back. The rhino was getting closer, and the driver was nothing more than the little bird sitting on its horn, steering my fate ever closer.

THREE

The car was a bit overwhelming. There were buttons for everything. Windows, seat positions, and even a television screen in the rear of the front seat headrests, which allowed me to have access to movies and shows all the Withouts watched. It was almost too much to take in.

As we rounded the last corner before the transport station, a statue came into view. I tore my attention away from the gadgets in the car to examine it. It wasn't something I saw often since it wasn't on my route to and from the plant. It was a historical staple. Something in me felt I should see it one last time.

At the center of a small roundabout, a white stone baby with tiny black numbers inscribed on the inside of her arm lay alone in a stone basket.

She was the first. Shiloh McGee. She'd been born with that strangely legible birthmark no one knew what to make of. Three days later, on the date so weirdly printed on her arm, she'd died.

It was a firestorm of media frenzy after that. Some people thought a nurse had murdered her. But they couldn't pin it on one. Not that the ones involved hadn't had their lives ruined over it. Our history books said one nurse had even killed herself over it.

When it happened again, over a year later, police thought a serial killer was on the loose. But it had been different that time. The date on the man's arm had been decades after his birth. And he'd lived all that time. What kind of serial killer put that amount of time into his murders? And who could manage to tattoo a baby without someone noticing? None of it made sense.

Over the years, it happened with more and more frequency. Supposedly, Withs currently made up about thirty percent of the population. Enough to do the danger-ous, dirty jobs to give the Withouts more longevity.

By the thirtieth anniversary of little Shiloh's death, society collapsed. The Withs and Withouts were separated by a revolution in the name of peace. Let the Withs do the dirty work, and they'd be compensated handsomely in the end. It seemed like a fair trade, at least to those who'd been alive at the time and hadn't had to live it out yet. When situ-ations were strictly theoretical, it was easy to agree.

A working government sprang from the ashes, enforcing order, divvying out work and funds. It was when our credit system started, while the Withouts kept their beloved money. We were given enough credits to survive, nothing more, while the Withouts wanted for nothing. Seemed like every single aspect of our lives were separated. By the time everything was in place, there wasn't much the Withs could do to even things out. "You'll get yours," they said. "At least you know when you'll die," as if that was some kind of comfort.

It was funny how no one acted nuts before, when everyone was a Without. It was an even playing field. But once that carrot was dangled, they all thought the grass was so much greener, so the Withs should gladly give up normal human rights without a thought. After all, they'd given up one of theirs. At least, it was how they felt anyway.

After that, Withs and Withouts never mixed. It was safer that way. Every time they did, fights broke out. The animosity among the two sects was too great. The Withs felt slighted, and the Withouts were so consumed by fear they couldn't see straight. That way, everyone was at least safe if not satisfied.

As we rounded the backside of the statue, I could see not everyone was satisfied.

Withs=slaves was emblazoned in dripping red paint on the baby's basket.

It was such an odd thing to see. Someone used their hard-earned credits for paint instead of food. How many days had they starved to accomplish that? And what was it even for?

Before I could think too much about it, the driver pulled into the parking lot of the station. I'd never been to the transport station. Never had a need. Withs never had much money to travel. We didn't get time off to do it, either.

Mom said she remembered when the station was built. She'd been just a girl, and it was a marvel of technology and science. Her dad had been on the line helping to build it. When it was finished, they'd even gone to the ribbon-cutting ceremony, like they were actually important people. Mom had a picture from the event. Actual photographs were something almost no Withs had. Cameras, printing, photopaper—they were luxuries in the face of eggs, milk, and bread. But they'd given the image to her parents as a gift for my grandfather's hard work.

The station looked old to me. They held the grand

opening about forty years ago. Sophie had been born almost seventy-five years prior. We'd been one of the last zones to get a transport station. When people needed transportation to the island, they had to take a train to the next zone so they could hop a transport. Like everything else in our zone, it was hard, but it worked. To be honest, I wasn't sure what prompted them to finally build it, except maybe to throw us a bone. Morale was a funny thing, and the smiles on the faces in the photograph Mom kept said the station did a number to boost it around here. Seeing the writing on that statue made me wonder if we couldn't use another.

The driver came around. Once he let me out, I saw dingy concrete steps beckoning me forward. I scowled, wondering why everything seemed to push me toward my death.

"This way, miss," the driver said as he ushered me through the steel double doors.

It wasn't about what I wanted. It never was. I was just expected to be a good little girl and march forward. What if I'd asked to stay? What if Jace had? We could all be together, here, at home. Would they let Mom and Dad take some time off? And that was where my dreams died. They'd never let my parents take time off. Not to mention the fact that no one got to stay home. They'd tried it at first, letting families stay together, but it was too hard. People started to feel slighted then. They worked their whole lives, but they never got anything for it.

The Withouts thought our lives were so simple. Black and white. But they missed the mark by a long shot. After all, we Withs never escaped death's presence either. If I thought about it, it was kind of funny. Not in a ha-ha kind of way, but in a I-just-won-the-lottery-and-got-hit-by-a-bus-on-the-way-to-collect kind of way. Not my favorite kind of humor to be honest.

The station wasn't huge inside, but certainly larger than our house. I'd heard of transport stations that were four stories tall and covered a city block. The one in the pamphlet of the island had a fountain inside it with running water and everything. I imagined the Withouts had fancy stations, too. They could go wherever they wanted, whenever they wanted. We used to gossip in school about how much the Withouts made, and what we'd do with all that money. It almost always revolved around chocolate, ice cream, and sweets. Once in a while, a soft blanket had been thrown in to mix things up.

Then, the conversation would devolve into what the Withouts actually did with their extra money. Traveling the world was something I imagined they'd do. Of course, none of us knew what actually went on in the world of the Withouts. Much like the vast majority probably didn't know what happened in our zones. After all, they never traveled here. So how would they?

Our transport station was just a small building. Four tubes total. We didn't have that many people coming and going. With a population of only about ten thousand, give or take, we weren't exactly a huge travel destination. I could just see the tourist flier. *Come one, come all, see the inciner-ator and stop by the recycling plant while you're at it!* Yeah, no. No one ever visited. Once someone came to Telos, they stayed until it was time to die.

The platform was empty, except for the driver and me. "No one else doing the death march today, I take it?" Not that I was surprised. What were the odds? Ten thousand people, three hundred and sixty-five days in the year—the math made my head hurt.

He frowned. Apparently, he had no sense of humor. I liked him a little less after that. Jace would've laughed or come back with something better. The thought of him had me excited to get this transition over with.

"Which tube, Sir Rhino?"

Again, he frowned. I realized I hadn't told him about the whole rhino-metaphor thing. I shrugged. He didn't need to know since it wasn't about him.

"Any one you choose."

The four tubes were lined up along the back wall, each with computer stations out front. Actual computers. Not like Frank. Properly built thinking machines. The urge to go to them was almost overwhelming, but Sir Rhino kept me on task with his cold, watchful eyes.

The idea was people coded the tube up and got inside, then it teleported them to the destination that was put in. The key with transport tubes was to code it properly. One misplaced backslash and a person could end up split between two places. That never ended well. I'd even heard of someone getting trapped in between. Some kids at school said they could hear her voice begging for help when they traveled. I'd demanded to know how they knew. After all, none of us had ever traveled anywhere, but they yelled at me for spoiling the fun. Jace had laughed and pulled me aside, telling me it was just a game.

But standing there in the tube, I wondered if I would hear her voice on the way to the island.

The driver stood at the screen. He typed in my destination before closing the door and patting a hand on the glass. "Ready?"

No. No, I wasn't ready. But I nodded anyway.

Purple light illuminated the tube, and a tingling sensation crawled all over my skin. I was keenly aware of a whooshing sound in my ears, but it didn't feel like I was moving.

I gaped at my hand. It seemed like I'd become a million tiny puzzle pieces. But these pieces were round. Tiny round pieces of slightly different colors. And if I held it farther from my face, they made a more cohesive picture.

"Trippy," I said aloud, then slammed my mouth shut, lest the ghost of the tubes answered me.

Suddenly, I felt like I'd been dropped out of the sky. I bent my knees, nearly going all the way down to my butt. The purple light faded and I blinked, trying to adjust to my new surroundings.

The door opened with a hiss, and a different man stood there. He was dressed in a crisp white blazer, white under-shirt, and white pants. A big, salesmen-like smile was plas-tered on his face as he held a well-moisturized hand out to me.

"Rarity Delman. Welcome to the island."

"Thanks, I—" I stopped dead at the sight of Jace, nearly tripping over the lip in the tube as I tried to get to him.

"Are you all right?" the welcome-wagon man asked.

I ignored him to focus on Jace. His arms were folded over his chest, and he laughed at me.

"You're a mess," he said.

"Oh, and you're Mr. I've Got it All Figured Out," I said as I hugged him. His arms were heavy against my back, and they felt good. Like coming home.

"You have a friend here, I see," the welcome-wagon man said.

"Thanks for the narration, Captain Obvious," I said, ticked he'd ruined our moment. I didn't need a guide. I had Jace.

The welcome wagon wasn't deterred, though. "Our

guests find it is easy enough to make friends here. I'd encourage you to do so as well, so you're not alone once one of you leaves."

"Leaves? Is that what the kids are calling it now?" I quipped.

The man didn't respond. He was good at ignoring me. Jace just smiled and shook his head. "Leave the poor guy alone."

"I'd rather he left us alone," I said quietly.

The guide smiled. "It's policy, Ms. Delman. Everyone gets a tour when they get here, along with a rundown of the rules."

"Rules on the island? What a disappointment." It wasn't the rules that bummed me out per se. The island was supposed to be this amazing Utopia, but it felt like a prison. A place I would never leave alive. The weight Jace's arm around my shoulders helped, but it didn't banish my dark thoughts as much as I needed.

"Rules help the place run smoothly, Ms. Delman. They aren't meant to restrict you. Make a request, and we'll be sure to execute it as safely as possible."

"Safely? What's the point? We've all come here to die."

"My... you're in a mood today," Jace said, frowning.

I shook my head, trying to clear the darkness. "Sorry. You're right. Why don't you play the third wheel and show me around for a bit, Mister..."

"Call me Finn." His smile never faded. I wondered if he even liked his job, or if he was just another With trying to make it until his turn on the island.

FINN SHOWED US THE SIGHTS. Jace filled me in on all the fun things to do in the various stations. He'd already been there for five days. Apparently, he'd made quite a few friends. I wasn't sure how I felt about that, considering I'd been slaving away at the incinerator while he was chumming it up with every Blondie McHalf Shirt that crossed his path.

As we walked down a wooded path, a space to our left opened. "You'll find a few volleyball courts here, if that's something you're interested in," Finn offered.

"Jace! Where you been? Come on and play a game. They're kicking our butts," a girl called, her giant boobs bouncing as she flounced our way.

Stopping when she saw me, she gave me a once over. "Who's your friend?"

"This is Rarity. The one I was telling you about." He appeared completely oblivious to the glare the new girl was giving me.

I stuck out my hand and smiled, not wanting to play games on Death Island. "Nice to meet you."

Frowning, she glanced dismissively at my hand. "Charmed." She turned to Jace. "You coming to play?"

He blinked, seeming to process the situation. "No, I don't think I will." He pushed on the small of my back, ushering me away.

"What the hell was that about?" he asked as we headed down the path, Finn in the lead.

"Seems she thought she had some claim on you," I said, trying to stifle my laughter.

"Why would she think that?" He sounded baffled, and I couldn't contain it anymore. A snort escaped, and he shoved me. "What?"

"Jace, come on. It's anything goes around here. Why wouldn't she?" I wasn't surprised. My best friend was a head taller than me, and I wasn't short. Years of manual labor at the incinerator had defined his muscles. Needless to say, he was built well. Short dark hair and dark eyes capped off a rather scrumptious package.

Of course, we respected the boundaries of friendship—most of the time. There had been a brush of the hand here, a hug that lasted just a little too long there, but nothing more. Now that we were together at the end, I wondered if we'd made a mistake and wasted the years we could have had as a couple. It had just never occurred to me to cross that line. Jace certainly hadn't proposed the idea, and it seemed safer to stay in friend territory. But I wasn't so sure now, especially after meeting Nasty McNoBoundaries.

But I couldn't have regrets this late in the game. Our friendship meant the world to us both. He wouldn't have met me at the station if it didn't.

"What have you done so far?" I asked as we continued to the next building. Finn kept talking, but I was barely listening. Jace and I could explore on our own to find activities easily enough. Finn had already taken us through the mall, the gaming center, and the food court. The latter had everything from fast food to so fancy I could barely make it out under the garnish sprig they put on the plates.

"After the spa, I'll take you to the university," Finn said.

"University? Hardly seems like two weeks is enough time to earn a degree," I said, snorting derisively.

"It's not about getting a degree. Instead, it's about trying something you've never done before such as painting, pottery, or music. Something fun."

"Is it all art?" I asked.

"No, there are several physics classes, engineering, robotics, and math. Anything you could want to learn," Finn answered.

The thought of computers, libraries, and answers

excited me. I had to hold myself back from running in that direction. "Impressive," I said, trying to sound disinterested but failing epically.

As we walked, I had no concept of how huge the island was. It seemed to span hundreds of miles, which were connected by the transport pods. Soon, the woods thinned and the trees changed to a more tropical landscape. Pine trees dissolved into palm trees, and pink flowers bloomed everywhere.

"This is the spa..." Finn gestured in front of himself, but I only saw plants. "They took an outdoor approach with this one."

Everything was surrounded by big green leaves and flowers in every shade of pink imaginable. The smells transported me to another place, and I almost felt like I could hear the ocean. I closed my eyes, trying to envision it lapping against my ankles just like Mom had said.

"I feel like I can hear the seagulls squawking," I said as I took everything in.

"That's because the beach is just on the other side of this," Finn said like it was no big deal.

"Can we see it?"

Before Finn could answer, Jace cut him short. "You know what? I'll take you over there a little later. Deal?"

It would be more special if it was just the two of us, but I was anxious to see what I'd only ever seen on TV. The television had been my protégé project before I built Frank. No one else on our street had one. Took two years to build it from parts I'd stolen from work. And another year to hack into a feed so we could watch it. Just like with Frank, my folks said nothing. They seemed to enjoy it once I'd hacked a few channels for us to watch.

The ocean had always felt like a fantasy when it came

on the fuzzy screen. Such a massive expanse of water was hard to comprehend.

"Well, if you don't want to see the beach, I'll take you to your room. You probably want to rest up after your trip."

"Lead the way, Mr. Honorable Third Wheel."

He ignored me as we walked for what seemed like ages. Seriously, the sun was already setting. Finally, we arrived at a series of buildings that butted up to a sandy beach.

"Is this where the rooms are?" I asked.

Finn's face fell, his hand going to his ear. "If you don't like it, we can make other arrangements. There are mountain dorms, and even a few virtual ones that can be set to any landscape, even space if you want. Just give me a moment to make the change, and we'll take a transport pod over there."

"Finn. Whoa. Slow your roll, man. I was just appreciating the view."

He blinked. "So..."

"This will be fine. Unless you have something a little less fancy? Something covered in ash and dirt with a lumpy mattress and a threadbare blanket to make me feel more at home?" I was only half kidding, but Jace jabbed me in the side with his elbow. It kind of hurt.

"Leave the poor guy alone," Jace said.

I cleared my throat. "Lead on, Finn. This will be perfect."

He took a hesitant step toward the glass double doors at the base of the tall, rectangular building that lined the beach. Well-groomed tropical plants hung over the sidewalk as we approached, and the atmosphere carried over into the lobby. A massive waterfall cascaded from the top floor down to the center of the building. When we stepped inside the glass elevator, we were behind it, watching the water from the inside.

"This place is amazing."

"My dorm is just the next building over," Jace said. I nodded, but I couldn't take in what he said. I was too distracted.

The elevator stopped in the middle of the building, and Finn gestured to a few doors down. "Here's your room. 420." He held out a golden key—one of those old-fashioned ones with a loop on top and two teeth on the bottom. "If you lose this, the people downstairs will be happy to replace it for you."

"Sure," I said absently.

"Okay. Well, I suppose that about ends our tour," Finn said as he handed me a card. "Should you need anything at all during your stay on the island, don't hesitate to call. No request is too grandiose, I assure you."

"Hey Finn, what's the most ridiculous thing you've ever been asked for?" I asked as he started to leave.

He turned and blinked as if I'd posed an unsolvable problem. "No request is ridiculous, Ms. Delman."

"Indulge me."

He nodded. "Once, someone asked me what the most ridiculous request I'd ever gotten was." He shook his head. "That was pretty silly, if I do say so myself." A smile tugged at the corner of his mouth as he dipped his head to bid me farewell.

"Nice," I said quietly to Jace when we were finally alone. "He seems swell."

"All the people who work here are like that. Don't let it get to you. Bunch of yes men if you ask me."

I squeezed Jace's hand. "Sounds like you need to take

your own advice." When I winked, he yanked on my arm, pulling me closer to him.

"Rarity." He gazed down at me, hooking a stray hair over my ear.

"What?" I breathed him in, and he smelled completely different from his normal scent. Not the smell of smoke, sweat, and caustic soap I'd come to love. He smelled...

"Are you wearing aftershave?" I blurted.

Smiling, he threw his arms around me and hugged me tightly, even tighter than when he'd left for the island. "God, I missed you."

"I missed you, too, Jace," I said as I opened the door to my room. It was every bit as extravagant as the rest of the building, and I had no idea how I'd actually sleep in there.

"This place is awesome, but the people here...they don't understand," Jace said.

I pulled back. "Don't understand what?"

"Me."

Now it was my turn to laugh. "Oh and I do, Mister Tall, Dark, and Brooding?"

He laughed again. "See? That's what I mean. You know exactly what to say. I hate that this is happening to us, but I'm glad you're by my side for it."

"Me too..." I hesitated. "But I don't want to focus on that. All I want to think about are these moments we have left together in this beautiful place."

"Then that's what we'll do. For the rest of our lives."

FOUR

Jace's sentiment was sweet, but he just wasn't the sit-around-and-moon-at-each-other kind of guy. The next morning, he took me to the gaming station. Apparently, the beach would have to wait.

"You'll get a kick out of this. It's extremely realistic." He was so excited his leg bounced while we rode the personal transport over there. It wasn't even a car like the one I'd taken to the station at home. It was this half-circle shaped driverless pod without a track. Plus, it was white. Could it be any more sterile?

"Don't people walk around here? Finn walked us all over. I liked it," I said while the beautiful scenery whizzed by.

"You can, and we will. The island is pretty spread out, so this is faster."

"You in a hurry?" I teased.

He blinked like I'd said something in Greek. "Rare, you're gonna love it. Trust me. It's such a rush."

I had to admit my curiosity was piqued. Getting hands-on with that type of technology was definitely worth putting the beach off for another day.

"They have all kinds of games. Puzzles, shooting, survivalist, old westerns, monsters. It's impossible to not find *something* you like." Jace talked fast, trying to convince me.

"Jace, you don't need to convince me. I'm actually kind of excited to see what Frank could've been." The mention of Frank brought my mind home, dampening my excitement a little.

Smiling, he nudged me with his shoulder. "You'll see. You're gonna love it."

As we raced toward the gaming station, I already knew I wouldn't hate it.

OF COURSE, we had to get suited up. I felt ridiculous in all that gear. I didn't even want to come out of the dressing room. From a design standpoint, the gear was essential to interacting with the game, and that level of interaction fascinated me. The flexibility of it. The possibilities were exciting. But from a player standpoint, I didn't love the shiny black body condom.

"Rare, what's taking you so long?" Jace said as he knocked on the door.

"I'm not so sure about this."

"Come on. I promise, I'll make it worth your while."

Squinting at the door, I warred with myself. I desperately wanted to see the game, but I did *not* want to be seen in the body condom. "All day at the spa," I demanded, testing the waters to see just how much I could get out of him.

"Deal," he said with a grin so big my eyes rolled themselves.

Against my better judgment, I sighed and pushed the door open. I tried to adjust my headgear as best I could, but it felt too big and heavy.

Jace pulled on my chinstrap, moving the thing around a bit. Suddenly, it fit more snuggly.

"Thanks," I said.

"You look good," he said. He swallowed hard before clearing his throat. I felt like an idiot. The black bodysuit didn't leave much to the imagination, and it made me feel like an otherworldly species the way the head-to-toe sensors shimmered when I moved. If I'd been the Without who'd designed this, I'd have taken comfort into account.

"I feel like an alien."

"You can be one if you like. There's a game—"

I cut him off. "Apparently, my tone didn't convey I don't particularly *like* feeling like an alien."

He grabbed my hand, then pulled me away from my safe space. "You don't even look like that in the game. It's totally customizable. Come check it out."

He pretty much shoved me into a booth before closing the door behind me. It reminded me of the dressing room, but more complicated. Instead of a mirror, there was a panel of buttons in front of me. I could handle this. Buttons. Technology. Slowly, the excitement of the game took over, and I started to relax.

"Jace?" I asked.

"Yeah, hang on." His voice startled me so much I hit my back on the inside of the door to my booth. Okay, maybe relaxed was pushing it a bit.

"Hey, you okay?"

"Why do you sound so close?"

"We both have mics and earpieces, ya' goon. They're in the headgear." Everything I was experiencing seriously threatened to blow my mind. I'd heard of headphones and electronics of that nature, but I never imagined how clear another person would sound. My homemade TV was pretty staticky, even on clear days when I could get a good signal. The headphones made it sound like he was in my head. It was bizarre in an exciting but also slightly uncomfortable way.

I could picture him shaking his head as I tried to slow my racing heart and regain my composure. Maybe a passerby would think I was in the throes of an intense game. One could only hope.

"Hey, there's a new one. It's called *Melting Point*. The sun is about to boil the earth and you have to save it. Sounds cool, right?"

"I dunno. Sounds tough."

"Okay, what about a racing game?"

"Like we'd get to drive cars?"

"Yup."

I didn't even try to hide my excitement at that. I'd never driven a car. In reality, I'd be horrible at it, but I didn't care. This was too fun to pass up.

"Yes, let's do that!"

His laughter filled my ears. "Okay. Buckle up, Buttercup."

The world around me dissolved, and I found myself dressed in a racing suit. I changed the color to pink by reaching out and touching a nearby color panel. Once I added purple accents, I examined myself in the mirror. Not too shabby for a first timer.

"Whenever you're ready, pick your car."

A garage-like setting surrounded me. A beautiful shiny red car rotated in front of me on its own accord. "If you don't want a car, just swipe right or left and another will take its place."

Swipe? Swipe what? When I waved my hand in the air, about sixteen cars went by in rapid succession. Perhaps a bit more finesse was needed.

I flicked my wrist a little more precisely, and only two cars went by. A slower movement brought only one. But it was a black, precocious-looking thing with a hood I could lay down on and an actual ornament. So I flipped through a few more until I found *the one*. A blue, two-seater convertible.

"Sometime today, Rare. I'm not getting any further from my date here," Jace said impatiently.

"These things take time."

"Just pick one and let's go. The fun part is out on the road!"

"Okay, how do I pick it?" I asked, feeling stupid. There wasn't a selection button.

"Walk over and get inside," he said flatly.

"Just walk over and get inside," I mocked while I cautiously made my way over there. "How am I not crashing into the side of that tiny room we're in?"

"Treadmills on the floor? I don't know. Don't think about it or it ruins the experience."

He was right. But the side of me that built Frank wanted to know how every tiny circuit worked. Everything about this was so immersive. It was absolutely amazing.

When I put my hand on the handle, it felt cool to the touch. I wanted to stand there and marvel at it some more, but Jace whistled impatiently in my ear.

In one fell swoop, I pulled the door open and sat inside.

After getting the seat adjusted and putting on my seat belt, I felt ready.

"Three years later..." Jace teased. "Let's go."

"How?"

"Start the car and drive."

Right... Just start the car and drive. Except I had no idea how to do that. No keys. No buttons except a dark screen on the center dashboard. Once I put my hands on the steering wheel, it lit up a soft blue under my fingers. The engine roared to life, and I immediately put my foot on the brake.

"Brake is the left pedal, right?"

"Correct. Left is brake, and right is gas. I'm already halfway down the track, I'll have you know. I got tired of waiting for you."

"No, you're not," I said as I watched the garage door in front of me rise to reveal a beautiful summer coastline with nothing but a winding road edged with clear blue water.

"You wanna make a bet?"

I mashed on the gas, tires squealing behind me before they finally got purchase and launched me out of the garage like a rocket. Hitting the asphalt, I rounded the first wide corner with no problems if swinging out into the opposite lane counted. There wasn't anyone coming at me, so it was fine.

"Where are you?" I asked, searching the road ahead.

"You're so far behind you're not even a speck in my rearview mirror," he teased.

I hit the gas on the straightaway, not even processing how fast I was going. Signs zipped by me, but the lines in the road were mesmerizing. They seemed to spell out a word.

I—M—M—O—R—T—A—L—I—T—Y.

Huh. That was a stupid message to have embedded in a

game on Death Island. Seemed cruel to remind everyone what they couldn't have. A message popped up in the bottom of my line of sight, and I couldn't help but read it as it scrolled across the dashboard. *Follow the immortal road.*

Man, they were really rubbing it in people's faces. I shrugged. Which one was the immortal road? Was I already on it? I zipped along the highway so fast I had no idea how I'd even see a turn-off, but I didn't want to slow down. I wanted to catch up to Jace. And besides, it was fun to drive fast and... the slow-moving car I came up on didn't stand a chance. I slammed into the rear of it. My body lurched forward, the sound of smashing glass and crunching metal filling my ears before my screen went black. I screamed, but it was so delayed it felt comical.

"Rare? You okay?"

I dazedly shook my head, breathing like I'd just run from a pack of lions. Because that was a thing I did. Run from lions. Hungry ones. I rolled my eyes at my stupidity.

"Rarity," Jace said again as the screen returned to life.

I was back in my car, but it wasn't moving. Covering my face, I peeked through my fingers. Everything was fine. I pulled the rearview mirror down to examine myself. Pink helmet in place. No blood. I was fine. What in the great green gravy had just happened?

Suddenly, the screen froze, and there was a knocking sound that felt unnatural for this beachy highway.

"Rarity?" Jace's voice was much further away. I blinked, bringing myself back to reality before I turned and opened the door to my game room. "Yeah?"

"What happened?"

"I crashed the car—smashed right into the car in front of me. I didn't even see it. Do you think they're okay?"

He took my shaking hands in his. "Rarity... it's not real.

It's just a game. And that's the beauty of it. If you die, you just start over." He glanced over my shoulder at the paused screen. "Maybe that's why I like playing. Because death doesn't mean anything here. Not like it does out there."

Maybe. But it had sure felt like it meant something. It had scared the ever-loving crap out of me.

"Maybe we should go do something else," he suggested.

"Sure."

"Let me just turn off the game. I'll be right out."

Waiting for my heart rate to settle down, I breathed deeply as he popped in and out of the room next to mine in no time.

Something in his hand jangled.

"What is that?" I asked.

"I think I finally got enough. Let's take them to the front desk."

"Enough what? Blood pressure points to earn a stroke?" But he didn't even acknowledge me. He just went on ahead, and I begrudgingly hurried to catch up to him.

"How can I help you?" a cheery woman behind a glass counter asked.

"I think I finally got enough of these." He dumped a handful of what looked like gold coins on the countertop. My jaw hung open. I'd never seen anything so valuable, and he'd just dumped them out like the trash we sorted at work.

"My, my. Congratulations. No one has gotten that many in quite a while. Well done, you." She seemed genuinely shocked when as she took in his haul, but I figured it must be an act to make the players feel good. That was what the whole island was about anyway—allowing people to feel on top of the world in their final days.

"You can take your pick from this case." She gestured toward a locked case over to the right.

"Jace, what are those?" I curiously asked.

"Tokens. You get them when you win a game." He eyed the case. "You go ahead. I'll pick something we'll both like."

"Okay," I said skeptically. Seemed like he was going to make a trade for something in that case. And what I saw in there wasn't crap either. Nothing like what went through the chutes at home. There were shiny gadgets I couldn't even comprehend.

"Rare, you trying to trap spiders?"

Slamming my mouth shut, I swallowed. I hadn't even realized it was hanging open.

Chuckling, he reached out to give me a little nudge. "Just let me take care of this, and I'll catch up with you. Go get changed."

I nodded, unable to process the enormity of Death Island. But maybe that was the point of the place.

I returned to the dressing room in a bit of a daze, then changed into comfortable clothes that were nicer than anything I'd ever owned. My dark hair even seemed shinier than it ever had after I'd washed it that morning with fancy shampoo and actual conditioner. It made me sad to think my parents wouldn't get to see me this way. Thriving on Death Island. The paradox of it threatened to make me mad, so I basically ran out of the dressing room like a bee was chasing me.

Luckily, Jace waited just outside my dressing room. How long had I been in there?

"What's up?" I asked, pretending I hadn't just stumbled like a crazy person into his line of sight.

He snorted, but left well enough alone. "Nothing. You hungry?"

"Starving."

"Let's get something to eat. I have some people you might like to meet."

Instead of heading straight for Jace's favorite eatery where they apparently served every type of meat cooked any way a person wanted it, he took me to a place that served all kinds of noodles in various cheesy sauces. I was in heaven.

The restaurant was nice, but not opulent like some we'd walked past. Gilded decorations said everything I needed to know about those places—the main being I didn't belong in there.

Jace didn't even wait for a table. Brushing past the guy waiting at the door, he headed to a table near the far corner. The view caught my eye first. Floor-to-ceiling windows showed the restaurant perched on the edge of a cliff, practically hanging off it, while the moon reflected off the water below.

Three people sat at the table, smiling warmly at Jace when we approached. The one who apparently couldn't afford an entire shirt wasn't there, much to my relief. All three guys were fairly attractive, and they seemed to be close to our age. Give or take five years. Okay, mostly give, but I wasn't the best judge of age.

"Where's Ben?" Jace asked as he pulled out my chair and then took the seat next to me.

"Went to the other side," the guy with piercing blue eyes said in an accent that made me want to swoon.

"Bummer. I didn't get to say goodbye," Jace said.

"Other side?" I asked, feeling dumb.

"Where you go for your last twenty-four hours. Apparently, it's a major bummer to see dead bodies all over the place. So, when you get close, they sequester you to a certain side of the island," the blue-eyed bombshell explained.

"What? What does that even mean?" Panic stricken, I swung my gaze to Jace. We would be separated for his last twenty-four hours? That was ridiculous. "You'll be alone..."

"Aww, that's sweet, Jacey." Needless to say, the other guy who spouted that line wasn't nearly as attractive, and his attitude was one hundred percent problematic. I glowered, and he snorted as he stabbed at his noodles.

Jace took my hand under the table, then squeezed it. "It'll be fine. Don't think about it now. Let's just enjoy the meal."

The guy next to Jace introduced himself as Brian. His date was in three days. He was fidgety and ate in spurts, shoveling food in like it was going out of style, then freezing like he couldn't remember what he'd been doing a moment ago. All I could think about was whether I'd handle the situation any better. Probably not.

Ben was from a logging zone. Before Withs and Withouts, logging had been one of the deadliest jobs in existence. But once Withs had been assigned to it, no one ever died. That didn't mean people weren't injured. But death always stayed just out of reach.

The snarky guy, Steve, glared down at his pasta while Ben regaled us with a tale of how he'd gotten so badly mangled he wasn't sure how he'd survived one day at work.

"You know, I tried to kill myself once." Steve scoffed. "Who am I kidding? It was more than once."

Everyone stopped what they were doing to stare at him. Food hung midair on our forks, dripping delicious sauce onto our plates. He'd done what?

"I was in the fishing zone. My friends constantly left for

the island. Soon, I was one of the oldest people left. My parents had gone years before, leaving me to fend for myself when I was only twelve."

I'd heard about the fishing zone. It wasn't like my zone, which wasn't so much dangerous as it was unappealing for the Withouts. Fishing and logging would claim the Withouts left and right. And the fishing zone had a pretty high turnover rate.

I studied him a little more closely. He did have the beginnings of grey around his ears, but he couldn't have been older than my folks. How long had he lived alone?

"Funny, but it never worked. Not once. Something always happened. Took a bottle of pills, but I puked them up immediately."

"We don't need details," Jace said, breaking the spell Steve had cast on the table.

"Right," Steve said, returning to stabbing at his food. "Point is, it never worked. And I had to wait my turn in the end. Just so I could die at exactly the right moment. And for what?"

"Hey, Steve, we're just trying to have a good time here," the blue-eyed bombshell said. I still hadn't caught his name.

"Yeah, whatever, Matt. Always the peacekeeper, eh? You and Jace make a nice couple," Steve said with a glare. Jace bristled, but Matt just shook his head.

"I don't know you, but it seems to me you'd get more sympathy if you didn't make everyone want to stab you in the eye." I always did have a knack for making friends.

Ben burst out laughing, but Steve threw his fork down and stormed off.

"Thanks for that. I haven't had a laugh like that in days," Ben said, a bit of a sparkle in his eyes as he moved across the table to Steve's spot so he could see us better.

Once Debbie Downer was gone, we had a good time laughing together and learning about each other. It was strange to hear about other zones and their ways of life. It was like nothing I'd ever experienced. Kids at school never wanted to socialize with Jace and me. We were outsiders together. Work was the same. Everyone was so different from us. Their dates were decades away. They had marriages to look forward to. Milestones. All we had was each other. Yet now, there were others like us. It was like finding something I hadn't known I was missing.

I ate until I couldn't sit up straight anymore. But when they brought out dessert, I obviously found room for it.

When I finally put my fork down in surrender, I pushed away from the table feeling completely gluttonous and delightful.

"Well, Jace. You told us she was lovely, but I thought for sure you were exaggerating. I must say, you undersold her." Jace cocked his head, but for once in his life, he was speechless. So was I. Well, almost.

"Why thank you, Matt. I think."

He nodded in my direction, then wiped his face with his napkin before tossing it on his plate and excusing himself. "See you tomorrow, I'm sure, chums."

"See ya," Ben and Jace said in unison.

"We should go, too."

Ben smiled. "Don't hang around on my account. You know I like to savor the good stuff."

Jace slapped his friend on the back. "Don't mope too much tonight. There's always someone in the game room to commiserate with." Ben nodded, and Jace gave him another slap before turning to me. "You ready?"

There was no bill to settle up. Everything was offered at no cost on the island, so we were free to go.

"Not sure I can move." Truth be told, I wasn't sure how I felt about leaving Ben. He was clearly distraught, but what exactly could I do for him? And how much of my precious time should I waste on a fruitless endeavor? When I thought about it like that, I sounded like the worst person on the face of the planet, so I decided to backspace that entire train of thought and just go with Jace.

Holding out a hand, he waited patiently for me to take it, then led me out. Maybe a walk would do me some good.

The path was smooth and sort of sandy with rocks on either side. The waves were gentler than I'd expected, lapping softly at the cliff below.

"Hey, thanks for playing games with me today."

"Sure. I might do it again." *If I can get my crap together*, I thought.

He chuckled. "Noted."

We walked in silence for a few beats, and I listened to the waves lapping at the shore, forgetting for a moment why we were there. It was bliss.

"I have something for you," Jace said, interrupting my thoughts.

"Oh, yeah?" I raised an eyebrow, skeptical of what he had in mind. Jace wasn't the thoughtful type except when he was drawing. He was strong, steady, and always there when I needed him. It wasn't like we had the means for grandiose gestures anyway. Every year for my birthday, he'd give me a stick figure drawing of himself that he'd deliberately made particularly elementary, then say my gift was him. After, he'd slap me on the back and say, "You're welcome." Every year, I'd laugh. It was perfect.

Needless to say, I wasn't sure what to expect when he handed me a black velvet rectangular box.

"What's this?"

"Well, since we don't have X-ray vision, open it up and see."

My eyebrow went up a little higher as I watched him. I feigned innocence as I carefully eased the box open, afraid something might jump out at me.

But it didn't. Inside was a beautiful rose-gold bracelet with the infinity symbol woven into the band. It was perfect in its simplicity.

"Where did you get this?" I asked, running my thumb along the band, almost afraid to take it out of the box. I'd never owned anything so fine. If I had, we'd probably have sold it for food.

"It's what I got for trading in my tokens. Back at the gaming station."

"What?" Honestly, I wasn't sure what I expected him to get. But this was not even close to what I'd imagined. Certainly not something meaningful.

He smiled. "This is something special." He took it out of the box, then clasped it onto my wrist. His hands were soft, warm, and everything I needed right then.

"Rarity, no matter what happens, I will always love you... and not just as a friend. I'm glad to have the chance to spend the rest of my life with you, and I'm mad as hell there isn't more time left."

I gazed into his dark green eyes. While that sparkle was still there, he wasn't kidding. He meant every word. I felt his statement wash over me, and I realized why the moment was so perfect. I was home.

I took his hands in mine, then rubbed my thumbs over the callouses on his palms. "I feel exactly the same way."

He smiled. "You could've been more eloquent. Like I

was. Don't you want this to be like a brilliant movie or something?"

I snorted, wanting to tell him he'd ruined the moment, but he hadn't. He'd made me laugh. Days away from our deaths, and he could still make me laugh. Home sure felt good.

FIVE

My room was so glamorous I couldn't get comfortable in it right away. I'd slept in a lounge chair out on the balcony the first night. It had suited me fine until Jace found out and insisted I at least try the bed.

"It's like laying on a cloud," he claimed.

"Why is that appealing? Clouds are wet and cold," I pointed out.

"You're being too literal."

I'd shrugged and acted non-committal. But when I'd stared at the huge bed with more pillows than any one person could ever need and a comforter that was so white I felt certain no one had ever used it before me, I couldn't help but wonder what such luxury felt like.

First, I showered. I didn't want to get the gleaming bed dirty. The shower was an experience in and of itself. Jets everywhere coming from all sides of the wall with temperature controls for each zone. Why were there zones in the shower? Like maybe my butt is cold but my head isn't, so fix it, shower water? I wasn't sure I'd ever get my head around the luxuries on the island.

The towel I dried off with was replaced daily, which felt like a waste. I'd hung the soft piece of fluff on the rack the first time I'd used it, but the next day, I found a new one folded neatly on the counter, every bit as soft and fresh as the first. I'd even spoken to Finn about it when I saw him. He'd just smiled and shrugged. "No sense using a dirty towel."

"But it's wasteful," I said. I'd used threadbare towels at home for years before they were replaced with slightly less raggedy towels. And even then, the fabric was repurposed for something else. Stuffing for a chair or whatever. If the Withouts were more...resourceful, would the Withs have to work as hard? The question threatened to let anger take the luxurious experience from me, so I stuffed it down, ignoring the issue altogether.

Once I was dressed in the satin robe hanging on the back of the bathroom door, I had nothing left to do but climb into that giant bed.

I pulled the shimmering robe tighter around myself. "Why would anyone want to sleep on a cloud?" I asked aloud before resigning myself to my fate.

I crossed the room in just a few steps, then stood beside the bed. Should I take the pillows off or just dive in? Before I could change my mind, I jumped up and landed face-first in the massive pile of pillows. I bounced only once before I was buried in them. It wasn't at all like sleeping on a cloud. It was lumpy. At least until I kicked all the pillows off.

I didn't intend to actually get under the covers. I felt I needed to keep that separation between my world and the island. I'd humor Jace by laying on it, but that was it.

But once I was on top of it, I was cold. I could've gotten the blanket I used outside, but it was easier just to get under the covers. And it wasn't at all like sleeping on a cloud. It was the softest, warmest, dreamiest thing I'd ever put my body up against. And that included Jace.

I couldn't help but think about what he'd said to me earlier. It wasn't fair that we had so little time left together. But as I lay there, I just couldn't bring myself to be upset about it. I stared out at the night sky as I listened to the ocean lap gently at the sand. I'd left the big French doors open. In fact, I'd left them open since the moment I'd gotten to the room. They were so big I wasn't sure I could close them by myself. There was no room for bitterness when I was surrounded by such comfort. And it occurred to me that maybe that was the whole purpose of the island.

THE DAYS SLIPPED through my fingers like water, and no matter how tightly I tried to hold onto them, they still leaked through. We spent time with puppies—one of my favorite things. Who knew the little poop shooters could be so much fun? When we snorkeled, I thought about Mom and how much she would love the island. We went back to the gaming wing about six thousand times. Okay, maybe not that many, but it felt like it. Each time, it was a new experience and I loved it. Sometimes, Jace's friends went with us, but the number dwindled as the week went on. One by one, they left for seclusion.

My favorite place was the Tech Wing. Jace tended to draw while I was in there, but he always stayed with me. Right next to me. Just like when we were back in my room. Servers buzzed along, and I always needed a coat in there. It felt like going home, but in a different way. Not in the familiar, warm way my parents felt. In an exciting, soul-satisfying way.

The workers there always said I was a natural, and they

let me take apart anything I wanted. They gave me access to things I'd never dreamed of back home, and I learned more in my time there than I had during my entire schooling in my zone. I could type any question I wanted and get some kind of answer.

Why hasn't a With been president?

Because Withs aren't eligible.

Why?

Laws instituted in 2235 by Thomas Underwell, a successor to BethAnne Mcumban dictated the Withs didn't have fair understanding of life for the Withouts.

Can a With change a law?

Yes. But it's a long, complex process of legislation. Details can be found below.

I didn't always like the answers. But they were there. It really was my own personal Utopia, except for the looming doom of my life, but whatever.

Nevertheless, we spent our days together, growing closer and closer, pushing the boundaries of our friendship a little more with each passing moment. Our friendship blossomed into something deeper. Something *more*.

With only three days left to go until Jace's date, we scheduled an activity he'd been dying to try—rock climbing.

One of the beautiful things about the island was access to every climate and terrain one could possibly want. They even had snow sports at the very top of the mountain Jace intended to climb.

It wasn't my cup of tea, but he wanted me to watch his feat of manliness, so I did. Rather than go digging on the computers in the technology wing, which was what I'd taken to doing when he hung out with his friends. At least before they'd started dwindling.

Two men strapped him into a harness. The straps got a bit personal on him, not leaving a lot to the imagination. I glanced away quickly, but Jace didn't notice. He was too busy pulling on ropes and watching them strap him in.

"You should come with me. I bet the view of this place will be beautiful at the top."

I shrugged. "You know I like to keep my feet firmly planted on the ground."

"The goal isn't to go flying, Rare. I plan to keep my feet planted." He took my hand and pulled me close, then planted a light peck on the end of my nose. "After you see how fun it is, you'll be begging to do it too."

"You want to make a bet? Tomorrow, we'll spend the day at the spa if I win," I challenged.

"No deal. We're going back to the gaming room." He winked, and I stood a little straighter.

"Game on. I'm going to cream you in that new game. I can feel it." They'd announced a fantasy game the other day, the object circled around archery skills, learning spells, and out thinking opponents. It looked like a lot of fun.

"Oh, you do, huh? I dunno, I've been brushing up on my aim at the range with Ben."

Ben had left just two days ago. He'd been the last one.

I cleared my throat. "Yeah, well. It'll take more than good aim to win that game." I nudged him with my shoulder. "Get going. I don't want to stand out here all day."

Jace flashed a smile, the kind that made me very aware of my tongue. I swallowed nervously. "See you from the top," he said.

The worker next to me pulled on the rope in his hands that was strapped to some kind of pulley system that connected to several metal contraptions at his waist. "Got you, Mr. Brown. Whenever you're ready."

Little by little, he pulled himself up the side of that sheer cliff face. Before long, his feet were over my head. Then they were a quarter of the way up. I squinted to try to see him.

"Dang, Jace. When did you become such a mountain goat?" I asked, shading my eyes from the sun.

"It's so beautiful from up here, Rare. I should've brought a canvas and some paints." With access to basically whatever he wanted, Jace had created some beautiful paintings during his stay on the island. He had a natural way of blending colors to create images so real it was almost haunting. He'd even done a portrait of me, and he asked that it be sent back to my parents. They said they'd do it, but I had no idea if they actually would. How would we ever know if they followed through?

"I bet. But then, I'd be waiting down here all day long."

"Some other place you'd rather be, Missy?" he asked as he found another handhold and hoisted himself up.

I glanced around at the beautiful day, the light breeze blowing the hair away from my face. "No, actually, I suppose there isn't."

He made it to the top with relative ease. We all clapped for him at the bottom, and he waved down at me. I waved back, beaming at his accomplishment. All right, so maybe he was right. It had looked like a little bit of fun. And I had to admit I was curious about what it looked like from the top.

"Changed your mind yet, Rare?" he shouted from the top.

"You wish," I lied. No way was I admitting he'd been right. I'd rather die four days early.

Jace chuckled, then slid easily off the relative safely of the cliff and began his descent back down the side of the mountain.

"How's the view from down there?" Jace asked, wiggling his butt.

I snorted. "Not so flattering in all that gear."

"Yeah, well, you like it and you—" He never finished his thought.

"Hang on there, Jace," the man who stood next to me said. Jace struggled with the gear, trying to work out some kind of jam in the linkage. For just that moment, he unhooked the gear to work it out. We both had our eyes on that when a sickening sound made me jerk my head up as the rope was jerked away from the man next to me, leaving Jace completely untethered.

I didn't see the rock go out from under him. I had no idea if it were a handhold or a foothold that crumbled beneath his weight. All I saw was half my heart falling from the side of the rock face.

SIX

My world ran red and white. Blood. I remembered blood. And lots of it. And the workers covered in it, their white uniforms stained crimson as they worked to save him.

I rushed to his side, but they pushed me away. "Jace, I'm here. Don't leave me. Not yet." His date was days away. He couldn't die early, could he? Accidents didn't happen. Not to Withs. This couldn't be happening, could it? It was all a nightmare. Right?

I pinched myself so hard I drew blood, but I still felt like I was in a fog. Workers rushed around me as a gurney suddenly appeared, and they lifted Jace onto it.

"Where are you taking him?" I demanded. Jace looked horribly grey, and it made me want to puke. It was too much. Everything was too much. When I swayed on my feet, one of the workers took my arm.

"Sit down, Ms. Delman. He's going to be all right. You can visit him in the hospital wing in a bit." I blinked up at her. How was she so clean? She seemed out of place.

"Here. Have some water." She held out a bottle to me, and I couldn't process. Jace had just fallen at least fifty feet, and she was offering me water? Her smile never faltered as I struggled to respond to her.

What was I supposed to do? Reach out and take it. Right. Still, such a simple act seemed Herculean in light of what I'd just witnessed. Movement behind her caught my eye, and I saw them wheeling Jace farther away from me.

I sprang to my feet, knocking the bottle of water to the ground. "No, you can't take him from me."

The transport pod was just big enough for the gurney, and a few workers who would hopefully keep him alive. They wheeled him inside it, all while pounding his chest, pushing meds with ridiculously long needles, and barking orders at each other. After the door to the pod sealed itself shut, they took off at lightning speed, leaving me in their wake.

"Jace," I screamed.

"Ms. Delman, your transport will be here momentarily. Just try to be patient."

I rounded on her. "Try to be patient? My best friend is dying—*before* his date, I might add—and you want me to be patient? I've had our last precious days stolen from me, and you're demanding patience?"

Her face softened into a well-schooled image of compassion. I would've believed her if she wasn't dressed in a white uniform declaring her an island worker. She was trained for this. She didn't give two watery craps about Jace or me. Not really. She cared about doing her job.

I shook my head and brushed past her, heading in the direction the copter went.

"If you'd just wait a moment," she called after me.

"Have it catch up with me, why don't you?" I yelled over my shoulder through gritted teeth. I had no idea where the hospital was. But I couldn't just sit there and wait for a transport. I had to move—to get closer to him.

I'd barely made it a hundred yards before the transport pod pulled up next to me. The door opened automatically, and I got into the driverless vehicle.

I sat inside. As the door clicked shut, it was like the weight of what had happened crashed down on me. I collapsed under wave after wave of uncontrollable sobbing. Except every time I closed my eyes, I saw Jace falling. Saw his ashen face as they wheeled him away. Saw his blood on the hands of total strangers.

So I forced my eyes open. The sobbing stopped, but the tears still flowed freely down my cheeks. Was this it? Could he really die on the island before his date?

The woman seemed to think he'd be fine. But she was probably trained to be reassuring, so people wouldn't freak out. Who wanted a crazy person ruining things for the other people on the island? Screaming and lost in her grief. Was that how I'd be in a few days when he died when he was supposed to? I shook the thought away. I didn't think about the time without him on purpose. It would be here soon enough.

I toyed with the bracelet he'd given me when I first got to the island. It felt like a lifetime had gone by since then. At the same time, it somehow felt as if it had happened only seconds before. Turned out our infinity would be cut even shorter. The thought made hot, angry tears trail down my face.

By the time the pod arrived at the hospital, I was a mess of anger, confusion, and fog.

"Welcome to the island hospital. Enjoy your stay," the transport vehicle said in a pleasant automated voice.

I jumped out and ran inside without responding to the

creepy voice. The grounds were well groomed, just like every other place on the island. Green grass and evenly trimmed bushes lined the sidewalks on both sides. Such a stark contrast to home with its dead bushes, overgrown trees, and weedy yards. Lawn care just wasn't a priority for anyone in our zone. Food. Fresh water. Finding slightly less holey clothes. Those things always seemed more important.

The glass door slid open with a bit of a whoosh as I approached, and chilly air spilled out, making goose bumps rise on my arms. I wouldn't think sterile would smell like anything. But the white-on-white hospital had a distinct odor of cleaner and illness that made me want to recoil. But I held fast to my mission—get to Jace.

Running to the front desk, I nearly crashed into it as I came to a screeching halt in front of a woman seated at a computer. She wore an all-white uniform not unlike the other workers on the island.

"Can I help you?" she asked with that same air of pleasantness.

"Jace Brown. Where is he?"

She typed more than it seemed was necessary for the little bit of information I'd given her, and I shifted impatiently.

I was just about to prompt her when she spoke up. "Ah, here he is. Sneaky little devil." I narrowed my eyes. Was she trying to joke with me? Now? "Go through those doors and to the elevator. He's on the third floor."

"Thanks," I said, suddenly willing to overlook the previous comment since she'd given me his location. Third floor. It wasn't the basement. So he wasn't dead. Right? Never mind the fact I was making a huge assumption about the morgue being in the basement. I would blindly cling to whatever hope was tossed my way, thank you very much.

When I crashed through the double doors, I nearly took out someone on the other side. But he was the one who said, "Excuse me," even though the incident was clearly my fault.

I couldn't acknowledge him. I couldn't waste precious time. I had to get to Jace. Now.

I mashed the button for the elevator with a shaking finger, and the damned thing took an eternity to come. Slow, deep breaths, I kept reminding myself. But the more times I said it, the more impatient I got for the elevator, so I jabbed the button three more times for good measure.

Finally, the world's slowest elevator arrived, and I climbed inside. Someone got off, and I nearly bowled them over trying to get in. I pushed the button for three, and the door stayed open. I pushed it again two more times for good measure. Finally, the door slid shut.

I swear I aged thirteen years in the amount of time it took that elevator to rise three floors. Six thousand deep breaths later, the doors opened, and there was another woman sitting at an identical desk to the one downstairs.

"Jace Brown." I called to her from across the room. No need to waste time walking up to her. Let her get started with all that typing.

Glancing at me, she nodded before getting to work. She was still scrolling through information when I got to her desk. What was so hard? It wasn't like he was in any kind of condition to move around on them.

"Oh honey, I'm sorry. I don't have that name here. When did he come in?"

"Just now. The lightning-fast transport pod brought him in." My voice shook as I tried to maintain control. It wasn't her fault. She was trying to help. *Don't bite her head off.*

"Oh, the pod. Then he's topside. Go up to the four-teenth floor. You'll find him there for sure."

"I..." I started to protest, but I realized it was futile. It didn't make sense to me. The pod was a ground vehicle. Why would he be at the top? But I didn't argue. She was the one looking at the screen, so she must've known better than me. I'd have to get back in that elevator. There were too many floors to take the stairs.

Molasses flowed faster in January than that elevator moved. When it finally dinged and the doors opened, I dove inside. Luckily, there was no one in it this time. But the button for the top floor wasn't lit up, and it wouldn't respond when I pushed it. Plus, as I examined at the panel, the fourteenth floor wasn't the top. So which one was it?

"You worthless piece of..." I frowned at the keypad in front of me. "You had *one* job." I pushed the button for fourteen harder than was necessary, and the doors closed.

I'd sung two verses of an old song Jace and I used to sing during our lunch breaks at work before we got yelled at by the time the doors opened again and dumped me off on the fourteenth floor. But as soon as they opened, I knew he wouldn't be there.

An identical desk greeted me on the other side of the elevator doors, but it was abandoned. No one mingled around on this floor or in beds in the rooms I walked past. Nothing beeped. I felt lucky the lights were on.

I had to go up one more to find him. She said topside, so that was where I was going. I needed stairs. Not more typing from some woman at a desk.

I ran to the double doors and pushed through them, thinking stairs would be in the corners of the hospital. Luckily for me, I was right. Unluckily for me, they required a key card to open the door to the top floor.

"Are you freaking kidding me?" I yelled, my voice echoing in the concrete stairwell.

If he were there, how on earth was I going to get to him if the floor was locked down?

Plopped down on the top step, I put my head in my hands. How had things gotten so out of control? This wasn't how things were supposed to play out. We were Withs. We weren't supposed to have such chaos in our lives. Suddenly, I felt the slightest hint of sympathy for the Withouts. They lived with this threat every minute of every day. It was no wonder they couldn't function normally and needed every indulgence to relieve the stress.

No. I didn't need indulgences. I needed a solution. Rising, I studied the steel door, trying it one more time for good measure. But it was locked good. And no amount of beating on it would make it budge. On the wall next to the door, a black screen and some kind of scanning device defied me.

I wondered if I could hack it. It wasn't all that different from Frank, right? Or the machines I'd dissected in the tech wing. Yes, they'd let me do that. More than once. And it was a blast. I'd learned quickly to use their screens to navigate and manipulate things on the island, as well as work in the tech wing. Here, in that hospital staring at their security measures, there was nothing I could do without one of those damned screens. I didn't think I could hack it by disconnecting wires. I'd need time and tools for that matter. And I was severely lacking in both.

I glared at the security measures, knowing Jace was behind that door. All I had to do was get inside. The rest would play out easily. Or so I told myself.

Deciding I wasn't getting anywhere trying to use my will to force the door to open, I went back down one floor. If nothing else, I could get some tools. Maybe even swipe a screen and hack the system, because clearly a few days in the tech wing made me an expert. Maybe it was the gravity of the situation, but I somehow knew I'd figure it out with the right tools or die trying. Heck, maybe inspiration would strike with a brilliant and safe way to get to him.

And strike it did. Right in my freaking face. Just as I was returning to the fourteenth floor, someone burst through the stairwell door, hitting me full on in the face. I careened back, smacking into the concrete wall behind me. The surprised man reached out to try to steady me.

"Oh my God, are you okay?" he asked as he produced a swath of gauze out of his pocket.

I held it to my nose, my eyes widening as I watched it turn red. "I'm fine." I spied the ID clipped to his pocket, and I couldn't help but wonder if that would work on the door upstairs.

"What are you doing in here?" he asked as he put pressure on my nose and eased me down to the ground.

As he reached for me, I couldn't help but notice the numbers emblazoned on his own arm in the white, short-sleeved scrubs he wore. He was a With. Just like me. All the workers here wore long sleeves. I'd never once seen a date on anyone. But it made sense they would be Withs. Without wouldn't want to deal with the likes of us. Serving people just wasn't on the top-ten most desired jobs list.

"You're a With." It slipped out of my mouth as he was tipping my head back, examining my nose. Not my most attractive angle.

"I am. But I've got a good long time before my date. Not like—" He stopped dead, realizing how his words sounded. "I mean…"

"Nope. No repairing that one, man. It's all right. The vultures aren't circling quite yet."

Chuckling nervously, he went back to poking at my

nose, which wasn't the most comfortable feeling in the world. "So, what were you doing in here?" he asked again, expertly trying to change the subject.

"Just looking for a friend of mine." The half-truth sounded a lot more convincing coming through the mound of gauze. Amazing how being slightly pathetic would make people not ask questions.

"Well, where are they? I can take you there after we get that looked at." The concern in his eyes told me he just wanted to help. But I couldn't let him take me away. I had to get closer to Jace.

"No, I'm fine. It'll quit in a second. Thank you." I held up my hand, trying to solidify my point. But I could tell by the way his eyebrow cocked toward his hairline that he wasn't buying it.

"At least let me go grab some supplies to help you clean up. I can even get you a new shirt if you want, so you don't have to go back to your room covered in blood."

I glanced down at myself. Was I really covered? I had no idea if it was all mine or mixed with Jace's. But I had no desire to change.

Still, I needed him to go. But not before I relieved the man of his ID. I eyed the badge, knowing I wasn't smooth in the least. Nope. I was the one who tripped over my own feet reaching for a toothbrush.

Thankfully, he wasn't watching me. He was studying my nose and the saturated gauze. "That gauze is toasted. Let me go get some more. I'll be right back."

As he stood to go, I leaned forward, pretending to be unprepared for him to step away from me. He leaned in to help me stabilize, and I snatched his ID right off him. I brushed against him for good measure to cover the jerking motion on his shirt, then quickly held the ID behind my back.

"You sure you don't want to come with me?" He eyed me, and I wondered if playing the unstable card was the smartest thing to do.

"I'm fine. Really. Going to get gauze is already too much fuss."

"It's the least I can do. I'm Brian."

"Rarity. Nice to meet you, Brian."

He smiled kindly, and it surprised me that I didn't even feel bad about stealing from him. He wanted to help me, and his badge would be how he did it. It didn't matter he might not approve.

He propped me up against the wall. I let him after I stashed his ID under my butt, then held the gauze against my nose with both hands to keep any possible suspicions at bay.

"I'll be right back. Don't go anywhere."

I chuckled, hoping it didn't sound too fake. "Where am I gonna go, Brian? Not exactly in marathon condition here."

"Maybe not, but something tells me you have no interest in sitting in the stairwell."

Well, his instincts were right on. "Well, it's not my first choice to spend time in my last few days, but I trust you won't keep me sitting here that long."

His expression made it clear he disapproved but appreciated the effort to make it positive, so I knew I had him.

"Fine. I'll be right back. I mean it."

"I believe you," I said. And I did. I didn't have any time at all to get up and make that black security screen work in my favor—all while trying not to leave a trail of blood drops from my mangled nose behind. No need to lead Brian right to me.

Reluctantly, he stood and went to the door. "Right back," he reiterated as he opened the door and turned to me.

I nodded. "I'll be here."

When he frowned, it was obvious he knew I lied, but he left against his better judgment. I thought he wanted to believe me, but his face told me he knew he shouldn't.

As soon as the door slammed home, I was taking the steps two at a time, trying not to fall on my face and make matters worse.

Peering over my shoulder as I reached the solid metal door, I jammed his ID into the slot above the scanner. Who needed tools when I had a keycard?

The screen lit up with a bunch of numbers made to look like buttons. Great. A code. I needed a freaking code. What exactly were they hiding behind this door that I needed security clearance level one million to get through?

I ground my teeth into oblivion.

The problem with security clearance codes was that they were nearly impossible to guess. There were so many different combinations of numbers. Statistically speaking, I'd never guess the right ones. If I'd had a screen or something from the Tech Wing, I might be in business, but all I had was Brian's ID card. Something I praised him for a moment ago, I found myself cursing at this new roadblock.

Then, the numbers on my arm caught my attention, and I decided to try them. Hastily, I punched in the last four numbers of my date, but the screen turned red and beeped threateningly at me.

"Crap on a cracker," I said through clenched teeth. Then I remembered seeing Brian's numbers on his arm and our conversation about it. When I typed them in to the keypad, it miraculously turned green.

"Thank you, Brian," I whispered as I yanked his ID free

and pulled the heavy door open, filing the six numbers away in my mind, hoping I wouldn't need them again.

As if the high-security entrance wasn't enough to deter me, I knew by the stark contrast of this floor to the rest of the hospital I wasn't supposed to be there. Where the décor downstairs was white, it was silver here. Silver doors against metal-lined walls and concrete floors formed a narrow hallway, making me wonder what was behind each. Sophisticated technology at every single doorway kept people like me out. Was lifesaving equipment so valuable they had to keep it under lock and key? How bad off was Jace that he needed to be up here? Would I ever get to talk to him again? We didn't even get to say goodbye.

The harsh fluorescent lighting flickering above my head didn't help the ambiance. Everything about the place screamed *run. Go. Leave. Now.*

I itched to follow my instincts, but the ones that knew Jace was somewhere inside held my feet in place.

As I stared down the seemingly endless hallway, I wondered how I would ever find him in such a place and what shape he'd be in. I only knew that as long as I drew breath, I'd look for him. I wouldn't let them win. I'd get my goodbye.

SEVEN

I couldn't just stand there and expect Jace to suddenly appear in front of me. I had to move.

One foot in front of the other, Rare. My breath thundered in my ears, and it made me feel conspicuous. But as I made my way to the first door, no one appeared.

Cautiously, I peeked in the long, narrow window. There were two beds with one patient in each. Bingo. I was on the right track. There were wires and tubes poking out of them in all directions, and I caught sight of a person dressed in blue tapping on a handheld screen like the ones I'd used in the tech wing.

I darted away from the window, as if my seeing her would bring her attention straight to me.

I wracked my brain for what I'd seen. Had any of them looked like Jace? I couldn't say for sure. Either way, I couldn't go barging in there with a nurse standing over the far bed.

Oh hey, I'm here to see my friend, nothing amiss here. Especially not a hot mess with a busted nose that stole some-

one's ID to be here. Derisively, I snorted at my lame thoughts.

As I moved farther down the hall, each room I peeked in appeared identical. Two beds, lots of machines, and a nurse keeping watch over the patients. If Jace were in one of these rooms, I'd never get in to see him. Would it be enough to know he was alive and well cared for? I tried to tell myself it was. Or it would be. But I could taste the lie just as easily as I realized there was something off in the air of that floor.

When I rounded a corner, a sign pointed toward the *Longevity Wing*—whatever that meant—so I followed it.

Why would Jace be in the Longevity Wing? He had less than three days left. Not long by anyone's standards. Trying to ignore my unanswered questions, I focused on finding Jace. I realized my nose had quit bleeding, and I needed some place to stash the sopping gauze. But there were no trash receptacles in the hall. There was nothing but metal and doors.

I peeked into the next room, my breath catching at the sight. Could the person in that bed possibly be him or was I seeing what I wanted? The patient's hair was almost exactly the same shade as Jace's, but it wasn't much to go on. His face was almost completely obstructed by tubes. My only advantage was there wasn't a watchful nurse around at the moment.

I took out Brian's ID card, praying he could get me inside. He'd gotten me this far, right?

The screen was just like the one outside, so I jammed the ID card into the slot and punched in the numbers, hoping beyond hope it would work. Lo and behold, the door clicked open. I slipped inside, holding it behind me so it wouldn't make a sound as it closed.

"Jace?" I asked as I approached the seemingly uncon-scious figure. His chest rose and fell almost mechanically. I chewed my bottom lip as I closed the distance. If it was him, at least he was alive. But would he be unconscious until his date? Did they save him just enough to unhook him at the appointed time? Anger rose in the back of my throat like bile as I took two more steps toward the unconscious figure.

"What on earth are *you* doing in here?"

The woman's voice startled me so badly I nearly jumped into bed with Jace.

"You can't be here," she said as she made her way around the second empty bed. She put herself between me and the only way out of the room. She was dressed in blue scrubs, her brown hair pulled into a tight bun that made me wonder if her face was really wrinkle free or if her hair was just that tight.

"I just..."

"You what?" she demanded. But she didn't seem angry or authoritarian. She seemed scared.

"I'm looking for my friend."

I glanced at the person on the bed. His eyes were closed and his hair was right, but seeing him up close, I realized it wasn't him. I'd blown my cover for no reason. It was over.

The tears came hard and fast, and there was nothing I could do to stop them.

The nurse's brown eyes filled with compassion, and she put a hand on my shoulder. "Oh, love. Who is he?"

Because all I could manage was that super embarrassing hiccup sob and couldn't form understandable words, I only shook my head.

The nurse half smirked before leading me toward the empty bed next to the poor unconscious soul I'd thought was Jace. Who was he? And where was his family? Why was he here? Why were there so many people here? What happened to them? Were they all hurt in accidents on the island? What exactly was the "Longevity Wing?" So many questions that never made it out of my mouth because of the incredibly flattering ugly crying.

"Here, sit down. Do you want some water?" She set her screen on the bed next to me, then reached for a glass pitcher and poured me some of the clearest water I'd ever seen.

I drank big gulps of water around the hiccups, willing the sobbing to stop. The nurse sat beside me, taking my hand as her eyes occasionally darted to the door. Deciding to ignore that, I focused on my own problems.

When my glass was empty, I stared at my lap. The nurse didn't pressure me to talk or leave, even though I could tell her stress level was at about a million percent. The fact she kept swallowing hard and glancing at the door were my only indications she was in panic mode. Probably because of me.

"His name is Jace Brown."

It had been so long since I'd spoken, my words startled her. Jumping, she scrambled for her screen. "Great. Let's start with his name." She went to work, jabbing away at the device. I marveled at how quickly she moved from screen to screen. Could I have been that skilled if I'd been allowed to do what I wanted instead of sorting trash? Was this what *she* wanted to be doing?

"What made you think he would be here?"

"The woman downstairs said he might be on the top floor."

Her breath hitched, but she covered it quickly. "Did she now? And how did you get in here?"

Blushing, I relinquished Brian's ID card without a

word. What was the point now? I'd been caught red-handed.

"Ah. I see. And your face?"

"Brian hit me with the door. I absconded with his credentials while he was off trying to get me some gauze. I feel a little bad about it, to be honest. But I needed to find Jace."

"You know, this would be funny if it weren't so terrifying." She chuckled, which got me giggling. And that led to full-on laughter from us both until a different kind of tears down our cheeks.

She took a deep breath. "Man, I haven't laughed like that in ages. What's your name?"

"Rarity."

"That's beautiful. I'm Max. It's a pleasure to meet you."

"Max, what are all these people doing here?" But as soon as the question was out, I regretted it. All the joy drained out of her, leaving the fear she'd had earlier when I came in.

"Let's just find Jace, okay? What happened to him?"

"He fell off the rock-climbing mountain."

"So he was a trauma. Okay. Here he is. Room two sixty-four. Looks like he's settled in and resting comfortably. They have him on accelerated recovery. He should be ready to go back to his room tonight. Not even twelve hours lost. Still, the island won't look kindly on having to take that kind of time from him. Particularly when he's so close to his date." Her green eyes were sad. "I'm sorry."

I couldn't believe my ears. It was the best news I'd heard since that sickening sound when he'd hit the ground. When I threw my arms around her, she breathed out a short laugh.

"Thank you. Are you sure? Because I've been told he was in three different places."

"Do you want to see him?"

"You can do that?" I blinked, suddenly aware of who might be watching our little exchange and starting to understand why she was so nervous.

"Of course. Here." She tapped on the screen, and it brought up a video feed. Jace wasn't even hooked up to any machines. He appeared to be sleeping. His face was only slightly bruised. He had one arm over his chest, the other down by his side. No casts, no breathing tubes. Only a simple IV in his arm with a heart monitor blinking constantly near his head.

"He's okay?" I asked, not sure I wanted to hear the answer.

"He's fine, love. He's probably just missing you."

"Why didn't they just tell me where he was in the first place?" I asked, baffled as I continued to watch his chest rise and fall, certain the next time it fell, it wouldn't rise again. But it always did.

"Traumas move around until they're stable. We don't get too many of those in up here. So the girls downstairs probably don't know how to track them properly." She was so nonchalant about it. Like, *duh, Rarity.*

"Thank you so much, Max. I won't forget this." I jumped from the bed, and her face grew even more frightened as she reached for me.

"Wait. What are you doing?"

"Going to him. Why?"

"Well, you're not going to just walk out of here, are you?"

"That was my plan...why?"

She glanced over my shoulder, then shoved me onto the bed more roughly than I'd expected from her.

"Hey, what—"

"Someone's coming."

When she threw the blanket over me, I started to protest, terror taking over.

"Just relax."

Someone she obviously thought would be a problem was coming and she wanted me to relax? Sure... no big deal.

"Maxine, everything all right in here?" The man's voice seemed friendly enough, but Max wasn't buying it. She was guarded as she stood in front of me.

I squeezed my eyes shut, hoping to block out the world or fake being unconscious. I was fairly sure I was epically failing at both.

"Yes, sir. Everything's fine. Just waiting for processing on this one."

Crap on a cracker, she was drawing attention to me?

"They haven't been through yet? She isn't even hooked up?"

"Not yet. They just rolled her in and left her here."

"How long has she been out?"

"Not long. They gave her the shot right before they left. We have time."

He hesitated, and I held my breath. "Well, if you're not concerned, I'll leave you to it. But ping them if they're not here in the next few minutes. In fact, I'll remind them on my way out."

"Oh no, that's fine, Michael. I'm sure they're just busy. I heard a bunch came in today. They're probably just backed up."

"I'll come back and check on you in a bit, just to make sure."

"If you want to. You certainly don't have to trouble yourself."

"I know that. You're perfectly competent. One of our

best. But that doesn't mean they should be taking advantage of you. I'll be back," he promised before I heard the door click shut.

"Come on," she whispered. "We have to get you out of here."

I sat up, throwing the blanket off me. "Why are you doing this?" I asked, baffled by the fact she would put her job on the line to save me. But from what exactly? I was a With in her last few days. I should've been invincible.

"Because you don't deserve this. Go find Jace and live the crap out of your last few days. For me. Okay?"

"What do you mean? What is happening to them?" I asked, but she pulled on my arm and dragged me toward the door.

"Never you mind. Spend your time getting back to Jace. Don't think another moment about this place. Okay?" She stared hard at me, and I could tell by her pleading eyes that it was important. "I'll get you out of here, but don't come back. Promise?"

"Max, I..."

"Promise," she insisted.

"Promise." What else could I do? I felt like I was missing an opportunity at a friendship and that didn't happen much. But I was probably already starting to smell sour, since my expiration date was so close. No need to put her through the heartache.

"Fine. Let's get you out of here." When she peeked out the window, she tensed. There must've been more activity out there than there was when I came in.

"No. This isn't going to work. You stay here. I'll be right back. If someone comes in, get back in that bed and pray."

"What—" But she didn't wait for me to finish my question. She darted out, and I watched her disappear around the corner.

Just to be safe, I got in bed and covered up. I didn't want them discovering me. But what if someone came in? What would they do to me? Would I be connected to machines like the poor soul next to me?

I couldn't even think about it without breathing like I'd just run five miles.

When I heard the door open, I squeezed my eyes shut harder than before, clutching the blanket close to my chin. Discreet, I know.

"Rarity," Max whispered as the door clicked shut behind her. Something landed on my lap, and I opened my eyes. "Put those on."

A set of blue scrubs like the ones she wore laid on the bed. "Hurry," she said, and I scrambled out of bed. Somehow, discretion wasn't a concern in that moment. Max was a nurse after all and I was in a bit of a time crunch, so I peeled off my bloody clothes and donned the scrubs.

"Take this, too." She handed me Brian's credentials, and I didn't know what to say.

"Okay. Go out the same way you came in. Down the hall there to the stairwell. Then go down to the second floor. That's where you'll find Jace. Remember his room number?"

"Two sixty-four."

She nodded. "I can't go with you. It would look weird. And if they found my room abandoned, I'd be sunk."

Once again, I threw my arms around her. "Thank you. For everything."

"Don't thank me yet. You're not out of here. Do your best to look casual as you walk toward the door."

"I didn't see anyone when I came in. Do you really think I will on my way out?"

Frowning, she nodded. What did she know that I didn't?

"Go. Before Michael sends someone to check on you."

"What will you tell him?" I nodded toward the empty bed, and she shrugged.

"I'll tell him they moved you to another room. You weren't stable or something. Happens all the time." She sounded more confident than she looked, but that could've been because I still stood in her room.

"Okay. Well, goodbye then." It seemed pathetic. I had no idea what she was saving me from or what it was costing her, but I got the distinct impression it was a lot.

"Goodbye, Rarity." A small smile pulled at the corner of her mouth. "The name suits you."

"Thanks. See you on the other side." She nodded as I took a breath and opened the door, stepping out into the hallway.

The door clicked shut softly behind me. As soon as I started walking away, a man popped out of the room two doors down from mine.

"Hello," he said, his voice distinctly familiar.

"Hello," I said as I kept walking down the hall, hoping he wouldn't acknowledge me more. Once I rounded the corner, I let out a breath I hadn't known I was holding. I was less than fifty steps to the stairwell door. No one was around. Forty. Thirty. Twenty. Ten.

A woman's voice stopped me dead in my tracks. "Hey, where are you going?"

Poke me in the eye with a hot iron. This was the last thing I needed. "I'm just going downstairs for some more supplies."

"What do you need? We should have everything up here."

Insistent little— "Gauze." Creative, I knew, but it was the only thing that came to mind. "The closet is empty and my patient's arm is oozing. I'll be right back."

"You know you're not supposed to leave the floor." What the... Did the nurses live here? Were they prisoners, too? What kind of hospital was this?

"I'll be right back. And my patient needs it. I thought we were supposed to make them our priority. No matter what."

Her eyes narrowed, but the sigh that escaped her told me she was buying it. "Fine. But if you get caught, don't expect me to rescue you."

"Fair enough. Put gauze on the supply list, will you?"

She snorted. "Why, is your screen broken? You do it."

Snotty little thing. Suddenly, I was glad I'd walked into Max's room instead of hers.

I closed the last ten feet to the door, then used Brian's credentials one last time to free me from the prison I'd wandered into.

Room 264. Jace. I was almost there.

EIGHT

I hesitated outside the door. Even though I'd seen him on the screen, I was still scared. Was he still there or had they moved him again? Was he stable? Would I find my best friend there? There was only one way to find out.

I pulled on the silver doorknob, then heaved the heavy door open to find Jace sitting up, alert, and only attached to an IV line. No breathing machines. No blood. Not even a heart monitor anymore. He'd changed since I saw him on the video. Rapid recovery indeed.

"You're a sight for sore eyes," he said, chipper as ever.

"Jace. You'll never believe—"

I was cut off by a doctor breezing into his room, a middle-aged man with a white lab coat and jet-black hair. He didn't even take notice of me. "Mr. Brown. I believe you're all set for release. One last check of your vitals and you'll be good to go. Try not to take any more nasty falls, okay?"

"Sure, Doc." Jace's tone changed to patronizing, and he rolled his eyes. The doctor didn't even notice, too busy flipping through things on his screen.

"Good. The nurse has the parameters for your release. As long as you hit them, you're good to go."

"Great. Hope I never see you again," Jace said.

That made the doctor finally look up and genuinely see his patient. "Yes. Me too, Mr. Brown."

The nurse came in just as the doctor left, and she looked me up and down. "That's an odd choice of wardrobe. Where did you get that?" the red-haired woman asked me as she pumped a blood pressure cuff on Jace's arm.

"Oh, it's a long story."

Her eyes narrowed, and Jace yelped as the cuff got bigger and bigger. "Watch it," he said.

She appeared startled, then released some of the air while turning her attention back to him. He silently questioned me, but I shook my head. Not there. Not then. Especially with Miss Sherlock Stick My Nose in Your Business Holmes between us.

The next several moments were tense. She listened to Jace's heart, made him take deep breaths, and generally fussed about him like he was some Prince of Persia. Finally, she unhooked his IV, put a bandage over the needle stick, and sighed.

"Well, you're free to go. Don't come back."

He stood gingerly, but he seemed pleased with how his body held him up. "You know, the doctor said the same thing. I'm beginning to think you guys don't like me."

Nurse Suspicious McNoseInMyBusiness didn't even crack a smile, nor did she say anything to dispute him.

"Yes. Well. The feeling is mutual," he said with very little humor as he grabbed my hand, sending tingles shooting up my arm. A smile I couldn't even hope to hide grew on my face, and the nurse glared at me even harder. "Come on, Rare. Let's get out of here."

"My pleasure," I said, meaning it with every fiber of my being.

We hurried to the elevator, and didn't speak as we rode down to the first floor. But when those doors opened, we could see the glass double doors beckoning us out of that prison. We exchanged a glance before we started to run flat out for the exit, laughing as we went. Jace was next to me, and he was fine. Everything was fine. The laughter bubbled out of me on its own accord as we nearly smacked into the glass doors before they slid open.

A transport pod waited for us at the curb, and we hopped inside.

"Did they order this for you, or are there always transport cars here?" I asked.

He shrugged without letting go of my hand. "Heck if I know." His smile never faded.

"I know I smacked my head pretty hard, but I could swear you weren't wearing that when we went hiking. And your nose..." Obviously, I wasn't winning any beauty contests any time soon. "What happened?"

I glanced around, unsure of the transport car and how much the powers-that-be could hear inside it.

I shook my head. "I'll tell you later. For now, tell me about what happened. How did you recover so fast?"

Jace gave a slight shake of his head. "Honestly, I don't know what happened. I remember being on the mountain. And then I was in that room and you were nowhere to be seen. But when I questioned them, they said I'd be free to go in a few hours and I could find you then."

"Did they tell you what happened?" I asked, wondering why they hadn't been more forthcoming.

"All they said was I fell during my rock-climbing expedition, and they were sorry I'd lost some of my time on the island."

"The medic on the mountain said the same thing to me." I gazed out the window, trying and failing to put the pieces together.

Jace followed my gaze. His voice dropped low, more bitterness than I was used to hearing from him in his tone. "Seems foolish to use all those resources on me just so I can die at the right moment, just a few days from now. What exactly do they hope I'll accomplish? It's not like I'm going to save the world or do something valuable with the time they've given me. I'm trapped on this island."

I tried not to be hurt by his raw words. "Trapped with me," I said quietly.

He jerked around and grabbed my hands, holding them tightly. "That isn't what I meant, and you know it."

"Well, what did you mean then?"

"I just meant why? Why do it at all unless they expect something from me."

"Something like what? Maybe it's just a policy they don't let people die until their appointed time."

"You're right. I know you are. But it just feels like a lot of pressure. Do you know what they'd give for that kind of technology back home?"

My mind wandered to my dad. A few years back, he got hurt at work. He'd been standing in the wrong place at the wrong time, and a load was dumped on him. He was out of work for a month, and his boss hated him for it. Like, genuinely hated him. Blamed him for their processing reduction. Dad nearly died, but they did just enough to save him. He had to do the rest on his own.

And yet, on this island, they saved Jace like it was nothing so he could live for two more days. What could our lives have been like if Dad had access to that kind of technology?

I tried to push the dark thoughts out of my head. With so little time left to our names, we shouldn't waste it on things we couldn't control. Or some sort of motivational poster like that. Right?

"I know." It was all I could think to say. Suddenly our last few days together seemed bleak and bitter. And that wasn't what they were supposed to be about.

I took a deep breath. "We can't let this ruin what time we have left together. We won't get these moments back. So let's just forget it and move on."

"Can we do that?" he asked, clearly hopeful we could.

"We have to." Our gazes dropped and we both gazed out our own windows, watching the scenery of the utopian island go by. But it wasn't utopian anymore, was it? We'd seen its underbelly, and it was hard to forget that kind of mix up.

As we bumped along, I realized I didn't get to tell him what I saw. But what had I seen? The Longevity Ward. Max. What could I say when I hadn't understood any of it?

When he stood, he interrupted my thoughts and basically dragged me out of the car. Apparently, we'd come to a stop, but I'd been so deep in my mind. I hadn't noticed.

We walked hand in hand toward my room, but he didn't press me. I didn't press him, either. It wasn't our normal comfortable silence, though. We were both trying to make sense of our circumstance and coming up desperately short.

My room was just as I'd left it all those hours ago. How much time had passed since we'd gone rock climbing? Night had fallen long ago, and exhaustion threatened to creep in at the back of my mind. But the questions circling in my head refused to release me.

I walked out to the balcony, and Jace trailed after me.

"Jace, I don't understand."

I leaned over the balcony, watching the stars above us twinkle in ways they never did back home. The sky was so clear here. Even when it rained, it was beautiful, smelled clean, and almost demanded we dance in it. But at what cost? Those people in the beds...what did it mean?

Jace put his hand on mine as he leaned on the rail next to me. "What don't you understand?"

The entire story of my search for him spilled out. He said nothing as I explained about finding the secured floor, seeing those people, Max and her fear of me being in there, and how Nurse Suspicious watched me, as if she knew where I'd been.

Jace frowned as he gazed over the water, watching it twinkle in the moonlight. "Did you know people can donate themselves to research?"

I sort of did, but it didn't seem like something people would actually do. "Research for what?"

"Immortality. But first, they're pushing the limits of our dates. They think if they can keep someone alive past their date, it'll be some key to immortality. The first step, so to speak. To the end of dates, Withs, and Withouts."

I started to speak, but the words wouldn't come, so my mouth hung open like some kind of super-attractive gaping seagull. "What?"

Jace snorted. "Yup. My parents are part of the program."

That was just as much of a shock as finding out people thought they could find immortality by doing what? Living in a vegetative state?

"I don't understand. How are they researching that? What are they doing to find immortality?"

"That's not really the important part, is it? What matters is they take Withs, like us, who have known expiration dates, and instead of sending them to the island, they spend their last two weeks in a coma, trying to be the one who unlocks the key to immortality." The disgust in his voice made the words heavy and hard to comprehend.

"And your parents are doing this?" His parents' dates were decades from now. Even long after my own parents. They'd outlive us all, unfortunately. Mom always said the mean ones lived forever.

"Yup. They tried to force me into it, but I said no." He snorted bitterly. "It was my last disappointment. They thought they could talk me into it right up until I left."

"Is that why you wouldn't talk to them?" I could sense the tension before he'd gone, but now I knew why. He didn't buy into their brainwashing.

He nodded. "They haven't even had any luck helping someone survive. And for what? To spend your whole life slaving away, to waste your last two weeks getting poked, prodded, and experimented on?" He scoffed. "No thanks. I just don't believe in what they're doing. Immortality is a myth. It's fiction. Everything dies. Eventually." He absentmindedly covered his own date with his hand. "Some sooner than others."

"But a world without dates. Without Withs or Withouts. Think of it."

"That's our past. We've evolved beyond it. And we will continue to do so until we destroy ourselves."

"But what are we evolving to, Jace? All Withs? Then what?"

"Who knows and who cares? We won't be here to see it." It was an attempt at a joke, but it fell flat.

He was right. Why should I spend my last moments on

this earth worrying about the choices of others? Who cared if what they were doing felt horribly wrong? They were doing it willingly. They knew what they were getting into, right?

"Exactly how much did they tell you about that volunteer research program?"

"Not much. Just that it would be painless, and we'd likely be in a coma for the last two weeks of our lives instead of living our best life on the island."

"So basically, they knock you out, do whatever they want to you in the name of finding immortality, and then you die on your date anyway, because all experiments thus far have failed?"

He nodded. "Pretty much."

"And your parents were gung-ho about this?"

"Yup. Awesome, huh?"

I shook my head. "Boy, we sure made a mess of this day, didn't we?"

He chuckled. "Speak for yourself. I went rock climbing."

I nudged him, and he returned the gesture. "So what do you want to do tomorrow?" I asked, trying to change the subject.

"Not dwell on today."

"Sounds ideal."

But was it? No. Not really at all. But it was the best we could do with the lemons we were given. That rhino was getting closer and closer. He almost took us out today, but we managed to jump out of the way. Unfortunately, I knew he was circling back around.

All I had to do was enjoy the time I had before he came barreling into me.

NINE

We decided to pretend the whole climbing incident hadn't happened. And we did pretty well with it for the most part. We were moody teenagers so we had our moments, but we still embraced the island life. After rock climbing, I made Jace do some things I wanted to do.

First, we played with puppies again. There was an entire area of baby animals, and puppies were there in force. We picked a bunch of Golden Retrievers and had a blast. Those little buggers were exhausting, climbing all over us, covering us in kisses, and never tiring of playing.

Then, we went to get massages. Jace said it was good to get the dog slobber cleaned off him, but it was obvious he enjoyed it, too. He lumbered out of there with his eyes at half mast, so we walked to the double hammocks where he took a nap.

But I couldn't sleep. In a matter of hours, they would take him from me. Take him to the other side of the island— to where people went to die.

"Jace?" I finally whispered after a while.

He groaned and rolled over, forgetting he was in a

hammock. In two shakes, he was flat on the ground with a face full of sugar white sand.

I tried and failed not to react. "Smooth," I said, giggling.

"What do you want? I was sleeping." Brushing himself off, he spit sand at the base of the palm tree.

"What about tomorrow?"

"What about it?" We'd been avoiding the conversation since his friends had mentioned the island's separation policy.

"Seems to me this is your time on the island, too, right?" He was so calm it was like I was watching someone else. Why wasn't he freaking the crap out, like I was inside?

"I guess," I said finally.

"So, tell them you want to be with me. It's one of your last requests. I can't see them denying you."

It was brilliant.

"Excuse me," I said, stopping a worker who was walking by. "Can you please get me in touch with Finn?"

"Of course," he said, pulling out a screen of his own. Finn appeared on the screen.

"Ms. Delman, what ridiculous request do you have for me today?" A small smile tugged at the corner of his mouth, making me smirk. Maybe he wasn't so bad after all.

"I'd like to accompany Jace in his transfer tonight."

Finn's face stayed noncommittal. As the beats passed, I wondered if he'd answer me at all. "I'll see what I can do," he said before the screen went black.

"What did that mean?" I asked, feeling a bit indignant. He'd hung up on me.

"No idea. But you tried. Now, let's enjoy what we have left of the day.

I tried hard not to panic. Not to think about the days without Jace. Not to obsess about Finn's non-answer. We went back to Jace's room and watched movies. They'd come for him at 11:30 to make the transfer. That way, he'd be settled by midnight on his date.

At 11:25, a rather jarring sob escaped me.

"Jeez, Rare. Next time you're gonna do your best impression of a dog, let me know first. You scared the crap out of me."

But his joke didn't make me laugh. In five minutes, I might have to say goodbye to my heart. How would I even form words for that?

Jace reached over to wipe the tears from my cheeks with his thumbs. "Rarity, we will be together again soon. I know it." He leaned in and kissed me. But it wasn't that soft kind of kiss that made birds sing. It was fierce. Hungry. Trying to satiate a desire we would never be able to quench.

A knock at the door made everything stop.

"Mr. Brown?" It was Finn.

"Yeah."

"Is Ms. Delman with you?" he asked.

Jace opened the door. "See for yourself, although if you don't let her come with me, she might punch you in the face."

That same smirk I'd seen on the video call spread. "You may accompany Mr. Brown. You'll be returned to your room after."

"Really?" Fresh tears streamed down my face as I threw myself at Finn, hugging him hard and sobbing into his shoulder.

"You're welcome," Finn said as he hesitantly returned my embrace. "Just don't get any snot on my shirt. I just had it cleaned."

"Fair enough," I said as I pulled away.

I clung to Jace's hand as we left his room. He held me

firm, but without the desperation I had. He was steady. Strong. Constant. Everything I needed.

I didn't absorb our surroundings as they shuffled us into a pod, then moved us across the island. We were together. I clung to that knowledge.

The building was almost exactly the same as the dorms. Gilded doors. Massive waterfall inside.

"You'll be on the third floor. If you choose to leave your room, just stay on the grounds. There's a beach and a pool."

"Games?" Jace asked.

"Games are in your room. To be sure, they're not as sophisticated as what's in the gaming center, but I think they're fun."

"Finn?"

"Yes, Ms. Delman."

"When is your date?"

He blinked. "How do you know I have one?"

"Please. I'm not stupid."

"No. I never thought that." Finn glanced at Jace, who shrugged. "My date is in twenty years, two months, and three days."

I nodded. "And are you happy doing this? Working on the island?"

"Today, I am. Thanks to you."

I was a bit speechless. The little bird riding on the rhino was likeable? What was this?

I cleared my throat. "Well, you're welcome."

Finn chuckled. "Enjoy your time here." He didn't add anything else, although the ominous promise hung in the air. I'd see him again soon. After.

But I wouldn't ruin the gift he'd given me by obsessing about that. No. I'd enjoy the crap out of every precious second I had with Jace.

Jace and I laid down on the couch together, snuggled in close. "Rare. If I die in my sleep, I want you to know I love you. Forever."

"I love you, too, Jace. Forever."

I was terrified to sleep. Scared I would miss something. Scared I wouldn't be there for his last breath. Wouldn't be holding his hand. Wouldn't be able to let him know he wasn't alone.

But by the time the clock under the TV blinked past 4 AM. I couldn't keep my eyes open anymore.

I woke up four hours later with a start.

"No," I breathed.

"No what?" Jace asked, sitting up slowly and forcing me to move.

"Oh, thank God."

"You thought you were rid of me already?"

"Bummer, huh? Thought I'd be able to spend the day staking out the best spot by the beach for my own date."

"Well, that'll have to wait."

"Thank God." I said again as I leaned in for a slow, light kiss. It was tingly, warm, and everything good in my life.

We spent the day playing video games, eating junk food, and laying by the beach.

Once darkness fell, time seemed to slow. We sat together on the couch, vowing not to go to sleep. He held my hand, and I realized I wanted more of him. In those last moments, I knew I'd never get another chance.

When I leaned forward, he watched me, eyeing me skeptically. "Whatcha doin?"

I didn't answer. I just went for it, kissing him deeply. His lips tasted like the glass of orange juice he'd left on the coffee table, a luxury for us back home. He hadn't shaved all day and his face was stubbly, but I didn't care. I felt my skin going raw from it, but it didn't matter. All that made sense was him. Here. Now.

I drank him in like I'd never be done. In my heart, I knew I wouldn't. In those moments, I lived fully, and my days without him would be dark and empty except for the ghosts of that kiss. That second. That time on that couch. Thank God I only had a few days left to survive. We'd be together again soon. Frankly, I wasn't sure what I thought of the afterlife, but my heart told me Jace would be there. And that was fine by me.

He crushed my body to his. He was just as hungry for me. We were two halves of the same whole. We'd spent our whole lives together, and it had taken us this long to realize just how precious our time together was.

He ran his fingers through my hair as we came up for air. "Rarity, I love you more than words could ever say."

"Me too."

He smiled devilishly. "I mean, I have more words than *that* to say about it."

I shoved him back playfully, and he pulled me back toward him. "You are truly a rarity."

"So I've been told."

"Oh, I'm sorry. Am I boring you?"

I crawled up into his lap, gazing into his face. "Never."

We dissolved into more kissing, then spent the rest of our time tangled on that couch. I thought about my best friend. About the man he'd become. How he saved me at work, how he made me laugh, how, after all these years, we genuinely loved each other.

I couldn't pinpoint the moment it happened, the moment I realized I loved him. Maybe I'd always known.

Was it that very first moment when he walked up beside me at preschool and declared I seemed pretty cool so we could we be friends? Or was it the day we named Killer Creek—which was really just a small creek behind our zone that we liked to make up stories about—and dared each other to go down to it? Neither of us did, by the way. Or maybe it was the day he fell. The day I thought I'd have to be without him.

In the end, it didn't really matter when, did it? All that mattered was that we loved each other.

Eventually, we snuggled into each other, and he held me while I rested my head on his chest.

"Don't go to sleep," I warned behind closed eyes that were so heavy from the lack of sleep the night before.

"No. I won't." He stroked my hair gently, making me relax even more.

I was losing him, and I knew it. That rhino was breathing down my back, and there was nothing I could do to put more distance between us. As much as I tried to fight it, I fell asleep in my best friend's arms for the last time.

TEN

I was dreaming. And even in the dream, I realized it wasn't real, but I didn't care. Jace and I were Withouts. We were married. And we traveled the world together without any cares at all.

Admittedly, the world was much smaller than I imagined, and it largely consisted of places I'd already seen or were borrowed from the island, but hey, it was a dream. Who was I to be picky?

"Where do you want to go next, my love?" Dream Jace asked. He held out a hand as if in that moment, we would teleport anywhere our hearts desired if I just took it.

Before I could react, he started to fade. "Rarity, take my hand. Come with me," he pleaded.

But I couldn't make my body move. No matter what I did, I couldn't reach for him. Just that quickly, my dream turned into a nightmare.

But he only smiled. "It's okay, Rare. I'll meet you there. You come when you're ready."

"I'm ready now," I said. "Take me with you. Please. Don't leave me here alone."

But he didn't answer me. He just faded away.

Slowly, I woke up just as Jace dissolved from my dream.

My neck hurt. But I didn't move. My head was on his chest. His arms were around my body. They were slack, but still heavy against my hip and legs. It was morning. I knew it with every piece of my existence. The sunlight streaming in from the double doors shone defiantly on my eyelids—ones I refused to open.

Morning. The day after Jace's date. As soon as I opened my eyes, I would begin my existence without him.

He still felt warm against me, not cold and stiff like I expected. It seemed wrong for him to be so inviting when he wasn't even with me anymore.

I held as still as I could, trying not to destroy the illusion. As long as I kept my eyes closed, Jace could still be alive. He could be here. We could still be together.

But then, the moment crumbled out from under me. He groaned so naturally I screamed and flew off his lap like he'd just zapped me with ten-thousand volts of electricity.

His scream joined mine as he shot off the couch, so we basically just yelled in each other's faces for about three seconds. Morning breath aplenty. It was great.

When we finally stopped, the silence in the room made my ears ring. We just gaped at each other without blinking for several seconds until he put his hands on my face—rather roughly I might add—and stared at me hard.

"*What* are you doing here?" he demanded.

I blinked, my heart beating about a thousand miles a minute. "I might ask you the same thing."

"Did you kill yourself?"

"What? No." I looked down at my wrists just to make sure, but then I felt utterly ridiculous for doing it. Of course

I hadn't offed myself. I couldn't. Steve had proven that. Several times.

"Then how are you here with me already?"

"You..." Putting my hand to his chest, I felt his heartbeat, strong and steady. "You didn't die."

"What do you mean I didn't die? That's not a thing."

Apparently, it *was* a thing. Right? He stood in front of me. I had my hands on him, and he held me in his. He was real. And he was still here.

"Did we get the date wrong?" he asked, and I ran to the massive TV screen in the living room, turning it on. It displayed the date and time at the bottom.

November 7, 2186 ,7:18 AM.

"It's the seventh." I stared hard at it, reading it and rereading it, unable to comprehend how this was possible.

I turned around to see Jace examining his arm. 11.6.86. The numbers we'd both memorized were still etched permanently into his skin.

"How is this possible?" he breathed as he came closer to the TV, eyes glued to the date.

"I don't know, but I'm scared to question it," I said. I watched him, fearful he'd disappear in right in front of me.

Suddenly, he started laughing. Not a quiet chuckle, more like a hysterical, possibly manic, laugh I knew other people would hear. But it was so contagious I joined in. We laughed until tears rolled down our faces, all at the fact Jace hadn't died.

My stomach hurt, and I clutched my side as I braced myself against the bookshelf near the TV.

"Shh. Someone will hear," I said, trying and failing miserably to be rational.

"I think someone already did."

He closed the distance between us, searching my eyes. "I didn't die."

"You didn't die," I said as he rubbed his thumbs against my cheek. Still, I resisted the urge to close my eyes and melt into him. It seemed like a dream. Like nothing was real. Questions raced through my mind as I tried to digest what it meant. He hadn't died. What would happen when my date came? Would he have to live without me? We'd done what they were trying to accomplish in the Longevity Ward without even trying. What exactly did that even mean? Was it a fluke? Would he die at any moment?

I shook my head, trying to clear it of the noise.

When he leaned in, I threw caution to the wind, leaping into his arms and kissing him with more passion than I had the night before, which I didn't think was possible. His lips were soft, warm, real, and full of life.

I pulled back and giggled. "You didn't die."

"No, my love. I didn't die."

We could've stayed like that all day long if someone hadn't picked that moment to knock at Jace's door.

ELEVEN

"Anyone here?" a man's voice asked.

"Yeah, hang on," I answered.

"What are you doing?" Jace asked, panicked.

"Well, *you* can't answer. You're supposed to be dead."

It was in that moment we realized they were there for him. The collection crew.

"Go hide," I urged.

"Ms. Delman, we need you to let us in. You can't let the body decompose too much." It was Finn. Would he help us? I didn't think so. He was nice, but he still had over twenty years until his date. I was willing to bet he wanted to keep his rather cushy job—not get sent to sort garbage for an incinerator.

"I'm coming," I said, trying to be noncommittal. I imagined myself breezily opening the door. I could do that, right?

I glanced over my shoulder, but I didn't see Jace. Hopefully, he'd gone to hide in the land of invisibility, because I swore that was the only way we were getting out of this one.

I took a deep breath as I stood with my hand on the

door. What would they do to him if they found him? Would they kill him? Take him for experiments? Celebrate with us? Maybe he'd be a celebrity. The first person to survive their date. The more I thought about it, the more I realized just how monumental it was.

It would be okay. We were together. Jace didn't die. That couldn't be for nothing. I comforted myself over and over as I turned the handle and opened the door.

I was greeted by Finn, along with two other men in white scrubs with a gurney and a black bag. Discreet, right?

"Hi, Finn. What's up?" Super breezy.

"We're here to collect the body of Jace Brown," one of the men in the scrubs said.

Finn held up a hand. "I'm sorry, you'll have to excuse my friend. He isn't used to interacting with..." He searched for the right phrase, so I filled one in for him.

"Live clientele?"

He gave the guy some serious side-eye. "Precisely."

"Well, I'm sorry, but he isn't here. He didn't come back last night." *Look distraught*, I told myself. "I was hoping to catch up with him here, but he must've died out there somewhere." I sniffled for effect, but I never was a great actor.

"Ms. Delman, we both know *that* isn't true. Please don't make me regret pulling strings to let you over here early." He cocked his head to the side, and I felt like a chided child.

Without waiting for an invitation, he stepped into Jace's room and I moved aside for him. The others followed him in like I'd welcomed them. *Sure, come in, sit down, put your feet up. Just don't find Jace, for the love of God.*

"So, where's Jace?" Finn said, his friendly tone fading. Crap on a cracker. I didn't want to be on his bad side. But what could I do? I couldn't give Jace up. What would they do to him? Images of the Longevity Ward haunted me.

When I didn't answer, Finn frowned. "Fine. We'll search the room. I've dealt with some strange things in my time on the island, Ms. Delman, but you, by far, are the strangest. I used to think that was a good thing." He walked away from me, and the two men went their way as well, leaving me standing with my back to the open door, feeling totally helpless.

"Survival is a funny thing. Isn't it, Finn?" I held Finn's gaze more confidently than I felt. "Know this about one of your strangest clients—I will never give up my family."

His eyebrows knitted. I could tell he hadn't understood, but I chose to plow forward anyway. He probably thought I was some unstable woman who'd done something strange with her best friend's dead body, which was why they didn't let survivors on this side of the island.

"Fair enough. Wait here while we search."

I bit my bottom lip, mentally trying to tell Jace they were coming so his spot better be the best freaking hiding place on the island.

The three men split up to start searching. Ridiculously, they bent and peered under the coffee table, which was in plain sight, but I'd give them credit for due diligence. They searched the kitchen and even opened the fridge.

"Wow, you guys must think he's pretty spectacular if he'd jam himself in the fridge."

The younger guy who'd opened the fridge turned to me with sad eyes. "You'd be surprised what we find."

Nope. Did *not* want to know what that meant. Not even a little bit.

Still, the questions bubbled up. "Do most people just... die? Or does something happen to them on their date?" Like falling from the side of a cliff, perhaps?

"Most people just go peacefully," he said, his sad

expression softening. "Some go a little crazy. That's when—"

I cut him off. "Nope. I know I asked, but I don't need to hear the weird stuff." I was fairly sure now that he'd planted the seed, I could come up with enough weird crap on my own.

Would I go peacefully? How would it be, now that Jace was still alive? Would he be there? Would they let him?

They must've seen the questions churning through my mind, because one of them stopped what he was doing.

"I'm sure you'll be fine. Most go in their sleep. Isn't that, right?" He turned to his cohort.

"Oh yeah," he said after closing the pantry. "Ninety percent are in their beds, sound asleep."

"Ninety percent, huh? That's really specific." I shouldn't be rude. They were just trying to comfort me. And if Jace were actually dead, maybe it would've comforted me. But seeing as he was living and breathing somewhere in that room, I wasn't looking for comfort for my own mortality. I just wanted to spend my last days with Jace. Which meant these guys had to go.

They ignored my sour mood, and the guy who'd been checking the cabinet came into the living room. "This one time, we found an old lady under the couch, remember? And she left us a note. *Good luck finding me, lads. Have fun.* And it turned out to be this weird scavenger hunt she left for us. Notes everywhere." The second guy chuckled a bit before he looked up with big brown eyes. "To be honest, I'm kinda sad we didn't know her in life."

"She sounds like fun," I said quietly, wondering if I would have the brain power to craft something like that in the hours before I died. Probably not, given the fact I had trouble thinking around that damned rhino and his tiny bird that were barreling toward me.

"Yeah. She was," he mused. I let the silence hang in the air, pretending I was deep in thought about the old woman. But really, I was panicking inside, hoping beyond hope they didn't find Jace.

"Hey," Finn yelled, sounding as if it came from the bathroom. What did Jace do, try to hide in the all-glass shower?

I ran toward the sound with them hot on my heels. Bursting into the bathroom, I found Jace in the closet with his hands up, mirroring Finn.

"Now, I don't want any trouble. This is probably just some misunderstanding," Finn said. He'd turned about three shades of white, and he swallowed hard.

Jace's eyes darted wildly to me, and I tried to give him a reassuring look. It wasn't time to panic. Right? Finn was a reasonable person.

"Let me just double check the date on your arm." Finn reached out for Jace tentatively, but Jace shook his head no.

"Come on, mate. It's not a big deal. I'm sure we just recorded the date wrong."

"But what if you didn't?" Jace asked, his voice shaking like the green gelatin in the buffet.

Finn cocked his head, clearly not sure what Jace meant by that. Then he shook his head. Facts were what they were. And the fact was, Jace was alive so the date must be recorded wrong. I could see his wheels turning, grinding, trying to click into place. Just like ours were.

"We did. I promise. Otherwise, you wouldn't be here. I know this must be freaky for you. I'll admit, this hasn't happened to me before, so I'm not quite sure what to do. But first thing's first, right? Let me just take a look at that arm." He was so friendly. It seemed clear to me he was just trying to do his job, and I wanted to help him. But Jace's instincts were telling him no, and I tended to trust Jace.

"Finn, is there any way the team can just move on to the next body?" I asked.

He jerked his head toward me as if he'd forgotten I was there. His coworkers stood behind me, watching the baffling scene unfold.

"Move on? No. I'm sorry, we can't just move on. Questions would be asked. And I'm afraid I have quite a lot of the same questions right about now." A small bit of that friendliness fell away as he turned back to Jace.

"I won't ask again, Mr. Brown. I like you two, I think. Although, I'll admit it's been a bit of a rollercoaster. Still, I'd prefer to do this nicely, so, if you would, please show me your arm." His voice got sterner with every word.

Jace swallowed hard, raising a brow at me. I didn't see any other options. We were outnumbered. By people who knew what they were doing. We weren't fighters. We were Withs. Rule followers. Slaves, if the graffiti on the transport station back home was to be believed. Jace was strong and he could certainly throw a punch, but against three guys? No way.

I shrugged and frowned, not sure what Jace was so afraid of. They seemed like they wanted to help. Like they were just as confused as we were, and they'd get it sorted.

Reluctantly, he held out his arm, and Finn frowned as he did. "Hmm. This is odd. I'm going to have to make a call. You stay here." He gestured at the men who'd come with him, and they pushed around me to stand in front of Jace.

When Finn stepped out to the balcony to make a call, I squeezed past the men and took Jace's hands in mine. "What do you think?" I whispered, knowing the lackeys could probably hear me. I almost felt bad thinking of them that way. They did seem nice, at least when they weren't imprisoning us.

"Nothing good," Jace said, keeping his eyes on the balcony.

"What are you so afraid of? What do you think they'll do to you?"

"Longevity," was all he got out before the leader came back in.

"Mr. Brown, I'm afraid I've had to call in another team. They've asked us to wait here until they arrive, to make sure you don't go anywhere."

"Where would I go?" Jace said, with a nervous laugh. It was a feeble attempt at keeping the situation light.

"Precisely," Finn said.

"Where will they take me?" Jace asked.

"I'm afraid I don't know. You're unprecedented. But I'm sure they'll have some questions for you." He turned his eyes to me. "For both of you."

"And then what?" I asked. "When the questions are answered, I mean. Will they let him go?"

Finn shook his head. "I don't know." He frowned. "But if I'm being honest, probably not. They'll want to monitor him closely."

"No," I screamed so loudly I startled the other two men. Jace was used to my outbursts so he didn't even flinch. "That's ridiculous. I have only five days left until my own date. The *least* you could do is let us spend them together." I couldn't let this miracle slip through my fingers just to have him become a vegetable in the Longevity Ward.

"Honestly, Ms. Delman, I have no idea what they'll do. I don't think it's time to panic just yet."

He was placating me, trying to keep me calm until I

became someone else's problem. Quickly, I approached him and stabbed my finger into his chest. "If you think for one second I will give up this bonus time we've been given without a fight, you've got another thing coming."

Finn stared down at me, unsure of what to do. He retreated a bit so I couldn't jab him anymore. "I assure you that we're not looking for a fight."

"All we were here for was a body, miss," the one who'd told me about the old lady said. "We're just trying to do our jobs."

"Well, maybe you're having an off day today. And maybe you turn your backs and let us slip out," I suggested.

The two lackeys glanced at each other, but Finn held firm. "No. We can't do that. I went out on a limb for you once and look where it got me. The call has already been made. The team will be here any second."

As if speaking about them willed them into existence, an entirely new group of people appeared in the bedroom doorway dressed like no one I'd seen on the island. They appeared ready for a fight in black long-sleeved jumpsuits, pads on elbows and knees, and thick gloves over their hands. Their faces were covered by something that resembled ski masks, but the fabric seemed a lot tougher than just knit cotton. It almost shimmered as they approached.

One of them approached without hesitation, then spoke in hushed tones to Finn.

"Mr. Brown," Finn said after a moment. "I leave you here. I wish you all the best." The sympathetic look in his eyes told me he meant it, but Jace was shooting him daggers, clearly not forgiving him for putting him in that spot.

The collection team left, leaving us alone with a bunch of rather intimidating ninja impersonators.

The one who'd spoken to Finn reached up and pulled

off her mask. Short blonde hair spilled around her face, and it surprised me that she was actually quite pretty. Somehow, it made her intimidating in a completely different way.

"Look, Jace. Can I call you Jace?" She didn't wait for an answer. "Let's just get out of here. There's no room. We can't talk. That's all we want to do. Let's chat. Find out what's going on. Once this is all cleared up, I'm sure you can go on your merry way."

"Bullshit," Jace challenged her with narrowed eyes, and I shifted uncomfortably. Somehow, I didn't think it was his most brilliant idea to cop an attitude with the blonde in kneepads.

She frowned. "Perhaps you're right. I shouldn't make promises I can't keep. I have no idea when or if they'll let you go. But..." She dipped her chin and looked directly at me with concern dripping from her down turned lips. "I can assure you that we will keep him comfortable and safe."

Now it was my turn to call foul on that ridiculous performance. She was using me to try to get him to calm down and comply. She was good, but I was better. In a super clumsy diarrhea-of-the-mouth kind of way.

"Oh, please. That's a worse load of crap than you just fed to Jace. All we want is to be together. Can you promise us that?"

She frowned. "I can promise you that you're coming with us. Willingly or not makes no difference to them." She gestured toward the seemingly impossible number of people who'd crowded into the room. It was a big bedroom, but not nearly big enough for the fifteen or so meatheads standing around, ready to spring into action.

"What'll it be?" She put her hands on her hips, shrugging like she couldn't care less what we decided. Like Jace wasn't the biggest thing to happen on this island *ever*.

I looked at Jace. In that moment, I shared his fear. What would they do to us? Him? Why was this happening?

The rhino was scratching the ground with his foot, kicking up dust behind him, and I was like some kind of deer in the headlights, too scared and stupid to get out of the way.

TWELVE

"Fine," Jace said, startling me out of my coming panic. "Let's go. But we go together."

"Fine," the woman agreed. The men converged on us, taking mine and Jace's arms roughly. "We'll want to talk to you, too."

"Hey, there's no need for that," I said as they grabbed me hard enough it hurt. "We said we'd come willingly, you oaf."

The men on either side of me didn't respond. Suddenly, I regretted calling the collectors lackeys. Because if ever there were such a person, these folks were it. Mindless drones who answered to the unfairly pretty blonde.

They muscled us out and into a black transport vehicle that was like nothing I'd seen on the island.

"This isn't terribly inconspicuous," I pointed out. "There'll be talk."

"From who? The people who are less than twenty-four hours until their date?" She smirked. "Let them talk to each other. What they saw dies with them."

They tossed us into the rear of the massive black vehicle, then climbed in behind us, sitting along the walls of the vehicle with us between them. At least they'd let us sit next to each other.

But we didn't dare speak. Who knew what they were looking for and how our words might incriminate us?

We couldn't see where we were going since the black vehicle didn't have any windows. The only light came from less-than-flattering running lights along the sides and floor, leading to the door.

It didn't take long to get wherever we were going, which was ideal, since I had nothing to do but stare at the meatheads around me. Blondie was sitting near the door, examining her nails closely. She'd even removed her gloves to do so. Of course, they were painted a sparkly shade of pink. Who was this woman? Barbie wasn't made to be a hard ass. What the heck?

Finally, the vehicle came to a stop, and I thought we were going to get out. I braced myself. Instead, we started going down as if we were in some massive elevator.

"Where are we going?" I asked, breaking the crushing silence. Unfortunately, because of the prolonged period of quiet, I had no concept of volume and ended up screaming it at them.

"Where you can give us some answers, Rarity."

"Wait, how do you know who *I* am? I never gave you my name."

"We know who Jace is. And you two are joined at the hip. Therefore, we know who you are."

She said it like it was the most obvious thing in the world. Of course they would know who we were. We'd been together since the moment I arrived on the island. No one ever questioned us, but I should've known they'd be watching.

The vehicle came to a stop. The door slid open, revealing absolutely nothing. I craned my head around a particularly big meathead, but I still couldn't see anything but darkness. It threatened to fuel my fear, but Jace leaned gently against me.

"It'll be okay. We'll be okay." I couldn't tell if he were saying it to me or himself. Maybe both of us.

Blondie stepped out, and lights came on brighter than the surface of the sun.

"I get the impression you want us disoriented. Because you're doing a great job at that," I said as I tried to shield my eyes, but I realized I couldn't use my hands since the meat-heads held both my arms.

It was so bright I couldn't see where we were going or even where Jace was. I had to keep my eyes closed and listen to the shuffling.

"Jace. You still with me?"

"Yeah. I'm here."

They muscled us along, and I heard a door open. They shoved me through, and it was blessedly dark in there. They tossed me rather unceremoniously in a chair, and I hesitated to open my eyes.

"Hey, warn a girl if you're going to turn on those surface-of-the-sun lights, okay?"

"Certainly, Ms. Delman." The voice was new, and I cautiously peeked from behind squinted eyes at him.

He wore a suit. Like an actual suit. Only the Withs who wanted to get fancied up dressed like that on the island. Who was this guy?

He had red hair and a thin build. After he sat across the table from me, he rested his ankle on his knee like he was bored.

"I'm happy to meet you. My name is Cedric."

"Cedric," I said, more to acknowledge him than give him any kind of approval. Maybe if I engaged with him, I could get us out of here faster. Us. I frantically surveyed the room, suddenly realizing I was alone. "Where's Jace?" I tried to stand, but the meatheads slammed me back down into my chair with more force than was necessary. My butt would hurt for days after that. It occurred to me that I only had days left, and now I'd be uncomfortable the entire time.

"Thanks for that," I said as I tried to adjust myself to a more comfortable position.

"Jace is in the room next door, answering the same questions you will be."

"Why not question us together? Isn't this a waste of time?"

"We thought you'd give more honest answers without the influence of your dear friend."

I narrowed my eyes. The way he said *dear friend* made me uncomfortable. "And who are you, Cedric? What's your role on the island?"

He smiled, but it didn't travel to his eyes. Good. He was dangerous. That was just peachy freaking keen. "I think, for now, I'll be the one asking the questions. If you don't mind."

"As a matter of fact—"

He cut my protest off. "What exactly happened last night? Tell me in detail."

"What do you mean? Nothing happened last night. Isn't that the point of why we're here? Something was supposed to happen, and it didn't." These guys were dumber than I thought. Dangerous and dumb was a bad combination. I glanced at the walls around us, wondering how on earth I could get myself out of this.

"But what did you do to make it happen?"

"What?" He thought we'd done something? "Like what?" I asked, completely baffled.

"You tell me."

"Look, we're not witches from the nineteen hundreds, okay. We're teenagers. What do you think we did last night? We made out on the couch and fell asleep."

Now it was his turn to glare. "You're lying. You can't tell me it was just a coincidence that your friend Jace over there skipped out on his date."

"Coincidence, miracle. You use whatever word you feel comfortable with."

If glares could pierce skin, I was fairly sure I'd have been nailed to that seat. But I just glowered right back at him. Jace and I hadn't done anything to deserve this third degree.

"You know, they were awfully apologetic when Jace's accident happened and they thought they were stealing time from us. Now you're holding us prisoner because you think we're magicians who cheated the With system? I still have two and a half days left. And I'd rather not spend them like this."

"Noted. I'm sure we won't be keeping you long."

"Wait, what the hell does that mean?" I demanded, but he didn't answer. Instead, he was flipping through a brown folder on his lap.

"Jace had an accident a few days ago? Can you tell me about that?"

"Why? I'm sure everything I know and more is in that folder on your lap."

"I'd like to hear it from you." He was trying to be friendly, but he fell way short of Finn.

"Fine. He fell off the side of the cliff. They brought him to the hospital, gave him some rapid-recovery crap, and sent him on his merry way." Something clicked in my mind when I said it aloud. "You think the rapid recovery extended his life?" The ramifications of that sent my mind whirling. That meant Jace could die at any moment, whenever the rapid recovery wore off anyway. He could die in the next room, alone. The thought made me want to go to him. To bust the meatheads in the teeth with my head and go to Jace, no matter the cost.

"It's one theory we have."

"If that's the case, you need to let me go to him. He can't die alone. He could be dead over there right now," I insisted, but he ignored me.

Instead, he chewed on his bottom lip, pondering the possibilities. "Perhaps you're telling the truth. If that's the case, Mr. Brown will need to be closely monitored." He stood. "We'll notify you of his passing.

Right before my eyes, he went to the door. Was this really happening? Was I so out of control? I wasn't ready to accept that. "Wait. What? What's happening? You can't keep us apart."

Then, that little twit of a man actually turned and laughed at me. "Oh, Ms. Delman, but I can. And I will. Have a pleasant rest of your life."

"Wait, just let me say goodbye to him," I pleaded. I actually begged.

And that compassionless pond scum didn't waver one bit. "I'm afraid we don't have time to waste for that, Ms. Delman. Mr. Brown is already being relocated to his new home. These gentlemen will show you out."

"No," I screamed as I stood and ran to the door. But it slammed in my face, and the meatheads just stared blankly at me. "Jace," I shouted, my voice echoing in the small space. I pounded on the door and yelled until my voice was raw, but it was to no avail.

Tears streamed down my face as I pounded the door until I couldn't feel my hands. I sank to the ground, sobbing into my knees.

"You about done?" one of the meatheads asked.

"Screw you," I spat.

"She's done," he said, and two of his men lifted me by my arms and carried me out of the room.

Once we were out in that bright light again, I fought against them. If I could just get free, I could get to Jace. "Jace," I screamed again, my voice hoarse, and not nearly as loud as it had been before.

"Hey, take a chill pill," one of the guys told me. I hauled off and kicked him square in the crotch. He crumpled to the ground. Score one for the scrappy girl.

The other guy took me more roughly by the arms, then lifted me off the ground. I kicked my legs furiously, hoping to connect with something important, but he held me out with freakishly long arms.

"If this is how you want to play it, that's fine by me. I like a good fight," the man said. He smiled at me, knowing he would win. Eventually.

"Just get her to the transport," the guy I'd kicked said through clenched teeth. "Before I do something I'll regret." The threat was palpable. But what did I care? I had just over two days left to live. So what if they tortured me. I needed Jace. He was alive. It was a miracle if you asked me, and they were keeping me from him.

I kicked, twisted, and even spat at the guy holding me. Not my best moment, I'll admit. But I missed him by a mile. Sharp spitting wasn't my forte.

"All right, you little spitfire. Into the transport you go," the man holding me said as he tossed me rather roughly into the back of the car. He closed the door and locked me in there alone. I heard nothing—no directions and no clue as to where I was going. The vehicle just started moving up and out of whatever rabbit hole I'd fallen into.

But unlike Alice, I was leaving Wonderland without a piece of my soul.

THE TRANSPORT STOPPED and opened the door at my building, letting the sunlight stream in. The transports didn't run on a track. There was nothing for me to follow back the way we'd come. I tried chasing after it for a bit, but it outpaced me before I even got to the edge of my building.

I stood with the sea air on my face, the sun on my skin, and soft green grass beneath my toes. But none of it meant anything. I was alone. And worse than I originally thought, Jace wasn't dead, but we were still apart. The thought filled me with a rage I hadn't known lived inside me, threatening to destroy my last days. To be honest, I didn't know how to fight it or make the best of it. At the moment, I didn't really want to do either of those things.

I wanted to wallow. I'd been screwed on the supposed utopian island. They'd ruined what was left of my life. And as I looked back at all the island had to offer, their promises turned to ash, just like I hoped to do to the island.

ALL RIGHT, I didn't burn the island down. Not even close. Instead, I went to a bar and decided to drown my sorrows. I wasn't much for drinking, but on an island with no rules, not even age limits on alcohol, I figured why not? Jace and I hadn't ventured down to the bar when he'd been here. We hadn't wanted to dull our senses. We wanted to soak up every moment together. And now...everything was too sharp. So sharp it cut me to the core. I needed to dull the pain.

A TV played behind the bar, but I didn't pay attention to it. Instead, I was drinking a particularly sweet concoction that I wasn't even sure what was in it. But it went down easy. The bartender recommended it for a first-time drinker. We didn't have luxuries like alcohol at home. Roughly fifty hours before I'd die, I thought I'd indulge in my first drink.

The bartender put a plate of food next to me that I hadn't ordered, and I picked at the French fries.

"Want to talk about it?" I looked up at him for the first time, wondering just how many people he comforted on the island. I didn't even have much time left here. Tomorrow at midnight, they'd move me to isolation. It was over.

"The love of my life didn't die. Instead, he's being held captive on this island somewhere where I can't get to him. I have two days left, and I'll be spending them without him."

The bartender's eyes widened, clearly sorry he'd opened that little can of worms and turned around. *Just as well*, I thought.

Until he turned the volume up on the TV. "This your man?"

When I dragged my eyes toward the screen, I swore a French fry fell out of my mouth because it was hanging open so far. Jace was on the screen. Not a live video of him, but his picture.

"What in the..." I trailed off as I listened to the reporter.

"Jace Brown is reportedly the only person in the world to outlive his date. What could this mean? Is it the end of the Withs as we know it? Dr. Hubert Wittel has some insight on this frightening development."

Frightening? "He's not some kind of sideshow freak," I mumbled as I picked up the fry that had landed on the bar.

"It's too early to know what exactly is happening with Mr. Brown. Right now, we think his rapid-recovery treatment from an incident on the island may have pushed his date back. While this has never happened before with other patrons of the island who were injured, it's a variable that needs to be given some attention."

Cedric had said the same thing. It was nothing new.

The reporter popped up on a split screen. "Dr. Wittel, what of the talk that Mr. Brown is the key to surviving our dates?"

I choked on my fry. Jace? The key to surviving? It was ridiculous. "For now, as I said, it's too early to leap to any dramatic conclusions. It's a waiting game as we wait to see if Mr. Brown dies on his own in the next few hours."

Dies on his own? Panic rose like bile in the back of my throat.

The shot returned to the newsroom and the main reporter, who looked visibly shaken. "We will keep you informed as more news from this alarming story breaks."

"Your man survived his date, huh? That's wild," the bartender said as he wiped out the inside of a glass with a white towel.

I took a deep breath, trying to calm myself. "Wild isn't quite the word I'd use to describe it."

"Sounds like they've really got it in for him. Tough break." He studied me sympathetically, and I knew he meant it. But he also knew something else I wasn't ready to admit. I was powerless. There was nothing I could do to help him. Was there?

The gears in my head struggled to clunk into place, searching for a solution. I had no time left. I couldn't pussy foot around. If I were going to act, it had to be quick. But what could I do? And how?

The rhino was circling me, stirring up dust, and making it impossible to see which direction to go or where the worst of it would come from.

THIRTEEN

I had one day left before I'd be taken into isolation. One day to take this pile of crap that was dumped on my head and make chocolate pie out of it.

I could do that, right? I almost snorted out loud as I sat in my room the next morning, debating how to proceed. I'd thought sleeping would help me see things clearer. Yeah, no. Things were as clear as mud in the morning light.

After fuming for a bit, I decided to go to the Tech Wing. I'd gotten answers there before. Hopefully, they wouldn't let me down when it mattered most.

On the way over, I made a mental list of things I needed to do. Get into that hospital. See Jace. After that, who knew? Maybe die in his arms. Great plan.

The thought of that made me reconsider my efforts. Would it be too much for him? But the thought was fleeting. I'd never once thought about not being with him on his date. He'd be with me on mine. If he were still alive.

He was all over the news. And as far as I could tell, he was still on this side of the dirt.

In my time on the island, I'd actually learned quite a bit

from the Tech Wing. As the transport pod stopped in front of the massive, grey rectangular building, I realized I felt more comfortable here than I had in most other places on the island. The Gaming Wing was fun, but it was stressful. The Tech Wing was where I could ask any questions I could think of and get answers.

But what questions should I ask?

When I walked up to the receptionist, she greeted me with a smile as always. "Ms. Delman, it's a pleasure to see you again. What can I help you with today?"

"I need a screen. That's it for now."

"Of course. Do you want one to take apart like before, or..."

"No. I need a fully functioning one. A fast one, please. I don't have much time left."

"Of course. Right away." Her fingers flicked across her own screen with a speed I wondered if I'd ever possess.

"Can I ask you something?"

"Of course." She stopped what she was doing, letting me know I had her attention. I'd always liked her. Even if she were paid to be nice to me, it never felt like she was.

"How did you get a job on the island?"

She smiled. "Well, to be honest, I'm not sure. How did you get your job back home?"

"Well, I certainly didn't choose it." Frankly, I didn't have a choice. It was where we lived, so that was what I did. But no one lived on the island, except the people who worked there. "Do you have family here?"

"I did. But the last of them died a year ago."

"I'm sorry." It was a natural response. She smiled sadly. It tried to pull the corners of her mouth up, but whatever she was thinking seemed too heavy to let that happen.

"Me too." She hesitated, as if she weren't sure she

should keep going, but she did anyway. "What makes you ask?"

"I just wondered how you got such a great job while I got stuck sorting trash into the incinerator."

She didn't even give me a sad smile. Nope. We were in full-on frown territory. "Every job has its hardships. And hopefully, its joys."

I thought about my job and my time with Jace. He could've been assigned a different department, but they honored our request to work together. She was right. It could've been worse.

"You're right. I'm sorry. I didn't mean anything by it."

She nodded. "I know. And do you know what? No one has ever asked me that before. It's always what I can do for them. And I'm sure when I get that close to my date, I'll be the same way. All the same, thank you."

"For what? Sticking my foot in it?"

She laughed, and it felt good to hear it. With everything that had happened, the sound felt foreign, exotic, and just plain good.

"Your screen is ready for you in room three."

"Thanks," I said before reluctantly walking away. It meant diving headfirst into my reality. Back to the place where nothing made sense, and I had no idea how to fix it.

I opened the screen, and it waited patiently for me to give a command. *Where is Jace Brown?* I typed into the search bar.

A series of articles popped up.

First Man to Survive Date Held at Island Hospital

Island Terror: Man Survives Date

Man Survives: What Does it Mean for You?

I clicked on the first article, but it didn't tell me anything I hadn't already known. There were no specifics.

Nothing helpful. Although I was willing to bet he was in that creepy place where Max worked.

I typed *Longevity Ward* into the search bar.

No results

I'd never gotten that before. The first day I came to the Tech Wing, they'd told me there weren't any secrets here. What was the point? We'd take the information to our graves anyway.

The hours clicked away, but I wasn't making progress. So I decided a more malicious approach might be prudent. I'd hacked the television feeds of the Withouts back home. This wouldn't be any different. Right?

I snorted as I searched for a way in. A weakness. Something that would get me the information I needed.

I started with the hospital. A comprehensive page gave me anything a normal person would want to know. Where it was located, what they offered, how many people worked there, and how many departments there were. But it lacked any information about the top floor and the goings-on up there. Basically everything I needed.

Then, I found a crumb. A little morsel. It didn't look like much. But I didn't need much. It was an employee login page. It meant nothing. Even if I did get in, I had no idea if I'd be able to find anything. But I'd done more with technology in my time on the island than I had in my whole life. And this was my time to be the person I could've been, if I hadn't been a With.

My fingers went to work, and I watched the screen light up. I was close. I could tell. *Login failed.* Once. Twice. I kept trying. Kept working to get around the firewall.

Until it worked. "Holy—"

"Ms. Delman?"

I actually screamed. I'd been so focused on hacking the

system right under their noses, I'd forgotten where I was and that I wasn't alone.

"I'm so sorry," Carolynn said. "I didn't mean to scare you."

I set the screen face down on the table in front of me. "No, I'm sorry. I was just focused."

"I could tell, but I just wondered if you were hungry. You've been here for hours. I'm happy to order you some food if you'll just tell me what you'd like."

"Hours? What time is it?"

"Two o'clock."

I frowned. I had ten hours to crack the code, then figure out how to use it to get to Jace. Not to mention figuring out how to duck the team that would take me to the death motel.

"Thanks, Carolynn. Can I check this screen out? Take it back to my room? I'm..." I couldn't form the words, but I held out my arm so she could see my date. Even though I was fairly sure she already knew it. I'd been in there enough times she must've figured I was getting pretty ripe.

"Of course. It's no problem. Take it with you." She made no mention of them getting it back. And I appreciated that. I didn't like having it thrown in my face that life went on after me.

I stood, tucking the screen under my arm. "Listen, I probably won't see you again."

Her face turned serious. "Thank you. For everything."

In that moment, she reached over and hugged me. I wanted to hug her back, but I was holding the screen, so I ended up giving her one of those super awkward one-arm hugs.

"See you on the other side," she said. I nodded and walked out of there, trying not to run.

The whole ride back to my room in the transport pod, I worked. The first thing I needed to do was turn off any tracking devices it had. But it was a matter of finding them and making sure I'd found them all. Frankly, it took longer than I wanted. But I couldn't risk them finding me if all this worked. And that was a monstrously large *if*.

Once I was reasonably sure I'd found all the things that could out me and turned them off, I went back to hacking the hospital. I got into their system, but I needed clearance to see what mattered.

At some point, I grabbed a snack out of the fridge and kept typing. Kept working. I sent signals to the server, trying to bait it to interact with me. All I needed was a connection. Over and over, it slapped my hand away. Until it worked. With a connection, I had access to a map of the hospital. Complete with color-coded names of who was in each room. While I wasn't sure what all the colors meant, I felt reasonably sure green meant life. Jace Brown was listed in green on the far side of the hospital.

I jumped up and shouted at the top of my lungs, holding my screen high in the air. *"Yes!"*

But my joy was short-lived. It was dark outside. When had that happened? The clock under the TV blinked one minute after eleven. That was a heaping helping of turd pie. They were coming at eleven thirty. And I was expected to be here.

The rhino was scratching the ground, but tonight, his charge would miss. Tomorrow, he'd have his day.

FOURTEEN

A black backpack hung in the closet next to a few other things I'd never used, including a silk robe. I snatched the bag down, then jammed it full of things we might need. Food. Flashlight. Knife. I even yanked the tie off that robe and stuck it in. Never knew when I might need to tie something, or someone, down...with silk. Only the finest for my prisoners, apparently.

By 11:25, I started to make my way out into the hallway. I opened my door just a crack and tried to see who was out there, but let's be honest. What could I really see through a crack? I ended up sticking my whole head out to get a good long look at the situation. A few stragglers were in the hall, but no one paid me any mind. They were all in their own worlds, with their own rhinos trailing behind them. More importantly, they weren't wearing the white uniforms of the ones who would take me to Death Motel.

Hiking the backpack up on my shoulder, I casually wandered out into the hall and down to the elevator.

My heart hammered so loud I was certain it was going to summon someone's attention to me. Then, several heartbeats too late, it occurred to me that the team could be on the other side of the elevator doors.

As the bell dinged, I panicked, wildly searching for somewhere to go. I moved next to a giant rectangular planter along the back wall, which offered absolutely zero coverage but somehow made my irrational mind feel better.

It wasn't the team on the other side of the door, though. But who was there was nearly as bad.

There was a couple against the wall of the elevator. The man had his hand up the woman's skirt, getting a handful of the bare ass I was getting an eyeful of. I uncomfortably averted my eyes, pretending if I didn't see it, it wasn't there.

.

She giggled as she leaned in and nibbled his ear. When he spied me over her shoulder, he nudged the woman off him. He grabbed her hand as he ushered her out, and it was then I recognized her. Fun fact: It's easier to see people's faces when their butts aren't hanging out.

The smile faded from her lips as she stopped. Carolynn stared, slack jawed, as I pushed past her and slid into the elevator. The stairs. Why in God's name hadn't I taken the stairs?

"Oh, Ms. Delman. I'm sorry. This isn't what it looks like," she said. She wasn't connecting the dots. She was too embarrassed to be caught with a resident. But I wasn't judging. I just wanted to get out of there.

"Hey, you do you," I said. I held my hands up, flashing my date at them. Mistake number six hundred thirty-two.

You could almost see recognition click into place as she stared at me, and I jerked my arms back to my sides.

"What time is it?" she asked.

"11:28," her man answered.

"Well, it was good seeing you again, Carolynn," I said

without meaning it even a little bit. I mashed the button on the elevator about six thousand times before the doors finally closed.

"Wait..." I heard her say before I was home free. Well, if this wasn't just I won the lottery and then got ran over by a transport pod eighteen times perfect. She knew. But I could tell her mind was having trouble putting it together. Maybe, just maybe, she'd brush it off and decide she was mistaken about when my day was.

And maybe chocolate would rain from the sky and wouldn't make us all fat.

I let a shaky breath go as the elevator arrived on the ground floor much faster than I wanted it to. Quickly, I took the pocketknife out of the backpack, flipped it open, and held it out, ready for the doors to open.

As ready as I could be, anyway. No way could I actually stab someone. Could I? All I knew for sure was I didn't want to have to. I prayed to whoever was listening that the other side of the door would be empty. That Carolynn didn't call anyone. That she chalked it up to a misunderstanding on her part.

The bell on the elevator dinged so loudly I thought the entire island would know where I was. Freaking thing echoed in my head as the doors slid open at a snail's pace.

I widened my stance and bent my knees, ready for a fight.

But there was no one there. Blessedly, I was all alone. The crickets chirped as I took several breaths, looking out into the night, breathing in the salty air, and watching the breeze shake the palm fronds.

It was peaceful. At least, if I wasn't running for my life.

The elevator dinged again. The doors started to close with me inside, so I snapped into action, sticking my hand out and stopping them. I quickly stepped off, trying to get my bearings.

As I stepped out into the night, I started to wonder how quickly they'd find me. It wasn't a matter of if—it was when. And would I make it to Jace before that happened?

Despite the fact they never openly scanned people, they always knew who we were when we walked up to a place, which gave the impression they knew where we were at all times. Jace theorized the transports kept tabs on us. And when we were out and about, the workers knew who we were.

I wondered about how deeply the technology went on the island. Were they tracking us with cameras and facial recognition software? If they were, it would be extremely hard to outmaneuver them.

I had to stay out of sight. That meant getting out of the open.

But just before I ducked off the path, I noticed a TV screen behind a glass wall. I remembered the gym from the first time I'd walked past it with Jace.

"Really, a gym?" I'd asked, wondering who in their right mind would want to work out during their last two weeks.

"Some people like to burn off steam that way. Maybe not you," he'd said as he poked at me.

"Just because I prefer a more sedentary lifestyle," I said. We'd worked hard, each in our own ways, ten hours a day, six days a week. We spent what little time off we had together. And that was that. Lather, rinse, repeat, until one of us came to our date. I just couldn't get my mind around why, when all the Withs suddenly had free time, they'd choose to spend it on a treadmill when they could walk on an actual beach.

"To each their own," Jace had said. "That's basically the

motto of this island. They're equipped to accommodate everyone."

But as I walked past it that night, I saw Jace's face on the TV and stopped dead in my tracks. His birthday and today's date were under his picture. I threw the glass door open, apparently throwing caution to the wind, and went inside.

"Ending the survival debate, researchers reported Jace Brown has finally died."

The words echoed in my mind. He what? One sentence drained all the purpose from my life, and I fell to my knees. But the reporter mercilessly kept talking.

"Doctors never figured out why he survived past his date, but they assure us that he is now at peace. Let's go over to the weather. Mike?"

My breath came in short bursts. Dead. How could he be dead? What would I do with myself now?

Unless...my mind whirled as I tried to put the pieces together. It was like someone had dumped a thousand-piece puzzle on my head, then gave me about thirty seconds to put it together.

What if he wasn't dead? What time was it? I pulled out the screen. 11:50. They'd be searching for me. Would they go so far as to discourage me from going after him? It felt like a leap, but then, the entire island was a bit on the unbelievable side.

What if it wasn't about me? What if they'd lost control? What if they had no idea why Jace was still alive and wanted to stem panic? Could they have just told everyone he was dead even if he was still alive?

Where did that leave me? With a heck of a lot of ifs on my plate and no answers.

What could I do? I pulled up the live map of the hospital, which displayed the names of the residents on the top floor. Brown was still there. And it was green. Green meant life, right? True, I was assuming, but it seemed logical.

I couldn't stand spending my last hours without him. I'd get to him or die trying—even if all I found was his body.

This was a fine bucket of turd if I'd ever seen one. The news anchors went about their late-night broadcast like they hadn't just sucked the air from my world. Fools.

Or maybe I was the fool. I stood in the middle of a glass-fronted gym while a crew was probably out searching for me. That couldn't be high on the intelligence list, could it?

I nervously glanced around. Going into the gym was a mistake. If someone walked in, I'd be trapped.

I had to get out of there. Keeping my head down, I hurried out and made my way through the bushes. It was a prickly situation, and I suddenly wished I'd put on long sleeves and pants, even though it was a comfortable seventy-five degrees outside.

Once I was scratched to ribbons, I popped out from behind them and hoped I could make my way without being spotted.

But how in the world could I do that without sticking close to the roads? By using my screen... Why hadn't I thought about it sooner? Probably because I had about point three seconds to figure out how to execute the non-plan I had going on.

I had a live map in my hands. It would lead me right to the hospital, even if I wasn't sure which direction to go. I just had to hope someone wasn't tracking the movements of it.

Suddenly, footsteps and voices caught my attention.

"Did you hear about Jace Brown?" Crouching behind the closest bush, I held my breath.

"What was that?"

A pair of workers stopped right in front of me. If I could see them, they'd be able to see me through the dappled foliage, so I did my best not to give them a reason to look my way.

One of them held a screen. "Who hasn't? Check this out. They're having a memorial for him in his home zone." That struck me as odd. Memorials were expensive and not often observed, particularly not in our zone. People just went on with their lives. Mom said it helped some people to stay busy like that. But I wondered if she still thought that on my date when she had no idea if I were still alive.

An owl hooted to my left, and the workers turned that way. The bird took flight, swooping down right toward me. Was he against me, too? Some kind of trained spy for the island? Could owls be trained to do that?

But no... he snatched a mouse off the grass about ten feet from me and flew the other direction.

I held my breath. Had they seen me?

"Damn mice. I keep telling them there's a rodent problem."

His friend chuckled. "Apparently, they're handling it with owls."

They started to walk on toward my building. I let out a breath, which brushed my backpack up against the bush I hid behind.

"What was that?" the guy without the screen said.

"It's probably just another mouse." The other never even glanced up from the screen as he scrolled through something that must have been rather riveting. Probably more lies about Jace. Or at least what I hoped were lies.

"No..." He stared right at me. Yellow light from the path

shone down on him, and I could see he had brown eyes. "I don't think it is."

I rose, then bolted through the clearing. "She's running." Captain Obvious to the rescue.

The one with the screen set off an alarm. Lights flashed, and sirens blared. Whelp, it was no secret where I was now. I just had to...outrun them. My favorite thing...honestly, how bad would it be to let them catch me?

No. That thought was fleeting, I promise. My will to live outweighed my hatred for running, but not by much.

I forced my legs to go faster. Concentrated on putting one foot in front of the other, suddenly glad I'd opted for sneakers instead of the nice sandals I preferred to wear around the island.

Suddenly, a net dropped out of the sky and landed to my right. I dodged left on instinct, but it missed me without my fancy footwork. Great, now they're dropping crap on my head. All because I didn't want to go to isolation? It felt extreme, but I wasn't making any bets that the next one would miss.

I had to get out of there.

But how? A silent helicopter shone a bright light down onto me. No hiding now. *Awesome.*

"We have you surrounded. We mean you no harm." I couldn't tell exactly where the booming voice was coming from, but I paid it no mind. *Run. Escape. Find Jace.* I was done following orders. Done explaining myself. My life lay ahead of me, and it started with getting answers about Jace.

I ducked into a group of trees, hoping the cover would shake the copters. Meanwhile, I spotted people on foot dressed a lot like the ones who'd kidnapped Jace and me. Meatheads. What were they doing here? I was certain people had tried to stay out of isolation before. Meatheads weren't for that. Or maybe they were. Maybe the runners needed a no-nonsense approach. Or maybe I'd gotten into deeper crap than I thought when I'd disabled the tracking on my screen. Whatever brought them there, I'd never outrun them. I needed an out. More than a blasted pock-etknife would give me, that was for sure.

The woods were thick, and it bought me a bit of time. But naturally, I tripped over a fallen branch and got a mouthful of leaves when I went down. It wasn't all roses and sunshine. But that's when it hit me to bury myself in the foliage.

I didn't have to dig that far. Where I hid was covered in leaves and twigs. I stowed the backpack high in one of the trees close enough I could see it, but not so close it would give me away. Then I laid under the branch I tripped over, hoping it would discourage them from stepping on me, and buried myself in leaves, gook, and moss.

This would work. It had to. My story didn't end here. I knew that like I knew how to breathe. At least for now. How ironic would it be if I died right in the leaves? It would take them forever to find me then, which would serve them right. The thought made me want to laugh, but with more hysteria than humor, so I decided I should probably get a handle on it.

But as the team filtered into the woods, doubt crept into my mind. "Turn on your infrared goggles. She's in here somewhere. I can feel it," a woman's voice said. That same one who came to Jace's room. The beauty queen enforcer.

Crap on a cracker. They had infrared goggles? They'd find me in a second. I struggled to calm my breathing, if for no other reason than I didn't want to look like some kind of leaf pile come to life.

They walked slowly, probably scanning high and low

for me. I had to think fast, but I couldn't. My brain was paralyzed by the fear of being found. If this were a fight-or-flight scenario, I'd be a deer in the freaking headlights.

"Group Alpha, scan the trees. Beta, scan the ground. Move," the woman commanded.

With every breath I took, their footsteps crunched closer and closer. The urge to scream bubbled in the back of my throat, and I swallowed hard to keep it down. I'd been manhandled by those jokers before, and I had no desire for an encore. Not my ideal way to spend my last moments, that was for sure.

One stopped to my left. I could've grabbed his ankle if I wanted to. Clutching the pocketknife to my chest, I tried to take shallow breaths.

As he stepped over the branch I'd tripped on, he came down on my hair. I fought the urge to cry out.

"Trees over here are clear, ma'am." The man's voice was deep and intimidating. He wasn't one of the men who'd spoken to me a few days ago. He was new. Awesome. There were more of them. A lot more by the sounds of the footsteps.

"Hey, I think I've got something over here," a voice far to my left shouted.

The tree searcher turned, digging his heel into my hair and took off running toward the sound. Whatever they saw, it wasn't me. Probably a fox or something. It didn't matter. That little creature saved my skin.

As their footsteps grew quieter in the distance, I stood, casting all the leaves off, grabbed the backpack, and ran in the opposite direction. One thing was for sure—my diligence paid off. They weren't tracking me with the screen I had.

As I ran, I knew I'd have to pop out of these woods

eventually. But when I did, I hoped that copter and everyone else hunting for me would be following those infrared sensors.

That rhino was bigger and stronger than I was. But he wasn't smarter. Chaos was his game, but I didn't come here to play it. I came here to leave him in his own dust.

FIFTEEN

The woods ended near the bottom of the mountain where Jace fell. I was getting my bearings. The hospital wasn't far from there. The map said it was just a few miles.

Creeping out into the relative open, I thought about what had gone down. Almost nothing I had done made my escape happen. Nothing. That net missed me, and their sensors didn't land on me. The only thing that had helped me was making sure they couldn't track me. But it was their bumbling that allowed me to escape. They knew where I was for a moment, and they hadn't found me. I couldn't let that happen again. They'd step up their game, and I had to stay ahead of them if I wanted to get out.

I realized the sun was rising. I'd spent the entire night running. And I'd spend what was left of my day running as well. I didn't have time to rest. I had hours left. Minutes maybe. I had to get to Jace.

But the more they hunted me, the more I wondered about Jace. Why the extreme measures to catch me? Did they need me to keep Jace in line?

I walked past where Jace had fallen, but I saw no sign of

the accident. No blood. No debris. Nothing. Someone else could climb there that day, and they'd never know what happened.

I kept walking, snacking on some dried fruit as I followed the map. Less than a mile to go. Which was good. The sun was up. Everyone else on the island would be, too. They wouldn't be able to hunt me so openly if they didn't want to disturb the guests. But I'd have a ton of new eyes on me. Potential helpers for the ones who hunted me. *Stay out of sight and get to Jace* became my mantra.

He fueled my fire. I had to get to him before I died. Then, a thought occurred to me. If everyone thought he was dead, and he wasn't, what were they doing to him? All bets were off. He had no protection. No rules. No limits. They'd kill him trying to find their key to survival if they had their way. Maybe they already had. I checked his name on the screen just to make myself feel better. Still green. Hopefully, that meant life. But I was starting to doubt even that. Maybe it meant what section he was in? Who knew? There were plenty of greens on the screen. But also a few reds and some purples as well.

No matter what any of it meant, I needed a plan.

If I just went stumbling into the hospital again, odds were I wouldn't be met with someone as kind as Max. I'd more likely run into that blonde on a power trip. I had to do my best to stack the deck in my favor. And when the crap hit the fan, I'd just do my best to tuck and roll.

Maybe I could find her. Ask her for help. But her warning to stay away didn't bode well for me or my faith she'd be happy to see me.

What could I do to stack the deck? To be honest, I had literally no idea what I could do besides hacking their system. But that wouldn't help me if someone tried to stop me. Jace and I lived hard and we'd even scrounged and found happiness in the little things, but we weren't fighters. We were Withs. We followed. Did what we were told, when we were told, so the Withouts could be happy.

I remembered the horror stories they told us when we went into the workforce together. Babies dying in their mother's arms. Whole families torn apart in the blink of an eye. People dying in horrific car accidents. Life was cruel to them, so the Withs worked hard to make it better.

We didn't have the fear of dying around every corner. All of us died one way or another, between 12:01 AM and 11:59 PM. That was the tradeoff. And the Withouts hated us for it.

We had our own reasons to hate them. They had a life free of responsibility. And now, Jace and I didn't fit into either world. So where did that put us?

Right now, it put me smack in the shadow of the looming hospital building. I swallowed the last of my dried fruit and contemplated what to do first. I had to think about this logically, not emotionally. Not exactly my forte, but I could give it a solid try, right?

I found a relatively safe spot to hide in some underbrush, then went to work on the hospital's security. Time ticked away as I worked to give myself the clearance I needed to navigate the floors. I felt like I was already two steps behind right out of the gate.

But not for long, I told myself as I watched most of the doors inside the hospital go from red to green for me. Today, I changed the game.

SIXTEEN

With the help of the screen, I opened the outer doors to the hospital easily. I decided not to take the front entrance. The map on my screen said there was a fire escape on the side of the building, so I started there, mentally preparing myself to climb over ten flights of stairs to get to the top, where Jace was supposed to be.

It was suffocating and stuffy in the stairwell, and I was completely out of breath and drenched in sweat by the time I got to the steel door leading to the experimental floor Max worked on where I hoped to find Jace or at least some clue to where he was.

The screen needed a little finessing to unlock that door. I'd gotten it to go yellow before I ever went into the hospital, but that didn't mean it would let me in. While I tried to sweet talk it, I glanced at the clock on the screen. It was already almost noon. Time ticked away on my date while I engaged in foreplay with a locked door.

I stood there far too long, and the longer it took me to dig into the system, the more anxious I got. Every time I thought I was getting close, the screen would give me an error code or tell me the path didn't exist.

"I'm standing right in front of the freaking path, you hunk of junk. It exists." My voice echoed through the stairwell, making me cringe. Would the people on that top floor have heard my little outburst?

I couldn't think past the sweat dripping into my eyes and occasionally onto the screen. I went and sat on the nearest step, trying and failing to find some comfort while I worked.

Then, I found a hidden icon. I didn't even do it on purpose. I'd gone down a rabbit hole of files marked for the hospital when I found something marked with an odd word. *He Xiangu.* When I tapped the icon, it opened up to a window requiring a password. The cursor blinked while I debated the best approach.

A workaround might fool the software, but I doubted it. Still, it was worth a shot. I tried every single workaround I'd learned in my brief time dabbling in technology and a few I made up on the fly. Every single time, it kicked me out. Frankly, I was surprised it didn't lock up completely after so many attempts.

Finally, I decided to try a long shot and type something into the password bar. But what? I tried *He Xaingu,* but it kicked it back.

Two attempts remaining flashed in purple on the screen. So, it did have its limits.

I decided to try it again, but all one word and lowercase. *hexaingu.* But that kicked back, too.

One attempt remaining.

I sighed. I was so close. The answers I needed were just on the other side of that door.

Out of blind frustration, I tried one more workaround.

It was messy and reckless and left pieces of myself behind, so they'd know I was there. But I was desperate. I didn't have time to be clean. And miracle of miracles, it worked. It opened a host of new data, including camera feeds. My brain warred with itself as I tried to decide what to do first. I could potentially see Jace in his room, just like Max had shown me. See if he were alive. I clicked on it, but it wanted more passwords. More time from me. So impatience won out, and I unlocked the door. Once I was inside, I realized I'd made stupid mistake number six hundred and thirty-five.

The world on the other side of the door was completely different from the stairwell. It was bustling with activity. The hall opened to a central desk I hadn't remembered from before. I wanted to look down at the floor plan to see where I'd popped out and where I'd been before. But there wasn't time for that. Someone was bound to spot me. It was a miracle no one had spotted me yet.

Damage control. I had to find a quiet spot to go over the videos, plans, and documents. That would give me a best-case scenario to get to Jace and find out of they'd been lying about him.

According to the map on my screen, Jace was in the far corner from where I was. I just had to make it there. But I hadn't planned on the floor being so busy. I'd gotten in and out fairly seamlessly last time with Max's help. It seemed like they'd doubled the staff since Jace became their prisoner. How in the world would I get back there without being seen?

The nurse at the desk was on the phone, and people moved back and forth in front of her constantly. Some wheeled unconscious patients across the floor while others hurried in the opposite direction. To my benefit, everyone seemed to be minding their business and no one looked my way. Yet.

I stuck close to the wall, knowing someone would see me soon if I didn't hightail it out of there. But I was afraid to just duck into one of the rooms. There were probably nurses and cameras in there. I'd be a sitting duck.

Not that I wasn't a sitting duck already out in front of God and everyone in the hallway, but whatever. Minor detail.

Unfortunately, I couldn't see anywhere suitable to hide. My option was to go back out and reassess. Maybe even find some blue scrubs so I could blend in like I did last time.

I felt better with a plan of attack in place. But, as I back-tracked, a man came into my path. He was looking down at his screen and hadn't seen me. But if I didn't do something, he'd crash into me. Panic made me push the door to my right open and duck inside. I held my breath as I turned around, fully expecting to be caught red-handed.

But no one came. No declaration of "what do you think you're doing," or "who are you?" In fact, it was dark in there. Enough light streamed through the vertical blinds on the windows that I could see it was an office. An empty office, thank my unlucky stars.

Would this be a good place to get my bearings? No, probably not. The owner of this office could come in at any moment. I hovered by the door, counting my breaths, waiting for that guy to pass by when I heard a woman's voice on the other side.

"No. Move him to three." The door opened, and I stood paralyzed. "Janice. Just make it happen. Move him. We need the room. With so many people giving themselves to the program, we're going to have to open the floor below. But that'll take time and preparation. For now, make do."

My body went boneless, and I slunk down while she was turned away from me. As silently as possible, I crawled under the nearby desk, hoping she'd just put stuff down and leave. She wouldn't camp out in here, would she?

I plastered myself against the back of the desk, praying to whoever was listening to become invisible. People could do that right? Will something into existence? Something like invisibility? Hey, stranger things had happened recently.

But, of course, I was quite possibly the unluckiest human on the face of the earth. She didn't just set something on the desk and leave. She sat in her chair before pulling it up to the desk. Her legs were so close to me that she nearly kicked me with those spiked heels. The only thing that saved me was the sheer size of the desk, which allowed me to get into the far corner and have the teeniest chance of going undetected.

Of course, the universe was not on my side. The urge to sneeze crept up on me like a determined slug trying to get to the grass on a hot day. I pinched my nose, trying to keep the betrayer at bay, but as soon as I let go, it came back in force.

Taking long, slow breaths through my mouth, I lost track of how long I fought with that sneeze. Maybe this was it. This is how I would die. I'd blow my brains out trying to keep a sneeze in. Just as I was about to give up the ghost and reveal myself, someone knocked on the woman's door.

"Jill, you're needed in eight."

"For what?" she asked, clearly not feeling the request at all.

"The nurse is struggling with the patient transfer, specifically completing the paperwork."

She pushed back rather forcefully from the desk, and I

hunched down as small as I could make myself. She was far enough away that if she glanced my direction, she'd see me.

"It's not that hard," she said. "Check the boxes on the screen and move on." Her voice moved toward the door as her impatience escalated.

"Well, the nurse is afraid to check the wrong boxes and mess something up. She says you didn't give them much training on what to do."

"Well, I didn't have time to. Things are happening fast with that girl missing. Everything is out of sorts." They knew I was missing? Of course they knew. Why wouldn't they? But why would they care in the Longevity Ward? Unless they'd pieced together that I would go there. They'd be watching for me. Boy, the special brand of turd labeled just for me was particularly rank today.

The door slammed shut behind her, and I let go of a breath I hadn't realized I was holding. I scrambled out from under the desk, eager to get out of there before that sour woman returned.

I opened the door slowly, peeking through the crack. There were people moving around, but they all had their heads down in their own screens, paying me no mind. All I had to do was make it to the door. It was about ten yards down the hall. No problem. I made it this far, right?

I decided to walk rather than crawl, thinking crawling would draw too much attention to myself. Blend in. Even though I wasn't wearing what everyone else was. That woman hadn't been in scrubs. Maybe I could play myself off as some kind of executive, like her. I looked down at my filthy hooded sweatshirt, thinking I might be overreaching just a bit. Maybe. I picked off a stray leaf leftover from burying myself in the woods and dropped it casually, as if that would help my case.

I walked slowly, measuring each step that brought me closer to my escape, each step that gave me more and more hope I'd do it. I'd make it out and be able to come back with a plan. A way to be undetected. A solution.

But less than ten feet from the door, someone came in through the very door I was heading toward. As I heard the handle click, I watched it open as if in slow motion and ducked into the room closest to me.

I didn't have to pull the door closed behind me. It slammed shut so loudly I cursed myself for choosing it. It was completely dark in there. No windows let any light in, and no light slithered in under the door.

In the darkness, sounds were louder, and I realized the sound of ragged breathing wasn't my own.

SEVENTEEN

Crap on a cracker. I had to get out of there. The ragged breathing slowed as I stayed still. Maybe the person hadn't seen me. Maybe they were hiding just like I was.

I reached up, trying to find the door handle, but I came up empty. All I felt was cool, smooth metal all around. At least until my hand found a button. Throwing caution to the wind, I pressed it and bathed the room in white light.

A girl with long, black hair huddled in the far corner. She started screaming like a banshee as soon as the light came on. Torn between covering my ears and turning the light back off, I was frozen in time for about a second, then I snapped the light back off.

"I'm sorry," I said, but her animalistic scream echoed in my mind. "Please, calm down," I begged.

I was shaking as I slid down into a seated position, waiting to see if she'd alerted anyone to my presence.

A precarious silence settled between us as I tried to decide what to do. She didn't seem to want to hurt me. She wasn't moving. All I could hear was her breathing.

I debated getting out my flashlight, but I was afraid to scare her again, so I just stayed still.

Eventually, when no one came to check on her, I figured it was safe to try to have a chat. "What's your name?"

No answer.

"I'm in trouble."

No answer.

"I need to find my friend Jace."

"Please don't turn the lights on again." Her voice was so quiet, such a low whisper, and it gave me goose bumps. Hearing nothing but a whisper in the dark had to be some kind of terrible omen, right?

I cleared my throat, trying not to let her know how creepy she was. "I won't. I'm sorry. I didn't mean to scare you."

"It hurts," she clarified.

"It hurts?"

"They use it. To control me."

None of that information was making her any less creepy. Not even a little bit. "Why would they need to control you?" I asked.

"Because I don't like it here."

Couldn't say I blamed her for that. "How long have you been here?"

"My parents donated me to the cause. I'm a With. My date is in one thousand, two hundred and seventy-eight days. And every day, I try to make it come sooner."

Bile rose in my throat. Every part of me revolted at the idea of what she'd just said. "How old are you?"

"Ten," she whispered, her voice never getting louder.

I wanted to hug her. To tell her it would be okay.

"What did they do to you?"

"What haven't they done? I miss the days when they let me sleep. Now they say they need me awake."

"Why?"

"So they know. Or something."

Know what? I wondered. How she reacted?

Whatever they'd done to her, it was pretty clear it was awful. I couldn't leave her here. I had to do something to help her.

"Come with us. Jace and me. We're leaving." I didn't think about how complicated it would be to take a ten-year-old who was hurt by any kind of light along with us. I just sprang into action.

But she didn't jump at the chance to escape like I expected her to. The silence that hung in the room dragged on so long I wasn't sure she was still there with me.

"Do you know what they'd do if they caught us? If they catch you?" The whisper was even quieter than before, making it sound more like a threat than a warning.

I didn't feel a need to answer that question. She knew full well I had no idea what they were capable of, whoever *they* were. If I did, I might not be trying to break Jace out in the first place. Sometimes, ignorance was bliss.

"No, you don't. Death would be better than what they'll do to you. You need to go. Leave Jace. Do it now."

"No. I would never do that," I said. "Jace and I..." What exactly were we? Soul mates? Two halves of the same heart? Despite how cheesy it sounded, I felt the truth of it. It was why I was crouched in that dark room with that creepy girl to begin with.

"Jace and I need each other."

"It's nice to have someone like that," the girl whispered. "I guess that's worth dying for. But is it worth living for if they catch you?"

That question was far too heavy for a ten-year-old. "I'm not leaving you here," I vowed.

"You have to." Fear tore at the edges of her whispers, making the hair on my arms stand up straight. When she came and took my hand, I nearly leapt right out of my skin. Ignoring my horribly uncompassionate reaction, she plowed forward.

"The nurse will be in soon to give me dinner. Go while you can. Free yourself. Make a change. It starts with you. I can feel it."

I frowned in the dark. "Change? No. You've got it all wrong. My date is today. I could die at any moment. I'm just here for Jace."

"None of us are here for change. And as long as that's the truth, they win. We're their captives. Too scared to fight back. To beaten to stand up. You must end this."

"And what exactly is *this*?" I asked, not sure a ten-year-old could answer me.

"The quest for longevity. To live beyond our dates. After that? Who knows? Immortality maybe." She laughed quietly, sadly, and I could tell she thought very little of the work being done there.

Well, at least we agreed on that. "I'm just trying to survive," I said, trying to make her see I wasn't what she needed. I could save her, but the thought of saving everyone on that floor was overwhelming. And when I really thought about the details—about possibly getting out of there with a girl who screamed like she was dying every time light touched her—was I so sure I could save her, too?

"You've got to do more than survive. You've got to find a way for all of us to *live*."

"In less than five hours? Sure. No problem. I'll get right on that."

Shoving me away from her, she scrambled to the corner. Just as I was recovering, the door swung in toward me and light streamed in from the hall. She whimpered as she tried to stay away from the direct beam, and I got a good look at her.

Her black hair was long and stringy, and she was thin as a rail. She wore a white knit hat on her head, the only thing that made her seem like a kid. Dark bags hung low under her eyes, but she never once looked at me. Never gave me away. I nodded to her, vowing I would come back for her. I wouldn't leave her there to be tortured like that. Would I?

"Go," the girl whispered.

The nurse moved about the room, setting a tray on a table near the bed I hadn't seen before. She never bothered to shut the door behind her, despite the fact she must've known the light hurt the poor girl.

"My, you're rather cranky today. Aren't you, Annabelle?"

Annabelle. A ten-year-old who had been trampled and broken by the rhino. Sadness, anger, disgust, and all the above swirled in my mind as I struggled to leave her there.

"Go," she said. But it wasn't a whisper this time. It was her best attempt at a shout.

It startled me into action, and I slipped out the open door while the nurse lectured her about being polite.

EIGHTEEN

Going back to the stairwell was automatic. I couldn't stop thinking about Annabelle. About the life her own parents sentenced her to. About what would make her need to stay in that torture chamber? What could possibly be worse than what they were already doing to her?

Questions swirled in my mind as I slipped unnoticed into the stairwell and down to the floor below. I decided to hide in one of the empty rooms instead of out in the open just in case someone came snooping around. I'd heard them say they were working to expand to that floor, and I didn't want to be caught unaware. Annabelle had given me an out for no reason at all. Except for some strange reason, she thought I could save the world.

I was no revolutionary. BethAnne Mcumban was the one who split the Withs and Withouts. The one who created our society as we knew it. The one who stopped the chaos things had dissolved to. She was a woman of change. I wondered what she'd think of how things were going. She died long before I was ever born as a With. She had cancer, and it was said her death was very slow and painful. Still, she never stopped working. To her dying day, she worked to make the lives of Withouts better. To bring balance, she said.

But who had she hurt in the process? Was it even possible to be a revolutionary without hurting someone? I didn't even want to know. I wasn't cut out for that responsibility. No. All I needed to do was save Jace before my own clock ran out. I'd make it up to Annabelle some other way. Maybe Jace could make her life easier. If I made it to him and told him about her, maybe he could put in a good word. He must be their golden child. Hopefully, that came with perks. Maybe, if I had time, I could hack the system and delist her for experimentation. Maybe.

First thing first, though. *Get to Jace.*

I pulled out the map and saw that in my attempt to safely flee, I'd positioned myself as far from Jace as I could get. He was on the complete other side of the floor. Clicking around a bit, I discovered something I hadn't seen before. He. Was. Alive. His vitals, the nurse's rotations, notes, everything was there. The relief I felt made my entire body wobbly, and I nearly melted right out of my chair and onto the floor. I was right. They'd lied. As that thought sank in, I was filled with new hope and vigor to get to him.

All I had to do was not die before I could make it happen. Easy, right?

It would be safer for me to walk to the other side from where I was, then take the stairwell up.

This time, I decided to try the video feeds, but his was blocked and needed more finessing than I had time for. It would take too much time to hack. The closer I got to midnight, the more likely it was I'd keel over at any second. Knowing he was there was enough for me. Feeds of the floor told me what I already knew. It was bustling. And I'd need a disguise.

Once I knew where he was, I set about searching for those blue scrubs. Lucky for me, the floor was empty. I assumed they'd already begun work to expand the Longevity Ward and relocated everyone. But then, where were the workers who should've been making it suitable for the work they were doing upstairs? It didn't matter much since it worked out in my favor.

Unfortunately for me, all I could find were white scrubs in the end. After searching the last room closest to the stairwell on the far side, I decided white would be better than what I had on. I also grabbed a surgical mask for good measure. No need for someone to recognize me offhand. No, people weren't wearing them when they were walking around, but maybe I could make it work. Quickly, I changed my clothes, jammed them into my pack, and stashed it just inside the stairwell. I imagined we'd need to make a fairly quick getaway. I kept the screen, though. Not only would it be helpful, but all the employees also had one. They all had their faces buried in them when I wandered around up there before. Maybe it would help me blend better. Maybe.

I steeled myself as best as I could before marching up the stairs and going into the unknown yet again.

Jace's room should be down the hall, the first right, and four doors down. When I made the turn, I nearly ran smack into a guy in blue scrubs.

"Watch where you're going." He carried a stack of used bedpans, and he nearly dumped them all over me. "I'd hate to spoil those white scrubs," he said with a smirk. I just blinked at him. "What are you doing wearing those anyway?"

"Got the blue ones dirty. This is all they had."

"And the mask? You worried you're going to catch a cold?" Snorting derisively, he kept talking. "Rookie. Here, you deal with these. I don't have time for them." He shoved the pans at me. Rather than let them crash to the floor and splash all over me, I took them. Dirty bedpans.

Speechlessly, I watched him walk away before storing the bedpans around the corner I'd just came from. Not my monkeys, not my circus.

A nurse sat at a small desk along the far wall. I ignored her as I hurried straight to Jace's room, screen in hand.

But the door wouldn't open. I tried my screen, but Jace's room was a bit of a dead zone. In hindsight, the darkened cameras should've tipped me off. Deciding it wasn't a great idea to just hover outside his door, I moved to the nurse's desk.

I swallowed hard before I interrupted the busy woman who was torn between typing on her screen and handling phone calls. "Yes, ma'am. Right away. I'll have Shoeman handle it. Of course." She hung up, but she didn't look up at me.

"Excuse me, can you let me into 1407? My clearance code isn't working."

Finally, she lifted her head. "What's your authorization?"

"I just need to change the bedpan."

Her face blanked, her brown eyes searching mine for the truth before confusion crinkled at the corners and her mouth drew down into a frown. She knew. I'd never get away with being so brazen. *Panic. Panic. Panic. Panic.*

"These long hours are killing me. I could swear you guys were just in there for those." She shook her head as she reached over and pushed a button on the screen.

"There you go. Get your screen fixed, okay? I don't have time to let you guys in all the time."

"Of course. Thank you," I said graciously as I ran to Jace's room.

A sigh of relief escaped me as I leaned against Jace's door. But that feeling didn't last. Nothing could've prepared me for what I saw inside that room.

NINETEEN

Machines beeped steadily as I stared at the boy I'd grown up with on the bed. He didn't even look at me. Dark circles under his eyes combined with that weird greyish tone to his skin and sunken cheeks made him appear as if he were on the verge of death. I fingered the bracelet he'd given me after our day playing games. It seemed so long ago. What had they done to him?

"Jace..." The whisper escaped me. He smiled, but he still didn't open his eyes.

Wires and tubes of all colors and sizes ran to and from his body.

I stood by the door, glued to my spot while I tried to decide what to do next. I'd expected him to be...maybe not well but functional at least. I wanted to talk to him. I needed him to talk to me. Tell me it would be okay. That he would be okay once I was gone. This wasn't at all how I'd pictured things.

Tears sprang to my eyes as he stirred. "Why are you just standing there? Do what you need and leave me alone." His tone was so bitter it made the tears fall faster. Who was he? What had they done to him?

Finally, he opened his eyes. The anger burning there was like nothing I'd ever seen before. Frankly, I had no desire to ever see it again. But as he processed what he was looking at, his expression changed to confusion before going back to anger.

"Look, whatever you guys are doing to me, this is a low blow. I draw the line at making me hallucinate."

"Jace, I'm not a hallucination. I'm here to..." To what? Say goodbye? He'd already done that. Suddenly, my good intentions turned to ash in my mouth. I shouldn't have come. I should've died alone. But even as I thought it, I knew it wasn't true. We weren't meant to be alone.

He blinked a few times while he watched me dissolve into a blubbering mess on the floor. "What's going on?" Sitting up with some considerable effort, he scrutinized me.

"Aren't you a hallucination?"

I wiped the snot off my face with the back of my arm. "No. I thought I needed to see you before I died, but not like this."

He frowned. "Come here."

I rose, went to his bedside, and then took his outstretched hand. "I feel you."

"I feel you." And in that moment, some of the regret I had fell away. But how could I leave him there suffering like that?

"They said you were dead."

"Who did?"

"The news. They said you died. Seems like your survival was creating a bit of a panic."

Just then, something beeped. Two succinct beeps, one

right after another. He glanced at the clock, and his eyes got big. "You shouldn't have come here."

The words hurt, and I jerked away from him. "Why?"

"It's midnight, and you're still alive. And you came right into the lion's den."

TWENTY

"What?" He must've been mistaken. Both of us couldn't have outlived our dates.

"You heard me."

"I lived?"

"You lived. Just like me. Now, please, don't end up like me. Get out." He was so harsh, but there was more to it than that. As I gazed into his sunken eyes, I saw fear. Fear for him or me, I wasn't sure.

I couldn't help the laugh that bubbled up inside me. I. Had. Lived. We could be together. But as I surveyed the room, saw the machines monitoring him and the evidence of what they'd done to him, I knew we couldn't do it here.

"You're coming with me."

"Now you're talking crazy."

"No, I'm not."

"Rare, listen to me. I can hardly walk. Get out. I will never forgive you if you waste the time you've been given. Go. Now."

He'd never spoken to me like that before, and it nearly made me cry. But I knew he wasn't speaking to me out of love—like I was to him. He spoke from fear. And fear made people stupid. Irrational. Hopeless. But I loved him too much to leave him in this situation.

"You're saying you'd just leave me here if the situation were reversed?" I suggested.

He didn't look at me. I could see the war raging inside him, so I decided to push.

"You're saying if the shoe was on the other foot, if you'd survived, too, you'd have left me to rot knowing they were torturing me in their quest for longer lives? You'd sentence me to that life? And you'd live it happily until the day you died, knowing you chose yourself over me?"

He pressed his lips together, making a fine line, and I noticed he was starting to get some stubble on his chin and his cheeks. It wasn't peach fuzz anymore. He was becoming a man. And I couldn't let that to go to waste.

"Quit that holier-than-thou attitude right now, or I will leave your butt to rot in here." I grabbed onto the railing at the edge of his bed, holding on for dear life and bracing for his response. If he wanted to drive me away, I may have given him an out. I bit my bottom lip, hoping he wouldn't press me.

"How did you get here?" The question was so quiet I wasn't even sure I'd heard him right.

"With a lot of running and a heaping helping of dumb luck."

"Do you think we can do this?" Hope threaded into his shaky voice, and I grabbed onto it with both hands.

I took his hand and held it tightly, hanging on to my life-line and hoping this new chance at life could be his. "Yes. I do. I'm not letting you rot in here. We lived." I laughed. "We lived. We're not wasting our lives as lab rats. We're getting out. And we're doing it now." I wanted to celebrate.

To kiss him. To scream from the hilltops that we were alive. But we didn't have time. Hopefully, we would later when we were safe. And together.

I looked around the room, searching for some answer. Something that would improve our situation. Inside one of the drawers by the sink, I found three silver cylinders that appeared very familiar. Just like the one they'd jammed into Jace's leg after he fell. On the side, it said *RapidHeal*. Jackpot.

Meanwhile, Jace sat up and started yanking at the wires. It took our situation from zero to sixty in about point three seconds. Alarms started sounding, and I knew the nurses would be on us like bees to their honey.

Thinking fast, I pushed one of the recently disconnected machines over to the door and jammed it under the doorknob.

"Dang it, that hurts," he said as he yanked the last few wires out of his arm. Blood streamed from the open wounds, and he struggled to stand. The grey hospital gown didn't do much to cover his body, which already looked like it had been put through the ringer after only a few days. How long had Annabelle been there? No wonder she looked like a living skeleton.

"Now what?" he asked.

There were no windows in his room, not even one on the outside. The only way out was through the door I'd just blocked, which was now being pounded on by the staff. "Jace, open up. This isn't going to accomplish anything."

"You wanna make a bet?" he shouted.

"Probably isn't smart to goad them on."

He shrugged as he sagged against the bed. I decided it was an appropriate time to use one of the cylinders, so I uncapped it, revealing a huge needle.

"What the hell do you plan to do with that?"

Rather than answer him, I jammed it into his leg. He cried out in pain, making the pounding on the door outside more urgent. "Jace, what's going on in there? If you're harming yourself, it won't do you any good. You're immortal, remember? You can't kill yourself."

"Says you," he said through clenched teeth. The color blossomed in his cheeks, and he sat straighter within seconds. "Anyway, why are you worried if you think I can't kill myself anyway?"

They answered with stronger ramming against the door.

"They're getting serious," he said. "We should go. Now."

Frustrated, I glared at the ceiling, but then spotted a ventilation duct. "There. We get out there."

After I pushed the bed under it, I hopped up. "Give me a boost, will ya?"

He jumped up, suddenly full of energy, and I wondered how long the shot would last. We didn't have access to it back home, so I didn't have a lot of experience with it. Hopefully, we'd be out of that prison before he crashed, if that was even a thing.

He hoisted me up. I yanked the cover off the vent and crawled inside, scrambling out of the way before he rather nimbly pulled himself up behind me.

"Now what?"

"Now we get out of here." Randomly, I picked a direction and started moving, knowing staying still would doom us.

"Hey, pull the vent closed behind you, will ya?" The last thing we needed was to tip them off to where we'd gone. Let them wonder for a minute or two at least.

I heard it click as I crawled through the vent.

"You could be a little quieter there, Twinkle Toes," Jace teased.

Easier said than done. Crawling through a steel vent was noisy. "I'm trying."

Somehow, he was sliding along much more quietly than I was as he brought up the rear. Or maybe I was just covering up his clunking with my own.

"They're gonna find us," he whispered.

"Just stop for a second," I said after we'd rounded a corner and gotten out of sight of our vent. I pulled out the screen and tried to see where we were, but Jace tapped me on the shoulder.

"I don't think this is a suitable place to camp."

I glanced up to see a cloud of something dark coming our way. "That can't be good," I said as I scrambled to stow the screen and get away.

We crawled the length of the vent when it ended at the top of a T. Our only option was to follow it left or right. But the dark cloud poured in on us from either direction.

"We have to get out of here," Jace said.

"Thanks, Captain Obvious," I said, wishing I had more of a weapon than my little pocketknife as I kicked the vent out beneath me.

Jace put a hand on my shoulder. It was the first time he'd reached for me since I found him. He resembled my old friend, not the scared and angry creature they'd made him. "Let me go first."

When I cocked an eyebrow, he insisted. "For all they know, this is just me. Let's see how they react. You could still get away."

"No way." I shook my head. "I'm not leaving you."

"We don't have time to debate it." He frowned. The

dark cloud was close enough to touch. We didn't have time to bicker.

He dropped out of the vent, and I watched him from above for about a half a second. He wanted me to be safe, but I had no idea what that cloud of crap would do and I was zero percent interested in finding out.

I dropped behind him to find total chaos below. People with gas masks and full gear ran in every direction. More than one was armed with a black rifle.

"Are they going to kill us?" I asked.

"No. They wouldn't. They need us too much."

Alarms began to blare as the smoke started to pour out of the vents. "Time to go," he said as he yanked my arm in a random direction.

A nurse slammed into my shoulder as we ran down the hall. Occasionally, I could see the door to the stairwell, at least when Jace would move his big head out of the way. We were close, but we still had about ten yards to go.

"Stop," a man's voice shouted. But there was no way we were stopping. We didn't have fancy gear like they did, and I wanted out of that smoky death trap.

"I'll shoot," he threatened. But Jace kept moving, kept pulling me toward the big silver door that led to our freedom. We just had to get to the stairs, and everything would be okay. I hoped. We could ignore the fact we were being pursued, and a steel door wouldn't stop them. One goal at a time. Get to the door. Out of the hospital. Then get off the island.

A high-pitched buzzing sound filled the air. Instinctually, I knew the rifles were armed and trained on us. "What are those, Jace?"

"Stunners," he shouted over his shoulder. "Don't let them hit you.

Five yards to go. So close. The first blast was a miss. It hit the wall we were running toward.

The second hit me in the leg, and it brought me down. "Jace, keep going!"

He dragged me behind him, and I desperately tried to keep up. We could almost touch the door when a third blast cut through the air.

Suddenly, in the middle of the chaos, a small girl covered in head-to-toe black with long hair stood calmly. Her arms outstretched as if she were commanding the world to stop. Annabelle. She positioned herself between us and the shooters, wearing the darkest sunglasses I'd ever seen. Could she even see out of them?

"Stop," she whisper-shouted. Everyone halted their movement for just that one second. The world held its breath while we waited to see what she would do.

"Annabelle," I said pleadingly. "Don't do anything stupid. Stand down. Come with us. Something. Don't stand in the crossfire."

"Go," she mouthed, and I couldn't bring myself to move. Jace, on the other hand, didn't need to be told twice. He tugged on my arm, freeing me from my spot. Well, except for my dead leg.

It made our progress slow. I didn't want to leave her. I kept looking back. As I watched, they took aim at her and mercilessly shot her over and over again with the blasts. Her scream was louder than anything I'd ever heard. It sounded like a dying animal, and it echoed over the chaos and straight to my heart.

Jace dragged me through the door, and it slammed behind us. We got away. Because of her.

"Is she dead?" I asked as we stood in the silence of the stairwell.

"We can't think about that now. We have to move."

He was still in escape mode, but I couldn't get my brain to click into that gear. We were safe because of her sacrifice.

"She was only ten, Jace."

"Rarity..." He took me by both shoulders, staring into my eyes. "Don't waste her sacrifice. Get your mind right, and let's go. There will be time for grieving later."

He was right. My head knew he was. But my heart...oh, how my heart cried out for her, broke for her life and what it wasn't.

"Look at me," Jace commanded. Tears pooled in my eyes before spilling over onto my cheeks. "Don't. Waste. Her sacrifice."

He was right. I didn't want to be trapped like she was. I wanted a life with Jace. A life that now had hers on my head. But still, it was better than being experimented on for the rest of time. Right?

Neither seemed terribly ideal, but I knew they'd be coming through that steel door at any moment. So living with the guilt seemed like the lesser of two evils.

When I finally nodded, he grabbed my hand and pulled me down the stairs. We took them two at a time.

"I need to block some of the doors, so they can't follow us." But taking the stairs and manipulating that screen was no easy feat. I nearly dropped it more than once.

"Here, in here." About four floors down, Jace yanked me out of the stairwell. "They'll think we went straight down. But if we cut across to another stairwell, we might throw them off."

I nodded as I hacked the system, locking doors at random and crashing everything I could get my mitts on.

A boom loud enough to rattle the walls rumbled from above us. "What was that?"

Jace shook his head without answering. We probably didn't want to know. The whole unit was going to hell in a handbasket because of us. Because of *me*.

I tried not to focus on it as I kept systematically shutting things down.

"Wait," Jace said. "Don't lock too many." Doors around us clunked as they locked, and I looked up.

We were at the stairwell. I'd left us a clear path to the exit. All we had to do was take it. Then, I'd lock the doors behind us and completely trash the system once we were out. They'd be untangling things for days. But I didn't have any satisfaction about it at all. I just felt heavy.

"Come on," Jace said as he held the door open to the stairwell. I nodded as I made my way down to the ground floor. They didn't get us. They couldn't by that point.

We walked toward the door, and I could see we were going to have a new problem. Instead of transparent glass, it had turned silver, as if a sheet of metal were drawn down in front of the door.

"What's this?" Jace asked.

"They're not giving up," I said as I moved through open windows on my screen, trying to find the right one.

"Shocker," he said as we stood in front of the doors.

I opened the window for the doors. It was red, giving me a massive error message. But I wasn't deterred. I just needed time. Would they give it to me, though?

My fingers danced across the screen, trying to woo the program into letting us out. But whoever fought me was good. It was frustrating just having that tiny screen. They were probably fighting me from behind a huge, powerful setup. I had to improvise a bit. And it was hurting me. Every time I gained an inch, they pushed back even more. Until finally, I went too far.

CRITICAL ERROR. WARNING.

"Well, that's just crap-your-pants fantastic," I said. Red lights flashed near the door.

"What did you do?"

"Nothing good," I said as I shifted my weight in front of the doors, trying to decide what to do.

A countdown clock started on my screen, and I knew *that* couldn't be good. "I think we need to get away."

"What?"

"Run," I said as I grabbed his hand. We took off as far away from the doors as I could get. In one fell swoop, I leapt over the desk with Jace close on my heels.

The explosion left a high-pitched ringing in my ears, and the dust cloud made it hard to breathe or see. But Jace held on tight to my hand and pulled me out from under the desk that shielded us from most of the shrapnel.

I still couldn't hear anything as lights flickered and grey dust hung in the air. The ringing didn't let up as we stepped through the now-broken doors and out into the sunlight.

We made it out. We survived. But we'd poked the rhino in the process. And he was madder than a hornet about it.

TWENTY-ONE

The choppers were on us like I'd soldered their lights to my butt. Sirens blared and people made their way in steady streams out of the buildings.

"Evacuate. Everyone to the transportation depot in a quick and orderly fashion." The overly cheery announcement was comical in the chaos.

"This way," Jace yelled, and I seriously appreciated the magic of that shot I'd given him. He had a heck of a lot more energy than I did. On the plus side, my leg was coming back to life and I was keeping up a little easier.

We went against the flow of people and quickly ducked into a building, even though everything in my mind screamed against doing it.

"They'll trap us in here," I said as I followed him anyway. The building was surprisingly empty. Evacuation was no joke on the island. One little explosion and they were all freaking out.

"I see your glass is half empty today, Rare," he said as he held my hand while peeking carefully around a corner.

I said nothing. All I could see were those people who'd

kidnapped us after his date. The ones in black. The ones who'd hunted me and nearly sniffed me out of the brush.

"These people...they're better equipped than us. They'll find us if we give them a chance."

"Well, we shouldn't give them a chance."

He opened a metal door with a clang, and the staircase inside led down in all directions.

"Jace, seriously, how are we not going to get trapped down there? Why don't you let me look at the map for a second?"

I pulled out my screen, but the genuine hurt in his eyes stayed my hand. "Just trust me, okay?" The bite to his tone made me regret questioning him. But he hadn't been out here running from them for the last few days. He'd been chained to a bed.

The apology I should've given him got stuck in my throat and he turned away, dragging me deeper into the basement of the building. Darkness closed in on us the deeper we went into the bowels of the structure, which wasn't helping my nerves at all. Even if I did keep peeking over my shoulder, there came a point where I couldn't see a dang thing.

I heard Jace open a door and pull me behind it before it closed.

"Jace?" I needed to hear his voice. Even though I could feel his hand on mine, I needed to know the darkness hadn't eaten him.

"Jace isn't here anymore," he said, his voice comically deep.

I smacked blindly at him, making no connections before giving up. "Good. Maybe you'll take me out of this hole he dragged me into."

"Sorry, princess. You're on your own there," he said,

using that same voice and trying not to laugh as he turned on a light.

"Figures," I said as I shoved him, moving him about an inch.

The room was fully furnished, complete with a television, a couch, some old-fashioned arcade games, a pool table, and pinball machines. It was a teenager's dream hangout spot.

"What *is* this place?" I asked, wondering if we should've spent more time exploring and less time in the game room.

He went to a mini fridge, then pulled out some water and even some snacks. I took them gratefully as I eyed the door behind us.

"It's just a hangout spot. But it's got a pretty excellent steel door on it. And it's got another great feature one of the guys showed me before you got here." He went back to the fridge, then pushed it aside with some effort. Dumbly, I just stood there and watched while I chewed my granola bar.

In the wall behind the fridge there was...nothing. I slouched, feeling a bit defeated. I wasn't even sure what I expected to see, but it wasn't more yellow wall that's for sure.

"Um...impressive?" I asked.

Jace held up one finger, then gave me a half smile. Raising an eyebrow, I crossed my arms over my chest, preparing to be amazed yet again.

He put his hand on what felt like a random spot on the wall. It wasn't even right side up. Just unceremoniously slapped against the wall like he and it were chums or something.

Just as I was about to give him a slow clap, the wall behind his hand started to glow and something behind him clicked. A sly smile grew from the corner of his mouth as he watched me. I had to admit I was curious.

As I stood there, the wall opened up like some kind of half door and revealed a tunnel behind it.

"Where does it go?" I asked, completely bewildered about the tunnel's existence and purpose.

"Anywhere you want. There are tunnels all over the island."

"For what?"

"Mostly for the workers to get around unseen."

Curiously, I cocked my head. I'd seen workers walking topside. Why would they need a system like this?

"But what for?"

"The guy who showed it to me said they use it to move stuff around. Food, supplies, things that might be unsightly to the residents."

"Unsightly?" I raised an eyebrow. I'd never heard him use a word like that before.

"His word."

"Clearly."

He frowned. "Well, are you coming or you just gonna stand there asking questions?" He stepped into the tunnel, and I had no other choice but to follow him.

"We'll never get out of here with all those people heading right where we need to be. Let them do their thing. We'll get out right after them."

The plan sounded good to me. But only if we could duck our hunters long enough to let them finish evacuating the island.

That got me thinking. Where would they send every-one? Certainly not to be with the Withouts. But the Withs would be outraged to be sent back to their zones to live out the remainder of their dates. Either way, I felt disaster looming like that spicy meal I regretted eating last week.

He pulled the door closed behind me. We were tossed into total darkness, but not for long. Jace produced a small flashlight he must've grabbed from inside and illuminated the entire tunnel, but not shedding much light on where we were.

Our footsteps echoed on the cement ground, and I found myself wanting to walk slower and slower as we dove deeper into the bowels of the island.

"Could we stop for a minute?" I asked finally.

He looked around. "Sure, but let's not camp out here."

"I just want to try to check up on them, see if they know where we are."

"Do you think they can track that screen?"

"I disabled that," I said as I pulled it out, trying to figure out what their next play was.

I opened up a file about the evacuation and scanned it quickly. I followed it to its origins. From there, I was able to hack into a classified debrief that was being updated as I went.

Several keywords stuck out to me. *Massive explosion. Several injured. No confirmed number yet. Annabelle Chesney, ten years old, no known surviving family, first confirmed permanent comatose.*

Permanent comatose. The worse echoed in my mind. People couldn't be killed before their dates, but they could cease to live. She would never wake up because of me. I forced myself to keep reading while my stomach churned with what I'd done.

Two missing. Jace Brown and Rarity Delman. Considered armed and dangerous. Capture alive.

Our pictures stared back at me as I blinked at the report.

I swallowed as I tried to comprehend the information. She'd never wake up again. And they weren't lying. A classified report would have no reason to be falsified. She'd done it for us, and now they were on the hunt.

I leaned the screen toward Jace. He frowned as we sat in the tunnel, our backs against the walls. "What now?" he asked.

To be honest, I had no idea. "Well, we either stick to your plan and try to get off the island after everyone's out, or we hide here indefinitely."

Either option made me want to puke.

"Rarity..." He took my hand, and I looked up into his face. It was covered in grime and dust, but looked more and more like his old self, which made my shoulders relax. "Tell me what happened."

"You were there. You saw what happened."

"No, before that. What made you decide to come for me?"

I chuckled. "What a silly question with a silly answer. I didn't want to be alone. I wanted to see you one more time before I died."

Smiling like I'd just handed him a cup of steaming hot cocoa, he dove into more questions. "Who was that girl and how did you know her?"

I frowned. "That's a bit more complicated."

"I'm listening."

I explained how she saved me. How she wanted me to save everyone. But instead, I'd hurt a bunch of them and stolen her chance at life outside that prison forever. I'd proved I was right and she was wrong. I was no revolutionary. I was too clumsy for that. Too selfish. To meek.

Jace laughed. He laughed out loud. In fact, it echoed off the walls of the tunnel. I held my hands up, begging him to stop, lest he bring the entire island down on our heads while he made fun of me.

"What, might I ask, is so funny?"

"Your pity party, that's what. You just single-handedly saved me from what was basically a maximum-security prison. And you're having a pity party."

"People were hurt, Jace. Badly. She'll never wake up because of me. She had over a thousand days left until her date."

"Annabelle, that was her name, right?" I nodded. "She did what she did willingly. She saved you on purpose. She made her choice. Now it's time to make yours."

"No. I don't accept that. I've never had a choice in any of this," I shouted, my anger getting the best of me. Jace made no effort to calm me down. Instead, he let my outrage wash over him. "I didn't get to pick being a With. The only choice I made was hacking my way into that hospital and leaving when I didn't die." I stopped short before my anger turned to hot tears. We were both scared. Both damaged by what had happened in the last few days. Both needing things the other wasn't whole enough to give.

"My turn to ask a question."

"Fair enough," he said, the laughter mostly gone from his voice.

I hesitated, not sure I wanted to give the question life. Once I heard the answer, there was no going back from it. "What did they do to you?"

Frowning, he turned away from me. "Some of it, I don't understand. Mercifully, they put me out for some of it. Then there were blood draws and pokes and moving this way and that. But some of it..." I heard the same fear I'd seen in his eyes trying to creep back into his voice. "Some of it doesn't bear repeating. Just know that it was horrible. And they'll sacrifice anything to figure out how to be like us. The drive to survive is not a pretty thing."

Silence strained the air, making it hard to breathe.

I squeezed my eyes shut, trying to shut all of it out. Annabelle. The Withouts. The choppers. The alarms. What they'd done to him. Everything.

But it didn't work. "Someone's coming," Jace said, interrupting my internal pit of doom.

He grabbed my hand, then yanked me to my feet. "Come on."

I needed more time. Time to find a map of the tunnels. Time to figure out what they were doing and what they intended to do with us. Time for everything. But I didn't have it. And I probably never would. They were coming down hard on our heads. All I could do was let him drag me away, hoping he'd know where they wouldn't be.

But I had the screen in my hand. I wasn't helpless. I'd proven that when I broke into that hospital. I'd held off looking at the map to show Jace I trusted him. Now it was my turn.

But the footsteps grew louder, and there wasn't time to get my bearings.

"This way," he said as he jerked me to the left down a passage I hadn't even noticed. I was too busy trying to get the screen up and make it work with that same hand.

"Jace, let go of me," I said, but he didn't respond. He just kept plowing forward, dragging me behind him.

But it was no use. I couldn't get him to listen. He was in rescue mode. Did I need that? Maybe. But as the glow from my screen lit our way, I thought maybe not.

"Jace," I said more sternly as I jerked my arm away. I

could hear the footsteps getting closer to us, and I was sure my voice would lead them straight to us. But I didn't want to be dragged anymore.

He stared, waiting for me to tell him what I wanted. But I had nothing. I looked down at the screen, letting my fingers dance across it. It was almost comforting to be doing something familiar while the world closed in on us. I searched for a map of the tunnels. It was remarkably easy to find *if* a person knew they were there.

"There's a closet down and to the left," I whispered. "Come on." I took off running, not trying to cover the sound of my feet at all. They already knew we were here.

I led him to the closet, which was about fifty feet down the tunnel and around the first corner.

We ducked inside, and I started stacking boxes in front of the door. "This will slow them down, but it won't stop them. If they figure out we're in here, we'll be trapped," he pointed out.

I didn't respond. No need to, really. He was right, after all. I could've just entombed us.

We could hear them outside. Their voices. Shouting. They sure weren't trying to be very inconspicuous.

"We know they came this way. Find them, you fools," the woman commanded. That blonde woman. Commando Barbie, Extreme Edition.

"What's her problem?" I whispered, but Jace didn't answer. Probably smart not to talk. She probably had the ears of a bloodhound. Wait, did they have good hearing? Or was that their sense of smell?

Mixed metaphors aside, I didn't want to find out what she had against me. I just wanted to get away from her. I listened to them scuffling around outside for at least three full minutes before the sounds became more distant.

Once it was quiet in our little closet again, I sagged against the wall and Jace seemed to do the same. We sat illuminated by his tiny flashlight, not exactly sure what to do since we'd escaped our fate...again.

"Now what?" he asked.

"We have *got* to get off this island."

TWENTY-TWO

Frankly, the truth went down about as nicely as a box of rocks. How in God's name were we going to get off the island?

"We can't keep running and hiding from them. We have to get away from them. For good."

I pulled up the map of the tunnel system. "I'll bet you dollars to donuts these tunnels lead to the transport tubes. We just have to find them. And hope they're empty when we get there." The evacuation was definitely pouring slime on our foolproof plan. But the tunnel closest to us did in fact lead straight to the station. It was odd because it seemed like when we came down into the tunnels from that hang out, we were a long way from it. But this made it look like it was right there. Just around the corner basically.

"What's wrong? Jace asked.

"Something doesn't feel right."

"Like you had some bad fish or what?"

"Like I just almost got blown up and I don't want it to happen again."

I studied the map, trying to reconcile it with what I

knew about the surface. The transport station was far from everything else on the island. Unsightly and nothing but practical, it didn't fit in with everything else. So it wouldn't make sense to have it so close to everything. Had we really walked that far in the dark? How far had we run from the blonde's goons?

"Let's just go take a look, I guess," I suggested. It wasn't that far. What could happen?

I nearly laughed out loud at my brazen thought. What could happen? I could nearly be blown up and become some lab rat for the rest of my life. But we shouldn't focus on the little things. Right?

Cautiously, we left our sanctuary and walked out into the tunnel. It was dark and quiet. If the blonde's goons were around, they were being awfully still. And since more than a few of them were mouth breathers, I wasn't sure they were capable of such silence.

"Which way, fearless leader?" Jace asked in a whisper.

I didn't answer. I just took off where the map said to go. But when I got there, it didn't feel right. There wasn't a hatch above like there was supposed to be. Maybe it was just a little farther down. I started to walk when I noticed a red dot shining on the side of the tunnel.

Jace grabbed my shoulder just before I passed by it. He didn't say a word, only shut off his flashlight and pulled me slowly away from it. As silently and slowly as possible, we retreated back to our closet.

"What was that?"

"A trap," Jace answered.

"How do you know that?"

"Rare, we haven't seen any other shining red dots in the tunnel. It was a trap. Trust me."

"Well, we'll never know now, will we?" Despite my sass,

I knew he was right. The whole thing was a trap. The map wasn't right. The longer I studied it, the more I understood what they'd done. My face fell.

"What?"

"The whole thing is a trap." I dropped the screen like a hot potato. "They can't track me, but they can hack me. They led us straight to that trap with a doctored map."

And just like that, our lifeline, our upper hand, was severed.

"Well, nothing like having a little glitter sprinkled on your pile of crap to make it sparkle," Jace said.

"That makes no sense," I said, glaring at the screen. I wanted to stomp on it. Pulverize it. But I couldn't bring myself to. It had gotten us this far. Now, I'd have to do the rest on my own. Which meant getting to the transport station. Once we were there, we could hack those screens easily enough. Assuming there wasn't a hoard of guards waiting for us or a huge mass of evacuees. How long would it take to evacuate the entire island? A couple of hundred residents, plus at least that many employees? One transport station with about ten tubes in it? It would take some time. I glanced down at the screen. It was almost morning. They'd had all night to get it done. Was it enough?

"Without a map, what's our best play?" I asked after I was done mourning the screen.

"I say we walk a bit, go topside to get our bearings, then keep going underground. Pop up occasionally to make sure we're going the right way until we get to the transport station. God knows we don't want to get tangled up in that evacuation. If we can time it right, they'll all be gone when we hit the station."

It all sounded perfectly logical. So logical it might work

if it wasn't for the blonde hound on our tail. "And the search team?"

"We'll deal with them if the time comes."

"When," I corrected.

"Oh ye of little faith." There was a glimmer in his eye that told me there was still hope for us. For our lives. For everything. I wanted to cling to it hard.

We were in this together. We'd be a team, no matter what.

Slowly, he opened the closet door and inched into the hall, shining the flashlight that I swore was bright enough to lead them straight to us. After the whole trap thing, I wished he'd snagged night-vision goggles, not a blasted flashlight, but beggars couldn't be choosers.

"Come on," he whispered as he made his way down the hall. Now that I'd seen the doctored map, I had no idea where the transport station was or how close we were to it. But it felt like we had a long way to go.

The first offshoot Jace decided to take was clear. It was dark when he poked his head out the door, and we found ourselves in the bowels of one of the fancy restaurants.

"Well, not there yet," he said as he closed the door and we backed away from the offshoot.

He turned in what felt like an arbitrary direction, and we kept going. We checked our position twice more, each time the location got a bit more remote. The last time, we ended up in a barn near the edges of main life on the island.

"We're heading the right way," Jace said as he closed the door and kept going the way we'd been going.

I didn't say anything—I just kept marching along behind him. For the first time in our lives, I didn't have anything to say. No joke to share with him. No jab at how he was acting like some kind of meathead superhero. No gratitude for being awesome. Just nothing.

It felt like the gravity of everything that had happened was crashing down on me, and the joy of surviving was being suffocated by the cost of doing so.

"Let's pop out here. We should be getting close." His voice brought my train of thought to a crashing halt, and I just nodded rather dumbly at him.

He didn't seem to notice as he approached the door. Turning a circular metal handle until it clunked, he then pushed the wall, opening what had been an invisible door only moments before. Well, invisible save for the circular handle.

"Well, well. What do we have here?" The man's voice made my blood run cold. I grasped for Jace's arm, wanting to pull him back into the tunnel. To slam the door in the stranger's face and take off in the opposite direction.

But Jace didn't do any of those things. He held up his hands as if he were giving up. As if he knew it was too late.

A low laugh rumbled through the air. I walked out behind Jace, who still had his hands up, palms out.

When I stepped out into the open, it wasn't like the other places we'd popped out. This tunnel entrance was in one of the gardens. I could see the blasted transport station from where we were. And it was empty. Not another soul waited for their turn to get off the island. We'd done it. Almost. So close. And yet. So far.

I sighed heavily, and the man turned his gaze on me. He was big, bearded, and dressed in black. One of the blonde's team. It was almost like they'd been waiting for us. Wonderful. Just what we needed. I hope he brought a side of cyanide with the crap sandwich he was serving us, because this wasn't going to go down easy.

"Oh, I'm sorry, little lady. Am I interrupting something important?" He aimed what looked like a laser pointer at me, and a tiny purple light beam lit up my chest. It was a stunner. If he deployed it, I'd be useless. They'd have me. But maybe Jace could get away.

By the alarmed expression on Jase's face, I didn't think he had any intention of leaving me. Hypocrite.

"Now, listen, seems to me that we can come to some kind of mutual understanding," Jace said as he took a small step to the left, putting himself slightly in front of me. He wasn't blocking the beam yet, but one more step would do it. The guy wasn't stupid, though. He saw what Jace was doing, and he knew he had his aim on the right target. I was valuable, and Jace had just proven it. Get one and the other would follow.

Crap on a cracker. "There'll be no negotiating. You're coming with me, or I will take you. Either way, I win in this scenario."

"See, that's where you're wrong. We can all be winners here. Just hear me out," Jace said, but even I could tell he had nothing. No reason for this guy to listen to him. No ace up his sleeve. He was just buying time, hoping something brilliant would come to him.

He shifted his weight a few inches more to the left. If the guy used the stunner, it would hit Jace, not me. It would get him in the arm, and I wondered how much damage it would do there. Typically, they were most effective with a chest shot. Knocked out the entire system that way. An arm shot wouldn't do any lasting damage, just like it had done to my leg during our hospital escape. It might just give us the distraction we needed.

But the guy saw what he was doing and shifted right along with him, keeping that damn purple light trained right on my chest. I wanted to put a hand over it. Scratch at it. *Something.* But I knew better than to move.

"Tell me about the woman. The blonde. What's got her panties in a wad?" I asked, trying to distract him.

"You mean Lieutenant Sunshine?"

I snorted. "Sunshine? You're kidding. That's not really her name is it?"

"Sonny for short," he confirmed.

"She ain't no ray of sunshine. She's a pain in the butt." It was possible antagonizing him wasn't my wisest move, but I was out of ideas, so I went to my comfort zone—sarcasm.

He laughed, a low, malicious sound that rumbled through my body and made goose bumps rise on my arms. "Well, you've certainly got her number. And I believe she's got yours."

Now it was my turn to laugh. "She doesn't know a thing about me."

"She knows more than you think. And you'd be a fool to underestimate her."

His ominous tone rang true. But I could be dangerous, too. At least, I thought I could.

"Yeah, well, she's clearly underestimated us, since we've gotten this far," Jace pointed out.

"Maybe. Or maybe she let you get this far. Maybe she's just getting tired of playing with her food, and she's ready to slice you up real nice." His smile broadened, and he revealed several gold teeth that shone under the light of Jace's flashlight.

When I wrinkled my nose in disgust, he smiled even wider. "What's wrong, pretty girl? Don't like my smile?"

"I never much cared for yellow. Much preferred riches be spent in a more practical way."

"Yeah, well, this was practical. Lost a few of my pearly

whites during training." He shrugged, and the light on my chest bobbled. He was relaxing.

"Who did that to you? Suzy Sunshine?" Jace asked, almost choking on her name.

The man turned his gaze toward Jace, and I knew it was my moment. I felt a rock beneath my toe. A big one. Bending slowly, I grabbed it. The meathead looked at me as I was standing back up, but he didn't question me. "If you must know, it was another of my men. He was trying to impress Sonny. But he got the raw end of the deal. Ripped his ear off with what was left of my teeth."

I grimaced, and he laughed again. "What's wrong, princess? Too gruesome for you?"

"No. I just thought you'd be a little pickier about your meat."

In that moment, I decided there'd been enough chatter. Enough delay. Any second someone else could come upon us and offer this idiot backup. Then we'd really be up Killer Creek without a paddle.

Two things happened at once. I hip-checked Jace, knocking him to the side, and launched the rock at Goldy. Jace went down, surprised by my attack, and I hit Goldy square in the face. He stumbled back as blood poured out of his nose, then went down like a sack of potatoes.

"Hey, good shot," Jace said, clearly impressed with my aim.

"Let's get out of here," I said, but Jace held back.

"Wait. I bet he has a screen we could use."

"Jace, I don't think we should waste any more time out in the open."

He didn't even look up at me as he went to the guy who I couldn't help but notice seemed very still. His eyes were open and more vacant than I would've preferred.

"Bingo." I saw Jace holding a screen and the stunner in his hands.

"Jace...is he..." I couldn't even finish the sentence. The guy wasn't moving. Like at all. Were my eyes playing tricks on me or was he not breathing? People couldn't die before their dates.

Compulsively, I went to him and pulled his sleeve back. He was a Without. Someone who'd chosen this life. He'd wanted to be a meathead. But that meant...what exactly had I done? I dropped his arm, and it made a sickening thud as it hit the ground.

"Don't think about it, Rare. Let's get out of here."

Don't think about it. Don't think about it. But I couldn't tear my eyes off him. I felt like I'd been responsible for Annabelle's fate, but not like this. This was different. I...no. I couldn't even form the words in my mind for what I'd done.

"Rarity. Let's go."

But I couldn't make my body move. My mind zeroed in on his forever blankly staring eyes. They were blue. With bushy brown eyebrows above them. Did he have a family? Someone who would miss him?

"What have I done?" I whispered, not entirely sure I wanted to hear the answer.

Jace tugged on my arm, but I was suddenly glued to the spot in the garden. "You did what you had to. We'd be on our way back to that hospital right now if it weren't for you. Or at least what's left of it. And now we're armed and ready to face whatever's waiting for us in that transportation center."

He sounded sure. Not an ounce of regret crept into his voice. But he hadn't thrown the stone. He hadn't dealt the final blow. A very selfish part of me wished he had. He'd handle it better. He'd know how to compartmentalize. All I knew how to do was look at the man. Look at what I'd done. Look at the life I'd claimed because what I needed was more important than him.

"Rarity. Look at me." Jace's voice felt distant. Like he was far away watching me. The only two people who existed in that moment were me and the guard. Jace was nothing more than a figment on the fringe of my existence.

At least until he grabbed me by the shoulders and started shaking me. That rattled something back into place. "Rarity. *Look* at me."

I dragged my eyes away from the guard if only to stop Jace from shaking me like that.

"You did what had to be done, Rarity. No one is coming for you. You have to rescue yourself. Do you think they've even broadcast the news in our sector?" He waited for me to answer, but words no longer existed in my brain. "I'm betting your parents don't even know you're alive. Otherwise the higher ups would have to do some serious explaining."

I tried to let that sink in. I did. But comprehension wasn't my jam at that moment.

"Rarity. My point is no one is coming for you. That guy wanted to lock you away forever to be nothing more than a science experiment for them. A guinea pig. Something to inject, poke, prod, cut, kill, and bring back to life an infinite amount of times until they got what they needed out of you. That would be your existence if you let them. Is that what you want?"

"Is this about what *I* want? Because I just prioritized my life over someone else's."

"And rightfully so, Rare. You could spend your entire life in their test tube and for what? What if they never found what they were looking for? But as sure as I'm standing here, I know they'll keep torturing us until we die. Only then will they stop. And I assure you, we will die someday. Even if they do figure out how to dodge their dates. I'd love to help your dad live longer, so your mom didn't have to spend those years alone. But would they want that sacrifice from me? From you? No. They wouldn't. Because in the end, we'll all die anyway."

"So why are we doing this? Why are we running, leaving a path of destruction in our wake? Shouldn't we be worthy of something to make these sacrifices?"

"We are. We are worthy of life. Of living. Not just surviving, not existing, but living. We were given this miracle. Let's not waste it chained to some fruitless cause." Taking my hands in his, he stared into my eyes. "Rarity. Come on. Live with me."

I looked at him. His green eyes had flecks of gold. And they were pleading with me to move. To leave the guard on the ground and get out of there. To put my life ahead of his. What's done is done and all that. Keep moving forward. But could I live with the person I was now? I was a killer. Forever more.

Something cool was in my hand. Hard and flat. And Jace's voice was in my ears again. Insistent. "Rarity, I need you to take this and get us into the transportation center, okay?"

I blinked at him, but he persisted, trying to break through to my mental agony.

The object in my hand got heavier. "Rarity. Please," he begged. He needed me to get us out of there. If I didn't, his life would be on my hands, too.

I looked down at the screen he'd pushed on me. Get us out. That was what I had to do. I scanned the area. It was dark outside still. No one had found us yet, but it wouldn't take long. Especially if anyone was trying to touch base with the dead guard. He'd be missed. And soon.

The screen came to life at my touch, shining brilliantly in my hands. As long as they thought it belonged to the guard, I should have free rein of the island. The thing was a beacon wanting to lead me out of there. Where exactly, I wasn't sure, but off the island was as far as my brain could take us.

"Jace. I don't think we can do this on our own." Suddenly, I realized my face was wet. When had I started crying?

"You're probably right. As soon as we get out of here, we'll figure something out. We'll get some help. From someone. It doesn't matter. Let's just get the hell out of here. Okay?"

Begging. He was begging me to move forward. To get him out of there. To choose him over the guard. And in that moment, I did.

TWENTY-THREE

Get out. That was my mission. I didn't need to think beyond it. Just get us off the island and away from the man I'd killed. Run.

Jace led us to a patch of bushes near the transport station. I squatted, trying to hide as best I could. I needed time with the screen. And he knew he had to give it to me.

He sat at the edge of the bush, blocking me from the sidewalk leading to the building, holding the stunner out, ready to take out anyone who walked up.

"How many people do you think you can take down with that thing?" I asked absently as I worked around the guard's security measures on his screen. They were a lot more sophisticated than the one I'd taken from the Tech Wing.

But once I was in that zone, I started to calm down. My fingers knew what to do, my mind clicked into place, and the spiral I'd started down didn't reverse, but it stopped.

"I don't know. As much as I'd like to try this thing out, I'm not sure I want to have to," Jace said, bringing me back to the present. The stunner. I'd asked him a question. Right.

"Mmm," I said, keeping my eyes on the screen and all the windows I'd opened. There was some serious stuff in there, just out in the open for God and everyone to see. It made me wonder what the heck he had on it that was actually hard to get to. Assignment sheets, plans, maps, security codes...I'd hit the jackpot with this guy.

I glanced over at where he laid on the sidewalk maybe ten yards away. Blood had made a shiny black circle around his head as it poured out of his nose.

"How's it coming," Jace asked as if he knew I was getting off task.

I shook my head, dropping my gaze down at the screen. "Fine."

Finding the digital controls for the transport station was easy enough. But something perplexing stopped me. Everything I opened indicated the station wasn't even locked. Would that make sense? They had just finished evacuating the island. Or were we walking into another trap?

I frowned at the screen as I tried three other ways to test the security of the station, all letting me in without me even trying.

"What's wrong?" Jace asked me.

"It seems too easy."

"Awesome. So what do you want to do?"

"I don't know what we can do. It seems like the station isn't even locked. We should just be able to walk in and leave."

"Great. Let's get going then." Without question, he stood and started toward the station. I watched him in wonder, wishing I had that kind of blind faith.

He turned toward where I still crouched in the bushes. "What are you waiting for?"

"Nothing," I said. I stood, bracing myself for some kind

of electric net to fall on my head and light my hair on fire. But nothing came. I took a step forward, expecting to spring some trap that would snap my foot right off my leg, but nothing happened. The grass was soft beneath my shoe. Maybe Jace was right. Maybe we could get out of there.

We hurried up the steps, Jace taking them two at a time. When he got to the glass double doors, he didn't even wait for me. He just yanked them open. Lo and behold, they gave way to him. They let him in.

I ran up the stairs next to him, ready for a fight. Ready to get shot at, stunned, hog tied, whatever. There had to be people inside, waiting to take us captive. Right?

But there weren't. The station was a ghost town. "How could they leave this place unmanned?" I asked skeptically, surveying the space.

Jace scanned the empty room with the stunner ready to take out anything that moved. "I don't know," he said through clenched teeth.

"Come on, let's get out of the doorway." I nudged him toward the tubes. "Maybe they shut everything down, so you can't use the tubes. Maybe that's why there's no one here. No reason to be."

"Except this is the way in and out. If we were going to get out of here, isn't this how we would do it?"

"We could take a boat, I guess," I suggested.

"But that would take forever. We'd be sitting ducks."

I shrugged as I crossed the room to the purple tubes. "I didn't say it was a good idea. There's a reason we're here instead of at the docks."

"If this doesn't work, we might find ourselves there yet," he said as he lowered the stunner and moved to the nearest tube.

The screen attached to the tube was dark, so Jace

touched it before I could stop him. It came to life right away, and something sank in the pit of my stomach.

No alarms went off. No men in black jumpsuits came crashing through the windows. Maybe I was just over-reacting.

"Where should we go?" Jace asked as he peered at the screen.

I moved to study it. We couldn't go home, at least not directly. They'd find us. They'd hurt my parents. As much as I needed them, we'd have to go the long way. Maybe taking the hunters on a wild goose chase would throw them off our trail.

"Anywhere but here."

"Sounds great to me," he said, then started to type on the screen.

"No, wait..." I wasn't sure what made me feel weird about the whole thing, but it all just seemed too easy. Like they wanted us to try this.

Jace's hands hovered over the screen. "Let me just try something." A red icon appeared on the guard's screen when I turned it on.

That couldn't be good.

When I opened it up, I saw that every single guard with a screen had been notified of activity in the transport station. "Well, that's just poke-yourself-in-the-eye perfect."

Jace looked at me, and I knew we had no time to lose. I had to hack the system and program it to take us where they couldn't follow us. If I could kill it while I was at it, I would. But that might take more time than I had.

"They're coming. Get in the tube," I said.

"Not without you."

"You know the drill, Jace. It's one at a time. I'll meet you there. I promise." I shoved him into the tube, and he reluctantly let me. I slammed the curved glass door closed, then went to work trying to find a way around the system. If I could use the guard's screen to send him off instead of the one attached to the tube, maybe, just maybe, we could evade them.

Seconds ticked by while I hacked the transport station, weaving this way and that to get around their security, which frankly wasn't nearly tight enough.

As soon as I gained access, I knew it wouldn't be enough. They would still know where we'd gone. The program was stronger than I'd thought.

"Fine. Have a little of this." I typed in a code of my own making. One that would burn everything behind it. There would be no trace of Jace when I was done. But would there be anything left for me to use to get out? I'd have to wait and see.

Stepping into the tube next to his, I sent him on his way. Immediately, the virus I set loose went to work. Now I was racing the clock. I typed in the command to send me behind Jace, but nothing happened.

"There she is," I heard shouted across the atrium. Panic threatened to stay my hands. But I somehow managed to push through and get back to work. I had seconds maybe until they hit the tube with something that would make me regret my life choices. All I had to do was be faster than them. I could do that, right? A self-trained coder with two weeks of real experience? Sure. I'd survived my date. I could do anything.

Before I could doubt myself, I actually managed to jumpstart my tube and get the heck out of there.

I held on to the screen while the world around me turned to a purple haze. I stared at the screen, knowing my work wasn't done. If they followed me, I'd be bringing the rhino right to my doorstep. And that was the last place that beast belonged. I would not have it trampling everything I held dear.

The virtual bombs I planted before I jumped would be going off any moment, rendering the entire station useless. They'd have to use choppers or boats to come after us now. And that was if they knew where we were going.

As the purple haze shifted, I hoped I'd done enough. That they wouldn't find us. And when we did eventually make our way home, it would be safe. For everyone.

When I found myself solidly in the strange tube, Jace was already stepping out of his and opening the door for mine.

"I was starting to worry something had happened."

"It got a bit squirrely back there."

"What happened?"

"They showed up."

"Before you got out? Did they see where you were going?"

"I don't think so. Even if they did, it will take them some time to get here now. They're traveling the old-fashioned way." I said it to comfort myself.

"Where are we?" Jace asked, scanning the unfamiliar station. It was bigger than ours, and decidedly better maintained.

"Some random station I picked from a list that popped up. We couldn't go home. Not directly. They'd find us." I'd made a last-minute judgment call, and I hoped it wouldn't kill us.

Jace nodded as we made no attempt to hide our smiles. We made it off the island. We'd outfoxed the rhino. But could we outrun it?

· · ·

PEOPLE. There was a substantial number of them in the station. Why were they here?

"This way, Withs. This way," someone was yelling.

I sidled up next to an older woman with graying hair and concern etched deep into her wrinkled face. "What's going on?" I asked.

"I don't think they know. That's the problem," she said, watching the guards with cloudy light blue eyes.

"Why are all these people here?" I asked as Jace stayed silent next to me.

"Same reason you are, dear. This group of evacuees was sent here." When I blinked at her, trying to form a response that wasn't some expletive about my cursed luck, she went on, apparently thinking I didn't understand. "From the island. Where we all came from?"

She said it like a question, and I worked to cover my tracks. "Of course," I said, glad it wasn't a lie. If they were from the island, they were liable to recognize Jace at least. His picture had been all over the news. We had to get out of there.

By the way the color had left his face, I knew he thought exactly the same thing.

"Listen, we've been hauled up here long enough. This isn't how I wanted to spend my last days," one of the men near the middle of the huge group of people shouted. He wasn't wrong. The evacuation had been initiated almost a full day ago. So they'd been cooling their heels in our dingy transport station for way too long, with their own clocks ticking down by the second. Didn't seem like the best idea to me.

"We understand. We just need to check and make sure we have everyone before we can move you to more comfortable accommodations," the guard said.

"Everyone is here already. Let's move this along. You've held us here for hours. The sun is up. I'm exhausted."

I glanced at Jace, who shrugged, seeming not sure what to do.

"There's just more people than we expected. New Withs are coming in. It just takes a second for us to get it together. We'll get you all scanned and transferred out, okay? Just a little patience will help make this entire process more pleasant." The guard glanced down at his screen, and I knew we were in trouble. Scanning everyone? They'd know who we were, and our game would be over before we could even get out of there.

We were up Killer Creek now. And that paddle was nowhere to be seen.

Jace was already scanning the guards. "There are only four guards. It'll take them forever to scan everyone. Frankly, it's no wonder they've been here so long. What's to keep us here," he whispered.

"Think we can sneak out?"

He shot me a sly grin. "I can. I don't know about you, Miss Twinkle Toes."

"Just because I fell in the incinerator chute *once* doesn't mean I'm a klutz," I objected.

He shrugged. "Once more than I did."

"Hush," I hissed. "There's enough people here to cover us up." I wasn't sure if I was saying it to him or myself.

We tried to move toward the door, but the pack pushed us forward—toward the guards who were scanning. "Now what?" I asked.

"Just stay close," Jace said, eyeing the crowd around us.

We kept trying to break free, but every time we gained an inch, someone would push us back, and we'd lose two. Before long, we were getting closer and closer to the scanning guards. They scanned the man right next to Jace.

"Give me your arm," the guard said to the man.

"This is ridiculous. I'm three days from my date. This is *not* how I want to be spending my time."

The guard didn't even look up as he held his screen over the man's arm. "Our apologies, sir. With any luck, we'll have you living it up again in no time."

The man scowled at the guard, and he wouldn't let up. "This is a violation of the contract the Withouts have with the Withs."

"Contract," I whispered, but Jace didn't answer. I never paid much attention to the politics of our society. I never thought about it that way. I just thought there were laws we had to follow. A contract implied a mutual agreement. I never knew we had a contract with them. The others. The Withouts.

The guard and the man went back and forth, the man refusing to give up once he'd been scanned. "You know, if you'd move aside, we could get this done a lot faster and get you on your way," the guard suggested.

"I will not until I know how you plan to make up for this lost time." The man became belligerent, and I wasn't sure I wanted to stand around and watch things unfold.

Good thing, because Jace shoved me past the scanning guard without being spotted. Unsure what to do, I clutched the edge of my hoodie sleeve, keeping my date securely concealed. I sidled up next to a few Withs who'd already been scanned and turned to face Jace, waiting for him to make his move.

Another guard stepped up, taking the scanner's place. "All right, your turn," he said to Jace without glancing at his face.

Jace held out his arm, and I held my breath. The guard was sure to recognize him. All he had to do was look up, see Jace's face, and we were sunk. But something was off. There was a lump under his sleeve.

"Please pull your sleeve back," the guard said, eyes still on his screen. There was a small flash of light, and the guard went down. If I hadn't been looking directly at Jace's arm, I might have missed it. I scanned the people near Jace, and they all took a step back.

Another guard rushed to the fallen man's aid. "What happened?" he asked.

Jace shrugged. "I don't know. He scanned my arm and went down."

"Fine. Move along." He turned to the guard dealing with the belligerent man. "We need more help in here."

The guard touched his ear, requesting reinforcements.

"We'll never get out of here once the cavalry arrives," I pointed out.

Jace pressed next to me, watching the guard he downed struggle to come around. "Then we need to get out before they get here."

TWENTY-FOUR

How quickly could they have more guards there? How much time did we have? I was betting none. And since we had no plan at all, it basically meant not enough.

"Fine, you lot get over along the back wall. When the rest of the guards get here, they'll take you to the next spot." The guard sounded confident, but I could see the fear in his eyes. There were four of them and about twenty-five Withs standing around waiting. Wasting their precious time.

We herded along the wall, while the last eight or so waited to be scanned. But the guards weren't scanning. Not with the one still unconscious.

"Come on, get this show on the road. We've got lives to live," one of the Withs who was still waiting to be scanned demanded.

"We've got a bit of a situation here, in case you missed it," the guard said, getting more than a bit snotty with the man.

Tensions rose as the two men squared off, standing chest to chest.

"I can't believe they haven't recognized you. We can't

get caught up in any of this. And we can't be herded along with them. We'll end up trapped again," I pointed out quietly to Jace.

"No, we won't. These guys will create enough of a distraction. Watch." He seemed so confident, but all I could see was chaos. Chaos brewing, and that was the last thing we needed. Chaos brought problems, and my plate was already overflowing with that fare, thank you very much.

While we all watched the two men size each other up, the woman to Jace's right fell to the ground. The thud she made was such a sickening sound I hesitated to look over. But I already knew. She was dead.

Jace knelt by her, picking up her arm. Today's date screamed back at us. She'd spent her last hours as a prisoner because of us. Because of our escape and the island's evacuation.

Before guilt could claim me, a woman next to her started screaming. A shrill, ear-splitting sound that made my heart race.

"No. That won't be me," the man who'd challenged the guard declared. He punched him in the face, sending him flat on his back. Then, the chaos I'd feared started.

The melee that unfolded was hard to process as the crowd descended on the four guards. It was different from what happened in the hospital. Less controlled. And that made it exponentially more frightening. They were throwing punches. Kicking. Stomping them. All four guards were on the ground, covering their heads with their hands in about three seconds flat. They were no match for the twenty-five angry Withs trapped in that transport station.

"No. We should help them," I insisted, not sure where the compassion for my captors came from.

"What?" Jace demanded, completely dumbfounded. Who could blame him? I kinda thought I was crazy too.

"They're just doing their jobs. They don't deserve to die for it."

I pushed my way to the head of the crowd, then grabbed onto one man's arm who'd been throwing quite a few punches at the guard he currently straddled.

"Stop," I said.

His eyes narrowed when he looked up at me. "Whose side are you on?"

I hesitated, glancing quickly at the crowd around me. At least they'd stopped beating the guards. Silence hung in the air for a brief moment. "Just don't kill them. Tie them up or something. Use them as leverage for when the other guards get here."

"Who says we'll still be here when the others get here?" the man throwing punches pointed out.

"I do. If you stay here and finish these guards, you'll still be here. These people move fast. You don't have time for this," I said.

"There is always time for justice," the man replied as he peered down at the unconscious guard. His face was already swelling to an unrecognizable state, and blood seeped from his mouth as it hung open.

Jace pulled on my arm, then yanked me away from the man dealing out 'justice.'

"This isn't justice," I said to Jace as he hauled me closer and closer to the doors. "This is fear."

"Call it what you want. I don't want any part of it. Get us the hell out of here."

He shoved me rather roughly in front of the transport tubes. "What if home is just like this?"

"Then we'll deal with it," he said.

I stared down at my screen as I plotted a course for us. We wouldn't go straight home. We couldn't. For the same reason we came here, instead of going home first. I couldn't lead them to my parents.

After I set the screen next to the tube, I got in. I didn't want them tracking me. We'd have to go to a nearby station and walk. Hopefully, they wouldn't find us that way.

I shut the door, watching as the crowd beat the life out of those four guards. More blood. More anger. More of all the things I didn't want. All started by us. By me.

As I watched the image fade and the purple haze descended on me, I wondered where we could go from here. What kind of future had we created in the days we didn't die?

TWENTY-FIVE

As we made the leap to the transport station, I held my breath, hoping it would be cleared out—that we wouldn't be jumping out of the frying pan and into the fire.

The more I thought about it, though, the more I decided I'd be surprised if our zone, or any zone close to us, was chosen for relocation of the Withs on the island. It was such an industrial sector. There was nowhere to put extra people. Nowhere comfortable for the Withs to go and spend the rest of their days. Although, I wasn't sure any of the zones had that. Except maybe the Withouts. Maybe that was where they would take everyone until they found us. Until the dust settled.

I snorted at the idea. The Withouts would just love that. The last time Withs and Withouts had mixed, the war that ensued killed over ten thousand people, explaining the mass die off that was predicted when so many people had been born with the same date.

New Withs would be reaching their time to go to the island every day. What would they do with them?

I shook my head as the purple haze cleared, and the

station came into view. Home. That was my main concern. Not other Withs. Not what they would do with them. They. Whoever *they* were. The ones with more control than we had. That was all I knew.

I stepped out carefully into the station, hearing a commotion coming from the far side of the room.

"Ooh, good play, Marley," a man's voice said through the laughter.

"Yeah, take your winnings. You'll need it," another man said. He didn't seem to be laughing.

Jace put his hand on my elbow. "Come on. Let's get out of here while they're busy."

As quietly as we could, we made our way closer to the guard station. Of course it was right next to the door. Where else would it be?

Closer and closer, we silently crept out in the open to our potential doom. If they spotted us, it was game over. They'd question what we were doing there, and we had no good reason to be. Nor was I the best at making up lies. I was liable to tell them a dragon chased us there rather than give them a perfectly reasonable answer.

Jace kept the stunner trained on the closest guard, but I knew it wouldn't be enough if they spotted us. Four trained guards on two untrained Withs with one stunner? I didn't like our odds.

We eyed the group as we made our way to the door. Deep into their game, they didn't see us inch past them and lean into the door. It clunked when Jace pushed it open and he froze, waiting for them to react.

"Ooooh," they simultaneously yelled. The one with his back to us threw his cards on the table. "That ain't right," he shouted as another guard dragged his haul toward him.

"Too bad, so sad, Gary," he said as he started organizing his loot.

Jace started moving again and slipped outside, pulling me behind him. He held onto the door so it didn't slam behind us, and we made our way into the night.

WE WALKED the unfamiliar zone in silence. It was known for making packaging, and it sent lots of waste our way for the incinerator.

We figured walking the streets would be too dangerous, so we quickly ducked into the woods. Someone would see us. Report us. And that was the last thing we needed. The zones weren't terribly close together. Although I'd burned any traces of us when we left and likely rendered the station unusable—sorry, fellow Withs—I still couldn't be sure they hadn't tracked us. They had someone good on the case. Maybe a few someones. We couldn't be too careful.

We had a long way to walk, but we were both exhausted. I didn't remember the last time I'd slept. Even though the sun was high in the sky, I wanted to drop.

"Maybe we should find somewhere to sleep," Jace suggested.

"Fine by me." I couldn't process the risks of that. Now that we were out of any immediate danger, the weight of everything that had happened pressed in on me. Annabelle, the guard, our escape, the evacuation, the woman who'd died at the station. All of it.

"Here, there's a hollowed-out tree we can sleep in. The trees in those woods were big. Old. I was willing to bet they'd seen the time before dates. They'd survived a lot. Somehow, I knew they would keep us safe.

Jace made a little cocoon for us out of the pack and his

jacket. It was small and we had to huddle together, but we made it work. And frankly, it was the best I'd felt since the day he survived and they took him from me.

He wrapped his arms around me as we curled up inside that tree, and we were both sleeping before we thought better of it. Jace and I were home. But it didn't look anything like his house or mine. It was big, but old. Clean, but worn. Neither of us seemed to care, though. We loved it. We were happy.

Jace was behind me with his hand on the small of my back while I stood at the sink looking out the window. A stream babbled along just outside, and a mountain towered above us in the distance. Was that Killer Creek? I shook my head, trying to make sense of what I saw.

"Meat supply is getting low. I'm going to go get us something."

"Okay, be careful," I said, like any loving wife would. Was that what we were? I glanced down at my hand, seeing a worn piece of twine tied to my ring finger. Was this our life? Had we escaped? Were we safe?

I never heard the front door close. All I heard were his screams. "Rarity," he yelled.

I ran to the door, horrified at the sight of dozens of copters hovering silently in the yard.

"We mean you no harm," they said.

"Oh yeah, and if you believe that, I've got a nice little plot of land on that perfect little island of yours to sell you," I said as I grabbed a shotgun by the door. When had I learned to shoot a gun?

"Rarity, don't do anything rash. Let's think about this," Jace said. Since when was he so complacent?

Ignoring the comment, I took aim at the copter closest to him. The shot rocked me back on my heels, and I emptied the chamber while I recovered, taking aim at another and another and another until all of them were in flames in our front yard.

I set the butt of the gun down on the front porch, surveying what I'd done rather proudly. "Well, Jace. What do you think of that *rash* behavior?"

But he didn't answer me. I peered out to where he'd been standing, but all I found was his destroyed body. He looked just as he had when he fell. Bloody, broken, and gone from this world.

What had I done?

I started to scream, but no sound came out of my mouth. I needed to yell, rail, cry, do something, but the more I tried, the more mute I stayed. I had no voice in all this. None at all.

I WOKE UP WITH A START, my heart hammering in my chest, and I could only hope I hadn't screamed out loud.

"Rare. It's okay. You're safe." Jace's voice cut through the pounding in my ears as I looked around wildly. The inside of the tree was dark and smelled of moss and mud.

Night had fallen while we slept. He was right. We were safe.

Sighing, I slumped back against the tree. "Maybe we should just stay here, Jace."

He chuckled. "Tempting, for sure. But I think we need help. We need food and supplies at a minimum."

"And my parents will have those?" My parents barely had two credits to rub together. They wouldn't be able to give us anything. But somehow, I knew they'd know what to do. They'd have an idea we weren't seeing. They always had ways to solve a problem as painlessly as possible. It was a skill I had yet to learn, and one we desperately needed at the moment.

"Well, no. But you know what I mean. They'll be able to help."

I did know. So I nodded. It was probably best to go under cover of night anyway. If we were lucky, we'd make it to their doorstep before the sun rose. It was true that luck wasn't on our side, but it was amazing what a little bit of sleep could do for my mental state. The protein bars we were munching on didn't hurt either. I felt almost human as we picked our way through those woods. And before I knew it, the map on my screen said we were just a mile from the edge of our zone. We were home.

IT WAS odd to be back at a place I never thought I'd see again. It was unsettling and comforting at the same time, and I didn't know what to do with all the feelings running through me.

We ducked behind familiar bushes that were so dead they barely offered enough coverage for us. Our zone wasn't as well-groomed as the island was. Not by a long shot. For the first time, I noticed how brown it was. How all the bushes that lined the homes were dead with sharp twigs sticking out of them. How the streets were crumbling from neglect and none of the streetlights actually worked, except for that one down on Main Street, near the grocery store.

We'd done it. We'd made it home before dawn.

It was almost like having my image of my childhood shattered. After living with the island's finery, was it okay to love such a dingy place?

"Is this weird?"

"Super weird," Jace said. "Who skulks around this time of night?"

I nudged him, and he didn't even break his stride. "I meant coming back here. Being home."

We turned down a dark alley that connected to the street that would take us home, and Jace shrugged. "I guess I never really felt at home here."

Surprised, I eyed him. "I always thought you were happy." I let more sadness creep into my voice than I meant to.

"I was happy. As happy as you can be as a slave to the Withouts." He shrugged again, and I blinked at him. Had we had the same life? We'd been so close. Such good friends. We loved each other, didn't we? I mean, to be fair, I hated my job. Something I'd been assigned to do, not chosen, like the Withouts got to do. It was slave labor for slave wages. But hearing him say it out loud made me feel like my whole picture of our life at home was a lie.

He crouched behind the corner of a building. "There isn't much cover on this street." He peeked out from behind the wall, but I didn't feel compelled to do the same. If we got spotted, our lives would be over.

"We'll have to cut through people's yards and hope they don't see us. Better than parading bold as we please down the sidewalk."

"Won't that cause more of a commotion?" I asked, eyeing the fences we'd have to leap over, the bushes we'd probably land in, and the trash cans to avoid.

"Nah. We've got this." He winked at me. I smiled in spite of myself. Despite everything that had happened, the life I'd taken, I was alive and home with Jace. It would be okay. Our happily ever after was in reach. Maybe we could grab my parents and go hide somewhere. Some other zone where we could start over. Maybe we could hide our dates and become Withouts. We'd have a fancy wedding and a honeymoon that would put the island to shame. Then, I'd work as a coder and he could be an artist. My parents could retire early and live however they wanted. We'd be alive and happy. Anything was possible, right?

I shook my head. I couldn't be mooning about our future right now. We were running for our lives. *Priorities, Rarity. Come on.*

He cut across the street and between two houses. The first house had no fence, so we easily cut through their yard. No lights were on, but that didn't really mean anything. It was just a few hours before dawn after all.

When we came to a fence, it wasn't so bad. Jace helped me over, and I landed on my feet. The grass was soft, so it didn't make any noise. It wasn't until the third fence that we had a problem.

I wasn't sure if Jace was getting tired. Or me. Maybe both. But either way, he didn't launch me quite high enough and I stumbled a bit, scrambling against the side of the fence.

"Shoot," I whispered as he struggled to keep me from falling on him.

"Get over," he said, less than encouragingly I might add.

"I'm trying." I grabbed the top of the fence and tried to get my legs under me, but it just wasn't working.

In the end, I gave up, landing in a heap on Jace. "Judges say, one out of ten points for that dismount."

"Harsh," I said as I stood. I thought I saw movement across the street. In the window of Jace's house. I froze, and he followed my gaze.

He frowned. "Keep moving. Come on." His tone was

cold and he held out his hands, ready to boost me over the fence.

"Maybe we should just go around."

"We can't. These guys share a fence with the Klein-man's, remember?" It was the longest fence in the world that backed right up to the next house. To go around, we'd have to go onto the other street and risk being seen. Through was the only way.

"Just hurry up about it. It'll be fine. I don't think your neighbors are up."

I hoped he was right as he basically tossed me over the fence this time. I landed flat on my butt in the hedges, causing even more racket.

I scrambled to get out of there and hide, but there was no place to do it.

Jace was up and over the fence in no time, landing on his feet beside me as I struggled to brush myself off and make myself look less like a crazy person with leaves and branches in her hair.

"Lucky shot," I grumbled.

He gently pulled a twig out of my mess of hair. "What-ever you say."

We stayed low to the ground as we made our way across the yard. When we jumped this last fence, we'd be in my yard. At home.

Jace held his hands out, ready to launch me into my own home. Into my safe space. "You ready?"

"No."

He nodded once. "Well, you better get ready." He glanced over his shoulder at the dark house behind us, and I knew he had no desire to linger in that yard.

The Johansens had never been nasty to us. In fact, they were great. But who knew what they'd do if they saw two people who were supposed to be dead poking around in their backyard. People did crazy things when they were scared. Frankly, it wasn't the crazy things I was worried about. It was the rational things—like calling authorities and reporting us—that would really put a cramp in our style.

I steeled myself and let him launch me over the fence, then landed on my feet in the grass of my own backyard. Nothing had changed in the time I'd been gone. I guess that shouldn't have surprised me. I'd only been gone a little over two weeks. But everything had changed for me. Everything. And somehow, the world at home kept turning. The grass was still that same greenish-brown color. The tree in the back was just as tall, with its branches hanging over into the neighbor's yard. He never minded, though. He always said it was nice that we shared our shade.

I hurried up to the back door, then lifted the mat. The silver key waited for me, like it always had. My folks put it there when Jace started having trouble with his parents. They wanted him to have a safe place to go if he needed it. They never made a big deal about it, just told him the key was there and he could use it any time. And he had. I'd come downstairs more than once to find him sleeping on the couch, a thin blanket my dad left in the hall closet draped over him.

It didn't surprise me that my folks hadn't moved the key. They were creatures of habit. And maybe it was too painful to move it. Too final.

"It's your key. You want to do the honors?" I asked.

He shook his head. "It's your homecoming. You do it."

Swallowing hard, I picked up the key. It slid easily into the lock, and I opened the door.

The kitchen was dark, but the smells of home filled my nose. I could feel my anxiety melting away. Lemon, fresh-baked bread, and a hint of Dad's soap had me gripping the nearest chair to hold myself up. This was real. I was standing in my kitchen after my date.

"You okay?" Jace whispered.

"Not really, no."

A dark figure filled the doorway, holding a baseball bat high. "Well, this isn't the place to get yourself together."

TWENTY-SIX

"Move along now," he said, and I froze.

"Mr. Delman, it's me," Jace offered.

Time stopped as we stared at each other.

"No. It can't be," Dad said, clearly trying to get a grip on himself.

"Turns out the dates don't mean much anymore," Jace wryly said.

I still hadn't found my voice when my dad's eyes landed on me. "Rare?" It came out a bit choked. Tears sprang to my eyes, breaking the spell that had frozen me to the spot.

"Daddy," I said as I went to him. The bat fell to the ground with a clatter. He threw his arms around me, then Jace when he joined us.

I didn't see Mom come downstairs, but I sure heard her when she started screaming. Quickly quieting, she threw her arms around us. We stood there together until none of us had any tears left to cry.

MOM MADE tea and we sat at the kitchen table, trying to

digest. "So they think you're the key to nullifying dates and want to use you to take the world back to the time before?" Mom asked.

"Apparently," I said as I held my mug between my hands, trying to hold on to that reality, not the one we were talking about.

"What do you need?" Dad asked.

Jace sighed. "For now? A place to hide. Maybe some advice on what to do and how to stay away from them."

Dad nodded and put a hand on Jace's arm, giving him a squeeze. "We'll figure this out. Together." My dad didn't make promises lightly. I knew he meant it. He would help us. They both would.

I sagged into my chair, feeling like I could relax for the first time in days. Everything would be okay.

My mom held my hand tightly. "You can stay here forever if you need."

I smiled weakly, but I didn't miss the look Jace and Dad shared. We couldn't stay forever. They'd find us. They'd hurt them. They'd do whatever it took to get to us. We had to move on. It was just a matter of when and where we could go that would be safe. And I was relying heavily on them to know the answers to those when-and-where questions that hung heavily in the air.

"Maybe not forever, but for now, we will keep you safe," Dad offered. "Why don't you go upstairs and get some sleep? You both look like zombies. In fact, are you sure you're still alive?" He grinned, and I rolled my eyes.

"Thanks, Dad. You always know just what to say to make a girl feel beautiful."

"And you stink. Maybe think about getting a shower while you're up there," he added. "Don't stink up the sheets in that room. Your mother just got it cleaned up."

I raised an eyebrow at Mom, and she waved me off. I knew she hadn't touched my room. Maybe she never would now. I'd offered her hope and I could only pray it wasn't cruel of me, because it was too late to take it back.

Leaving Jace at the table with my folks, I hugged both my parents hard and made my way upstairs. To my old life.

The bathroom I shared with my parents was unchanged. Small but clean with a showerhead sticking out of the wall, a curtain hung across it, a toilet, and a single sink crammed into a space barely big enough for me to stand with my arms outstretched.

But it was so much better than the bathroom on the island. It was mine. It had washed away so many of my tears. It had watched me grow and change. As I stood there, looking in the tarnished mirror, I wondered if it even recognized me. I wasn't sure I recognized myself. My hair was a mess with more than just twigs caught in it. In fact, I was fairly sure a bird had taken up residence on the left side.

My hoodie was full of holes and streaks of dirt, my shoes were full of sand, and my socks were a color that once resembled white but now looked more greyish.

My parents didn't have enough to keep four people alive for long. Their rations would quickly run short. And people were bound to notice Jace and me holed up in the house, no matter how careful we were. But I didn't want to think about those problems now, so I stripped off my clothes and stepped into the shower.

As I stood there, scrubbing my skin, trying to get the island, Sonny, the hospital, the guard, Annabelle, and every-thing else off me, I started to realize something. I couldn't scrub hard enough to find the girl I'd been before my date. She wasn't there anymore. Maybe she *had* died that day. Maybe Jace had, too.

But in that moment, as the chilly water made goose bumps all over my skin, it didn't matter. I was home. And everything would be okay.

WHILE MY PARENTS were at work, we spent the day in the house napping and being bored together. It was heaven. Jace found his stash of charcoal, then did some drawing. I poked around Frank, getting back to my roots.

"We should have a plan," Jace said absently as he smudged what he was working on with the side of his hand. "We can't squat here for the rest of our lives. Sonny's gang isn't stupid. Okay, well, maybe they are, but Sonny isn't. They'll come here looking for us. And if we're here, think what they'll do to your parents. We need to go. Sooner rather than later. But where? And to what end?"

I frowned. I knew that. The hard truths were riding on the back of that rhino, ready to bowl me over any moment.

"Fine, we can talk about it with my folks when they get home. Dad will have some thoughts on what to do."

Jace nodded, and I was relieved I'd put him off. For now. I knew I couldn't run from the rhino forever. Or maybe I could. He'd proven to be easier to outmaneuver than I originally thought. Maybe I'd live a nice long life and die of natural causes at the ripe old age of ninety-nine. Every day that passed and I didn't die, it became even more of a possibility.

Maybe I could lose the rhino in his own cloud of confusion. It was all in the execution. And while I hid away in my own little oasis, I had no desire to make the first move. And that, I learned the hard way, was a deadly mistake.

TWENTY-SEVEN

That night, we didn't talk to my parents about a plan. Dad had clearly had an exhausting day. He was hunched over, wearing a dark expression when he walked in the door. Mom entered just behind him, ready to be there if he needed, but not so close it seemed like she was helping him.

"What happened?" I asked as he made his way to the couch. Mom sat down near him seeming just as bleak.

"Nothing. Just a run-in at work." He smiled, but it looked a bit more like a grimace. That could mean anything. It wasn't like working at the incinerator was risk free.

Dad appeared defeated. He laid his head against the back cushion and closed his eyes. Mom watched him, waiting for him to break the ice.

"I guess we're just gonna sit here in uncomfortable silence for the night? Cuz that's not really my idea of a party."

Jace elbowed me, Mom glared at me, and Dad just grunted. They were all against me, apparently. But I still wanted to know what happened.

"They questioned us," Dad finally said.

"About what?" It wasn't time to panic. Not yet. My parents could've been questioned about any number of things. They were management at the incinerator.

I looked back and forth between my parents. My rocks. Mom was wringing her hands like I'd never seen before. And Dad had leaned forward with his head down, refusing to look up at either Jace or me.

"They came. They're here." It hit me like a blast from a stunner. They'd found us.

"They did. But I don't think they know you're here at the house yet. They think you're on your way," Dad said.

"Who questioned you?" Jace asked.

"She didn't give her name. But she looked like—"

I cut him off. "Barbie on steroids."

Dad's face scrunched, and I frowned. Sunshine was here to rain flaming turds down on our heads.

"How did you..." Dad started to ask, but he never got the chance to finish his sentence.

The doorbell sounded, and everyone froze.

"What was that?" I asked as Dad tensed.

His face was stony, and he'd launched himself off the couch faster than I thought he could. He didn't look at me as he watched the door, as if it might reveal who was behind it. "Probably just a neighbor at the front door who needs something." A halfhearted chuckle escaped him. "The other day, Eric was over here with some freshly made brownies. Can you believe that? Said he felt bad we'd lost you and Jace so close together. They wanted to do something nice for us."

I looked at Mom, but she didn't make eye contact either. She was watching Dad.

"It was a lot of sugar and chocolate," Mom said quietly. "Must've cost them a lot of credits."

Dad nodded. "You all get to the basement. Stay quiet."

Mom herded us as quietly as possible across the room as someone knocked on the door.

"Just a minute," Dad called.

She pushed us into the stairwell, then hugged me hard. "If things go south, there's a storm cellar door on the far wall. Use that to get away. But only if things go south."

"Mom. Nothing is going to happen. It's a neighbor. Nothing more." But the words sounded hollow even to me.

She didn't nod or smile. She kissed me hard on the forehead, then squeezed Jace's hand. "Keep her safe."

"Always, Mrs. D."

"I mean it."

"Me too," he said.

"I love you, Rarity. And you too, Jace."

She was saying goodbye all over again, and I hated every second of it. She closed the door silently, then left us to our own devices at the top of the basement stairs.

Jace and I waited just behind the door, too desperate for information to bother taking cover in the basement.

"It sounds like my parents," Jace said, none too happy to hear their voices.

"Maybe it just sounds like them. Maybe it's not actually them."

"And maybe I'll sprout wings and fly us out of here," Jace said, more than a little sarcasm dripping from his tone.

Then, he did one of those things that in hindsight, people wished they could undo. That they cringed while watching, knowing it wouldn't end well. He opened the door a crack.

Obviously, once the door was opened, I wanted to see too. And I didn't like what I saw one bit. Jace was right. His parents were standing in the doorway. By the way my dad greeted them, his back stiff, frown deep on his face, I knew they weren't here to give my folks their condolences.

"Come out and discuss it like professional adults, Martin," Jace's dad implored my own father.

"To what end, Greg? Why would I leave the safety of my own home when you've shown up here with an army? How dare you bring this down upon my head?"

"How dare *you* bring them into your home?" his mother accused in her high-pitched squeaky voice. She even dared to poke a finger at my father's chest.

Jace was so tense it was obvious he was about to snap so I pulled the door shut as quietly and forcefully as I could.

"Jace, we have to go. Mom said there was a cellar door. They must've added it after I left."

"With what credits?"

"Maybe the bonus they got from my date? Who knows?"

Most people spent their bonus on food so they could take a year off work or whatever. But not my parents. They had the foresight to put in a security system and a way out of the basement.

I'd have to worry about gratitude later. I made my way to the far wall. No cellar door leapt out at me. It looked just the same as it had when I'd lived there.

"Do you see anything?" I asked.

Jace moved some shelves out of the way, less than noiselessly, and there it was behind our small collection of Christmas decorations and canned goods Mom saved for a rainy day.

The door looked old. Like it had always been there. Maybe they hadn't put it in. Maybe they'd just never told me about it. Unfortunately, now wasn't the time to get answers.

We scrambled up the stairs, then struggled to push the heavy door open. Jace couldn't do it himself, so I had to help. Together, we managed to get it open. Once on the outside, I saw why. It was buried beneath my mother's neglected garden in the back of the house. The only seeds she ever planted were ones from the fruits and vegetables we got from the store with our credits. Sometimes, we'd get free cucumbers or something. Other times, nothing would pop up. Now I knew why. The dirt was awfully shallow here. But she tended those plants meticulously. Always making sure the spot was covered.

"Come on," Jace said as he pulled me around to the front.

My instincts were screaming at me to run. Leave. Get out of there. But I let Jace drag me to the scene. My heart wanted to know what was happening and if they would leave my parents alone.

They were out on the lawn by the time we jammed ourselves into a nearby bush. Big black jeeps were parked out front, lights shining on the house, lighting up the yard like it was noon. Armed guards dressed in black stood along the front of the house and surrounded mine and Jace's parents.

Sonny walked up to them, a big automatic gun slung over her shoulder. "That's not a gun. It's a laser shooter. One of the games I played used them. I didn't think they were real. They're state of the art. They can do anything from stun a person to melt the skin right off their body." Jace seemed a bit less scared than I would've liked and a bit more impressed than I felt comfortable with.

I had a lot of questions. How had they made such a weapon and why did Sonny have it here? But I couldn't bring any of them to life. I was frozen to my spot, watching helplessly as my parents were at Commando Barbie's mercy.

Jace stayed perfectly still beside me, like a mousetrap about ready to spring.

"You know, I don't know what to think," Sonny said. Our parents said nothing, but Jace's were clearly more nervous than mine. They shifted their weight, and Jace's mom fidgeted with the bottom of her shirt. My parents just stood there, not making eye contact with Sonny.

"Should I believe the over-ambitious couple who claims the kids I'm hunting were here? Or should I believe the couple who seems to have true care for the traitors?" She seemed relaxed as she clasped her hands behind her back and paced in front of our parents, who were lined up like they were getting some kind of disciplinary action. Maybe they were. Question was—how far would Sonny take it?

"Listen," my mom ventured, and I sucked in a breath. What was she doing? "Maybe we could help you? Speak to your supervisor? I know you must be under a lot of pressure to find them. Like we told you at work today, we didn't even know they were alive. *Believe* me, we want to see them out of harm's way." She was alarmingly convincing, and Sonny even stopped walking to face her. Woman to woman.

"You didn't even know they were alive..." Sonny repeated, seemingly unmoved by my mother's plea. "For someone who learned earlier today their daughter is a freaking miracle, you seem very...unshaken."

"Jace, we should go," I whispered, but I didn't mean it. I wanted to see how this ended. I wanted to see Sonny and her minions leave my parents alone. And truth be told, I wanted to see Jace's parents hauled away. They wanted someone to experiment on, take them instead of us.

But Jace ignored my warning, and I was secretly glad he

did. We both stayed stock still as the scene in front of us unfolded.

"Forgive me," my mom said. "I'm trying to maintain composure, given the..." She glanced around at the guards in her yard, the cars lined up outside her home, and the weapons they all held. "Situation."

"Fair enough." Sonny still seemed skeptical. "You're doing quite well with that, for a...what exactly is your job in this sector?"

"Floor Supervisor," she answered.

"Ah. I see. So you're used to maintaining composure then." Sonny stalked back over to Jace's parents, and they lost a bit of their color in the harsh light of the headlights. "So, as a supervisor, what would you have me do with a couple of overreaching climbers?"

"Nothing, ma'am."

She turned back to my mom, an expression of sheer confusion on her face. "Nothing?"

"No. Doing nothing allows them no forward movement in their climb. Possibly the most frustrating thing of all for them." It made sense. I bought it anyway.

But it was clear Sonny wasn't having it. "These people brought the big guns to your doorstep. And you still protect them?"

My mother said nothing. And that was where my dad stepped in. "Listen, Emily is right. This is all entirely unnecessary. We'd be more than happy to cooperate with you in the right way."

"And what exactly is the right way, Mr. Delman?" Sonny challenged.

He eyed her up and down before answering. "Without weapons for one thing."

"The two we hunt have proven to be violent. In fact, Rarity killed a guard a few days ago."

I blanched. That was a detail I hadn't deliberately hidden from my parents, but it didn't exactly come up in conversation either. Now they knew. The people I loved most in the world knew I was a killer.

But neither reacted at all. They weren't horrified, and they didn't spring to my defense either. Had they processed what she said? Maybe they thought she was just saying things to get a rise out of them. What would they say when they found out it was true?

"Without knowing the circumstances, it's hard to pass judgment on the situation," my dad eventually said, apparently playing along with Sonny's game.

"Circumstances? The circumstance was that we found him dead on the sidewalk, his screen missing. She killed him, then used his screen to get off the island."

Mom's face was turning red, but she bit her bottom lip.

A man in black stomped up behind Sonny, holding objects that took the wind out of my sails.

"What's this?" she asked as she looked down at some of my dirty clothes.

"Those are clothes she left behind. It means nothing," Mom said, sounding a bit too defensive.

"And this?" Sonny held up the screen I'd taken from the guard.

Mom and Dad said nothing, but the vindictive look on Jace's parents' faces made me want to hurl myself at them both.

"Yes. That's what I thought. I'm afraid I've seen enough," Sonny said abruptly as she stood in front of Jace's parents. She lazily put a hand on the gun that hung from her shoulder, but my dad didn't miss the gesture and tensed.

He held my mom's hand tightly as they both watched the blonde woman who held their lives in her hands.

But they couldn't die, right? Their dates were years away. No way would she go that far.

The world slowed down in that moment while I was cruelly glued to my hiding place in that bush. I could do nothing to move anything. I even held my breath as I watched Sonny raise the weapon. She pointed it at Jace's parents first, but then swept across them while they cowered and flinched away.

While she did, she adjusted a dial on the side of the gun. Jace's grip on my arm tightened. "No," he whispered. But the command did nothing to stop her. Not a thing.

A strange warm pulse cut through the air. I closed my eyes, just for a moment, but when I opened them, my parents laid motionless on the grass next to Jace's parents, who'd gone from white to green.

Jace's hand clamped over my mouth as a scream escaped me. I closed my eyes again, but the image was burned onto the inside of my eyelids. They were gone. Before their dates. They'd become one of the few. A true rarity.

"I'm afraid traitors breed traitors," Sonny said as she tossed the weapon back over her shoulder.

A woman in all black rushed up with a rectangular scanner in her hands, then ran it over my parents.

"No brain activity, ma'am. Should I have them sent to the facility?"

My heart froze. The facility. Where Withs who were too hurt to recover went, but not hurt enough to die. Accidents happened more often than the Withouts liked to admit. Those people never got to the island. Never got their two weeks. They made the ultimate sacrifice and never got a dang thing for it.

"Yes, that will be fine." There was no emotion in her voice as the woman hailed a couple of goons pushing stretchers behind them. In an instant, my parents were loaded up and pushed into the back of a black van. They were gone.

Jace's mother looked like she was about to throw up, and I hoped she did. All over Sonny.

The anger building inside me grew hotter by the moment as I watched them, squirming under Jace's vice-like grip.

"You, on the other hand, you had better prove useful to me. Because if there's one thing I hate more than traitors, it's parasites."

TWENTY-EIGHT

The shaking started small. So small I thought it was me at first. But then, I realized it was Jace. I was holding on to his arm with a death grip, and he trembled beneath my hand. His face was strained, eyebrows knitted together, jaw clenched.

"Find them," Sonny commanded, then the guards dispersed. Most went to their cars, but a small team went back inside the house to search more thoroughly. I cringed at every single crash they made as I wondered what else they were taking from me. What childhood memory was being crushed beneath their black boots?

Jace's shaking was too much, and I let him go. It felt like he was rattling my brain.

"Jace, let's go. They're leaving. Now's our chance." It didn't even sound like my voice. It was obviously someone much more rational and present. Because I wasn't there. I was in a place that never saw such horrors, and I planned to stay there for the rest of my life.

But he didn't speak. Instead, he took a step away from the bush. I followed him at first. But step after step, he got farther and farther from the bush, and his intent became clear.

He was stalking toward his parents.

They stood in the yard, unmoving, while the majority of the guards, including Sonny, went to their vehicles. Everyone had their backs to him. He hadn't been seen. Yet.

I wanted to call out to him. But I knew the second I did, we'd be sunk. They'd see us, and my parents' sacrifice would be wasted. But if he lashed out at his parents, wouldn't that do the exact same thing?

Jace had nothing but his bare hands as he clenched them into white-knuckled fists at his sides. He slowly closed the distance between him and his parents. In that moment, though, I knew it would be enough. His rage consumed him in a way I now understood. If they'd minded their business, my parents would still be alive. They'd willingly sacrificed them. And they were plainly terrible people. It wasn't fair.

A tear escaped my eye as I stood paralyzed, watching Jace get closer and closer to his parents, who still had their backs to him.

The worst part was, I didn't know what I hoped for. Their dates would keep him from killing them, but part of me still wanted him to end them, like my parents had been ended. Except I wanted him to make them hurt. To drag it out. To punish them for what they'd done to my life. But another part of me wanted to run. The smallest part of me didn't want it to end here. Didn't want to give up. And that was what his revenge would do. Sonny would like nothing more than for us to show ourselves right here, right now.

Suddenly, my feet were loosed and I darted out ahead of Jace. Understanding washed over me, and I knew. Sonny did that to them so we would come out. We'd played right into her hands. And if I didn't stop him, she'd see her victory walking willingly into the open.

I said nothing as I positioned myself between Jace and his father's back. I held my hands out, but Jace's green eyes didn't see me. They were focused above me. On his dad's head. I had no idea what he planned to do—strangle him? Bash his head? Would he finish his mother off, too? The one who gave him life? Would he have the stomach for it?

It didn't matter. All that mattered was that I stopped him.

But there was no sign of himself in his eyes. They were cold, hard, and unrecognizable as he got closer to me. I held my ground, though, and he actually bumped into me.

He blinked, and the hard look was replaced by confusion as he peered down at me.

"Not like this," I whispered so quietly I wasn't even sure he heard me.

"What?" Jace's father asked, turning to the side. We froze as his mother looked at her husband.

"I didn't say anything," she said, and they both pivoted to watch the guards leave, their headlights slowly dimming.

I shook as I watched the van with my parents inside drive away. Never to be seen again. I wanted to run after them. To put my arms around them. Sob for them. But I couldn't. I wasn't allowed to grieve for them. Not then. Maybe not ever.

In that moment, we needed to get away. Or their deaths would've been in vain. And I wouldn't allow that.

Jace looked around, his eyes falling on my parents. I feared it would rekindle his rage, but sadness made him sag. Grief was heavy, and he wore it on his shoulders like a million-pound boulder. He eyed the guards, the house, and finally me.

Taking my hands, he gave a short nod. I glanced over my shoulders at his parents. I shouldn't have, but I did.

"I saved you once. It won't happen again," I whispered.

Then we took off, our feet flying beneath us.

"Hey, they're here," his father yelled like the ding bat he was.

The sound was deafening as gunfire erupted all around us. In an instant, the guards were out of their trucks and descending on us with stunners landing all around us.

"They couldn't hit the broad side of a barn," I gasped as we ran.

"Let's hope," Jace said as he pulled me along the back fence and to the street behind us.

The cars were on us like dark on night, so we darted away, back between the houses. But guards on foot met us in that direction.

"Come on," Jace said, jerking me out toward the street.

"They're everywhere," I shouted above the noise of the stunners hitting the trees, homes, and ground all around us.

"They wouldn't be if you'd kept your mouth shut," he yelled.

"If you want to throw stones, maybe you should've left one of the hundreds of times I suggested we do so, before you went walking up to your folks with some kind of death wish."

He didn't answer as he yanked a storm grate open. "Come on," he said as he pulled on my hand. I didn't even have time to put on the brakes or consider what might be down there.

I basically made a controlled fall into the drain, using the ladder, and Jace didn't do much better. I narrowly missed having a one-hundred-and-eighty pound man on my head as I stepped away from the ladder.

"Go," he yelled, his voice echoing down the sewer system. As if I needed encouragement.

I shook my head as I took off running in the darkness, not sure where to go, but just trying to get away from there. Neither of us had a flashlight. I had to admit, it was pretty freaking dark. I felt the damp, slimy wall with my hand and ran along it until I ran smack into an adjacent wall, deciding that wasn't a great plan.

"Why don't you lead?" I suggested as I rubbed my forehead.

"Just hang on for a second," he said. He was tense, but so was I. We were being chased by people who wanted to end our lives as we knew them.

The stone path we ran on was narrow. Water flowed next to us, making it hard to hear anything at all. The light was what we saw first. Light from their flashlights as they hunted us. They were in the sewer with us.

Well, if that wasn't icing on my rancid death cake, I didn't know what was.

Jace didn't have to say anything. I turned around and started back the way we came. No need to end up back at our original storm drain, where there was sure to be a team of guards waiting to apprehend us.

But we didn't get far. That cursed light off in the distance bounced off the far wall, and I stopped dead. Jace crashed into me, and I nearly fell into the water.

"Turn off your lights. Turn on your night vision goggles and set your stunners to heat seeking." The command echoed off the walls, telling us just how close the teams were.

I didn't need to see the fear in Jace's eyes. I felt it. It crushed us both under the threat of what our future could be.

"Quietly now," Jace said as he sat on the edge, easing his legs into the mystery water.

I tried not to think about what was in the water as I eased in as quietly as I could. The shock of the cold nearly made me gasp, and I bit down on my bottom lip as I sank down to my neck. I could touch, but not easily. The current threatened to carry me away, and I clung to Jace's hand. He seemed anchored much more easily.

I knew we'd have to go all the way under. But the thought of all that crap, literally, floating in the water, into my eyes, mouth, ears...I swallowed hard, stifling the gag that rose in the back of my throat.

Jace yanked down on my hand. Slipping beneath the surface of the water, I squeezed my eyes shut. I went all the way to the bottom, hoping my air bubbles would go unnoticed as Jace and I sat facing each other, holding hands, at the bottom of the sewer.

I thought about other things. Anything besides the fact I was surrounded by turd water. Something brushed against my arm, and I stifled a yelp. Jace squeezed my hands, and I anchored myself to him.

I remembered the time before when we were—well, what were we? Happier? More carefree? Sort of. We had our dates barreling down on us, our deaths staring us in the faces. But it was much more abstract than someone chasing us with stunners. As sewage water floated all around me, I realized ignorance really was bliss.

Jace ran his thumb along the back of my hand, and I thought about our time on the island. A maddening glimpse into what our lives could've been, but it was such a glorious time. Time together to do what we wanted, when we wanted. We'd never known a life like that, and as we sat at the bottom of Crap Creek, I didn't think we'd ever know that again.

My lungs screamed for air, and I dared to open my eyes —probably giving myself a host of eye infections and para- sites—and peer up at the surface, but I couldn't see anything through the dark water. I couldn't even see Jace sitting in front of me. He held on to my hands all the same, not moving. Not relaxing. Just there. Letting me know I wasn't alone. And if he could do it, so could I.

It was a mind game. How long could I stay there, in that freezing water, holding my breath? How long before I needed to go to the surface and reveal myself? Would I drown? Or would my body take over and force itself up?

How long had it been? Thirty seconds? Three minutes? I couldn't say. Time was so weirdly relative when I held my breath underwater. It seemed like an eternity, but in reality, mere seconds had gone by. I knew it wasn't enough time. If I popped up, they would see me. They'd be right there, right within arm's reach.

But if I didn't go up soon, I'd gulp in a lungful of the poop lagoon. Jace gave my hands two squeezes, and I didn't need any more encouragement than that.

Slowly, we went to the surface. As much as I wanted to dramatically break the surface and gulp in air, I knew if we made noise, we'd be discovered.

I tilted my face back and stuck my nose above the water, but it was still too close to the surface. I needed to get my mouth out. Needed that gulping breath. So I stood a little taller, stuck my lips out like some kind of needy chick, and sucked in air. I was sure it was a good look for me.

Air filled my lungs and cleared my mind. Nothing existed except air.

Jace tapped on my shoulder. Without thinking, I stood all the way up so I could see him.

"They're gone," he whispered just loudly enough for me to hear. The sound of the water drowned out everything else.

We were safe. They'd gone by without finding us. But we were also completely and utterly alone.

TWENTY-NINE

We didn't speak. Not at first. We hauled ourselves out of the water, covered in slime and filth, which was probably supposed to be some poetic mirror of how we both felt about our situation, but I found it more annoying than anything else. After all, I was covered in literal crap. Everything was most definitely *not* coming up roses.

I sat on the ledge, my feet crossed under me, so I could be out of the water completely. Jace stood next to me, shaking. At first, I thought he was just cold. Or maybe coming down off the adrenaline rush.

But then, I saw him literally biting back something, his face contorted by what could only be anger. He started pacing in the darkness. A few times, I heard him stumble and expected him to fall back into the cesspool.

Finally, I couldn't take it anymore, and I broke the silence. "What now?" My voice echoed in the dark space, even though I'd barely spoken above a whisper.

"Now? I don't have any. Freaking. Idea," he whispered, clearly frustrated with our current situation.

I let him pace around a bit more, trying to decide what

to do. Calm him down, find a safe place, get cleaned up, assess our situation—the possibilities were endless.

"Why didn't you let me kill them? Why did you get in my way?" His accusation cut my train of thought so short my hamster was definitely not on the wheel anymore.

I couldn't see him, but I felt like he was glaring at me. It made my skin feel crawly, and I rubbed my arms.

"Because I didn't want to live like a lab rat for the rest of my life."

"You ruined everything." The accusation stung, so, naturally, I ran with it. I did ruin everything. I didn't die. If I'd died, none of this would've happened. If I hadn't decided to go on some heroic mission to save him, none of this would've happened. If I'd gone off, kept to myself, my parents would still be functional, and Jace would be completely oblivious in his hospital hell. At least I would be safe. But instead, I wanted him with me. And now, my parents had lost all semblance of life because of it.

"Because of *you*, we're being hunted in our own home."

To my completely stable mind, that statement was what put me over the edge.

I exploded. "Where do you get off putting that on me? I didn't see you protesting coming here. I didn't see you coming up with any ideas for what to do or how to stay safe. All I saw *you* doing was attacking your parents, which would've made *my* folks' sacrifice worthless."

I was standing. When had I stood up? In my mind, I was chest to chest with him, facing him down. But I didn't have the guts to reach out and see if he was really there. The darkness made both of us a little more bold.

"I'm the one who said we should go. Somehow, *you* heard 'oh okay, let's march out into the middle of the group of people who want to take us captive and try to kill a couple of people while we're at it. That'll go great. No one will even notice while we what—strangle them to unconsciousness since they can't be killed before their date?'"

The words bounced back at me rather loudly, and I winced. If the guards were still in this section of the tunnel, they'd be on us. And soon.

Silence hung between us, and it weighed me down even more. Sagging under it, I sank back down to the ground. I stunk. I couldn't stand myself. But I had nowhere to go. No way to escape. I just had to sit in my own filth.

I felt Jace sit next to me, and I wondered how he knew where the heck I was. He hadn't even kicked or stumbled over me.

"What do you want to do," he asked quietly.

What did I want to do? "I want to go home. I want everything to be fine. I want there to be no dates, and I want my parents to be okay." Ugly crying wasn't attractive on me, so I was pretty grateful for the darkness as I sobbed the words.

I felt him reach for my hand, but he fumbled around a bit, groping my thigh, then jabbing me in the side before I finally reached for him with both hands.

"I want that, too." It solved nothing. But somehow, the acknowledgment made me feel better. Like I wasn't alone. It certainly didn't make it okay. But it did help me to stop sobbing uncontrollably, which was a major bonus in my book.

I took a few shuddering breaths, and he squeezed my hand. "I think we should make some changes and get the heck out of here," he suggested.

"Changes?"

"To our appearance."

I chewed on that for a beat. How could we do that? I

knew there were some programs coming out that would allow people to project images onto themselves, allowing them to completely change how they looked. They were testing hair color, eye color, and makeup at the moment, but the potential the technology held was exciting and terrifying at the same time. Thing was, we didn't have access to any of that. I didn't even have a screen anymore.

"How do you propose we do that?"

I felt him shrug. "The old-fashioned way. We get some dye, scissors, change our clothes, and then head for the hills so to speak."

Getting those things would mean going topside. Exposing ourselves. But then again, we'd have to do that anyway. Neither of us had food or supplies of any kind. We didn't even have a flashlight. While we were up there, why not get some things that might give us some freedom?

"Okay, but what about my parents?" I asked, breathing life to something I couldn't get my mind off. Sonny had them now. They were being tortured in the name of science.

"What about them, Rare?" he asked gently.

"I think we should try to save them."

Jace sighed. "You heard her. They're out for good, Rare. They're at the facility. I'm sorry. But even if we did save them, we couldn't care for them. Not like they can. Even if by some miracle we managed to get two unconscious bodies out undetected, how would we feed them? Keep them hydrated? It's not practical. Unfortunately, I don't think rescuing them is a good option."

I wanted to scream at him, to rail against his truths. They were awful, and therefore they couldn't be true. Right? I needed time to think. Time to come up with a plan. I couldn't abandon them. Not yet.

"I think we should hang around here for a bit."

"What? How can you say that? We should get as far away from this place as we can."

"If we stay here, we might learn what their plan is, so we can stay ahead of them. Hide right under their noses, ya know?" With every word, I talked faster and faster, getting excited about potentially having the upper hand. "They'll never expect us to squat here. And that's why it'll work."

"Just like hanging out on the island worked for us?" Jace snapped.

"That's low."

He didn't apologize, but he didn't take it any further either.

"Fine. Where do you suggest we go?"

He sighed so hard I felt the breeze from it on my arm. "Let's just take one thing at a time. First, we get cleaned up and make it so we don't stick out so much."

I agreed to that, but I had no idea how we would go about accomplishing that. Turned out Jace had some practical suggestions.

Slowly, we made our way to a grate. Light streamed in, illuminating the ladder below. At some point, the sun had risen.

"You wait here. I'll go up and gather supplies."

"What? No way. I'm going with you."

"No. We're too conspicuous as a pair. They're looking for both of us. If it's just a dumb kid wandering around, they won't give me a second glance."

"A dumb kid covered in goo?" Getting a good look at him in the light made me think this plan wasn't going to work at all. His skin was at least a shade darker than it should be, and I didn't even want to think about why.

He shrugged. "Maybe I'll run through a hose or something. I'll work it out. Anyway, the point is that you stay here. Stay hidden."

"And if you don't come back?"

"Stay hidden."

I wanted to defy him. To tell him I wasn't leaving him. I'd worked too hard to be with him. It didn't matter what our differences were now—we were all we had. But he was serious. He already had his hand on the ladder. I knew he wouldn't hear any more about it. He was going, and I would wait.

"Jace Brown, there will come a day when you demand too much of me, and I will say no."

He smiled widely, knowing he'd won. He even leaned forward, planting the smallest kiss on the end of my poo-covered nose. "But it's not today."

He turned and climbed up the ladder. I mumbled, hating myself as I watched him go. "No. It's not today."

I WASN'T sure how long I waited for him. Frankly, I needed to get myself a watch. Just add it to the extensive list of things I needed—like to get rid of the people hunting me, lunch, a safe place to exist, and maybe a watch.

My stomach growled loudly, and I put my hand on it. "I swear to God, if you give us away, I'll never give you anything good to eat again," I whispered. It didn't help. My defiant body wanted food, and I had nothing for it.

The light streaming in started to wane. I'd been sitting there a while. Would he come back? What if he didn't? How long should I wait?

As if in answer to my question, the grate above me scraped back. I scuttled into the darkness like some kind of creature of the night. If it were a guard, I didn't want to be spotted.

A man with a backpack, dressed in jeans and a dark hoodie, descended the ladder, so I pulled back more. Who the heck would be climbing around in the sewers from my neighborhood? Probably some dumb kid meeting up with his friends. Just what I needed—to get caught in the middle of a bunch of bored teenagers out for trouble. Boy, would I give it to them.

"Rare?" The whisper was so quiet I wasn't sure if I'd heard it or just wished it.

"Rarity, where are you?" The voice came louder this time, more concerned.

"Jace?" I asked, not revealing my position yet.

But I didn't have to. He shone a flashlight right at me, blinding me. I held up a hand, and he moved the beam down. He looked like a different person, except for his hair. He was clean, for one thing, which I didn't appreciate. I still smelled like the bottom of a sewer, thank you very much.

"Hey," he said, like it was totally normal to rendezvous at midday in the sewer. "I thought maybe they got you."

I shook my head. "I haven't seen anyone. *I* thought you were some hoodlum."

"Good. That's the point. There's a hose up there not far that you can use to clean up. I suggest you do that first. Then we'll worry about clothes and your hair."

Go topside. Could I do that? "Did you see anyone? Did anyone see you?"

"Yes. And yes. But by the time they did, they didn't look twice at me."

"Even while you were using someone's hose to wash?" Skeptical didn't even begin to describe how I felt about this. He'd made it, but what were the odds I could do it, too?

He shrugged. "No one was home."

"And they're still not home?"

"Not when I walked by a few minutes ago."

Where would they be at that time? "Do you think they evacuated the neighborhood?"

"No. I saw people at the store."

"And by the way, how did you get so much stuff without credits?"

"Got creative."

"Creative?"

"I swiped it. What do you want?"

He actually seemed a little guilty. But really, how else were we going to get the things we needed? Not like we had my folks as a resource anymore.

"No, you're right." It was all I could say. After all, I couldn't tell him he'd done the right thing. He stole stuff. But he didn't need to feel bad about it either.

He brought the pack in front of him and dug into it, producing a bar of soap. Actual soap.

"Here. Go get clean. You'll feel better."

"If I don't get killed," I grumbled as I pocketed the soap and scaled the ladder. But when I got to the top, the grate was so heavy I couldn't budge it.

"A little help?"

"Always coming to your rescue, huh?" he teased.

"I've rescued you enough times. It's about time you pulled your weight around here."

When I got to the bottom, I stepped aside. He climbed up quickly. "I suppose it is," he said when he got back down, gesturing for me to go up.

He climbed up behind me. "When you're done, just holler down and I'll let you in."

I nodded. "If I don't come back—"

He cut me off. "I know girls take longer showers than boys, but don't take forever, okay?"

"Okay," I said, and he slid the grate back into place.

The sun was high in the sky, telling me it was past lunchtime. People would be at work, so maybe I could get cleaned up without being spotted. Time was marching on without my parents. It had been more than twelve hours since they'd had their lives stolen in my front yard. We'd spent that long running and hiding from Sonny and her gang. We hadn't slept or eaten. How much longer could we do it? I could feel our time running out, backing us into a dark, sewer-filled corner, and I didn't like it one bit.

The grate was in town. We were surrounded by businesses. Where was I supposed to find a hose here?

But Jace was right. Just across the street, in an alley, a hose was connected to a faucet. The alley even offered a small amount of privacy.

I darted into it as quickly as I could, and I hoped I could be done with it as quickly as possible.

Grabbing the end of the hose, I scurried behind the dumpster and waited. Of course I hadn't thought to turn the dang thing on, so I had to leave my relative safety to turn the water on. When I did, I heard voices, so I jammed myself behind the dumpster, making myself one with the brick wall behind me.

"This patrol is useless. Those two kids are long gone by now," a man's voice said.

"Maybe. Maybe not," a deeper man's voice said.

"What are you talking about? Her parents are essentially dead. His clearly don't support him. They have nothing here. They're gone."

"Sonny doesn't think so."

"Yeah, well, maybe Sonny doesn't know everything,"

the first guy said. I nearly choked. Their voices became more distant as they passed by the alley where I was hiding.

"Say that to her face sometime, why don't you?"

"I don't have a death wish."

I hid there for a long time, making sure they weren't circling back around. It seemed Sonny thought we'd stick around. Maybe Jace was right. Maybe we should go. But that little detail was so valuable to me, so what else could we learn if we just stayed a little bit longer? Moving on meant abandoning my parents. Not to mention the fact we had nowhere to go.

Wanting to get back to Jace, I hurried up and did the fastest cleaning job I could. I ditched my clothes in the dumpster, then changed into the new stuff Jace snagged for me. It looked a lot like what he had. Jeans and a grey hoodie. Inconspicuous. Gender neutral. Maybe, if we were lucky, we could get away with this.

All that was left was to get back to the drain. But after seeing the guards, I hesitated to run out into the middle of the street. Creeping to the edge of the alley, I looked both ways. The street was totally deserted. A breeze blew my hood away from my face, and I pulled the strings tighter around it.

With nothing left to do, I darted out to the grate and hissed for Jace.

"Coming, sweetie," he said in a singsong voice.

"Jace," I scolded, but he ignored me.

He moved the grate, and I basically climbed over him to get off the street. "Jeez, let me get out of the way at least."

"I saw guards, Jace."

"You what?"

"I saw them. They were patrolling. They walked by the alley when I was trying to get cleaned up."

"Did they see you?" Suddenly, he was serious, like it hadn't been life and death two seconds ago when I was trying to get out of the open.

"No. They seemed unconvinced we were still here. But apparently, Sonny thinks we're hanging around."

"So we should go. She'll keep combing the city for us," Jace said, more assured of himself than ever.

"Go where? And how for that matter?"

"We have legs. We can walk just about anywhere," he pointed out.

"I know, but if we stay here, just for a few days, maybe we can get some information. How helpful is it that we know she's still looking for us?"

Jace shrugged. "Not very to be honest. We could've correctly assumed that on our own."

"I guess, but maybe if we hung around, we'd hear something more valuable. Like how they plan to catch us. Or what they plan to do with us. Or how we can get to my folks."

"Rare." Jace hesitated, but I could tell by the way he frowned he didn't agree. "We've been over your parents. I love them, too. But they wouldn't want us throwing everything away to go after them. What good would it do?"

"They'll be away from *them*..." I spat the word like it was some kind of curse.

Frowning, Jace reached for my hand. "Rare. They're at the facility. That isn't us-or-them territory. It's neutral ground. They're not in pain. They're not even there. You heard the woman say they were brain dead."

I broke down. I wasn't sure what triggered it. Maybe him saying they were brain dead. Maybe it was the thought of them lying in the facility alongside so many others just like them. Not a hospital, but not a graveyard either. In between. Neutral.

The sobs came in heaving gulps, and Jace pulled me close to him, crushing me against his chest. He was my rock. He held me close and let me cry, saying nothing as he ran his hand across my back. There weren't words to make it better. Nothing that could magically erase everything that had happened and give them their existence back.

Time didn't ebb and flow in that moment. All I knew was my grief, and it consumed me in a way I didn't fully understand.

Eventually, the tears stopped. I didn't have any left. My body betrayed me.

Jace finally pulled away from me, brushing the soaked strands of hair away from my face. "I think we should stay put, but just for a few days. Just until we can figure out where to go. Sound good?"

I nodded. It was all I could manage.

Jace smiled sadly. He held up a pair of shiny new scissors, trying to distract me. "Now, let's cut that hair."

THIRTY

Darkness surrounded me, and I found myself back in my parents' yard. The guards were there. Jace's folks were there, and Sonny was there with her rifle over her shoulder.

"Jace, we should go," I said, but I didn't mean it. Not this time. Maybe not the first time either. This time would be different, though. I would save them. I wouldn't watch them lose their lives again.

But even as I thought the words, Sonny swept the rifle around and shot them both, melting their skin right off their bodies, reducing them to piles of red goo.

But this time, instead of Jace advancing on his parents, I did. I picked up a rock and moved in on them, the rage building inside me was more than I could control.

Jace's dad was taller than me, but it didn't matter in my dream. No one saw me approach. Sonny walked back to her car. The guards dispersed. It was just me, my dead parents in a heap on the ground, and Jace's living ones with their backs to me.

The rock was heavy in my hand, and I pooled all my rage into it as I swung it at the back of Jace's father's head. A terrifyingly satisfying crunch filled my ears, and he turned to look at me. But it wasn't Jace's dad. It was my own father.

Blood dripped down the side of his face from his ear. Confusion pulled the corners of his lips into a slight frown. "Honey, why did you do that?"

I looked over at Jace's mother, who wasn't his mother at all anymore, but the guard I'd killed. He glared at me as well as he could with a bashed-in face. "What have you done?" the dead guard demanded to know.

A scream burbled up inside me, but when I opened my mouth, no sound came out. My father crumpled to the ground and I backed up, but no matter how many steps I took, I couldn't move away from what I'd done. It stuck to me like fly paper.

My breaths came in short bursts as I dropped the rock, then promptly tripped over it as I tried to get away, to escape what I'd done. But I couldn't. My father's unseeing eyes never blinked, never turned away from me, never stopped asking me why.

"Rare." The voice was soft and almost imperceptible. So I scrambled back, on all fours now, trying to get away, but always keeping my eyes on my dad and the guard, who never stopped staring at me no matter where I moved or what I did.

"Mom," I cried out, wondering where she'd gone. But she didn't answer me. No one did. The guards, the cars, the house—they were all gone. All that existed in the world was me and the dead bodies I'd created.

"Rarity..." The voice came louder, and I gasped. I blinked, trying to comprehend the scene around me.

A dull light glowed by the far wall. I was lying on the ground, but I had a blanket. Jace had apparently abandoned his.

"You okay?" he asked.

I swallowed hard, as if that would help clear away everything that had happened.

"No. Not really."

He didn't say anything. What could he? I licked my lips, tasting the desire to kill his parents like they were standing right in front of me. "*I won't save you again.*" I heard my own words echo back in my mind. But did I mean I would be the one to wield the rock? Certainly felt that way in my dream. But then to see the disappointment on my dad's face turned my stomach.

"I need some air." I stood, and so did Jace.

"Okay." Without asking any questions, he climbed up the ladder and moved the grate for me. The dim morning light streamed in as he backed down the ladder. We'd slept the whole night in safety. I wasn't sure if I should be relieved or filled with dread. More time had passed. More time in which the world kept turning without my parents in it.

"Be careful. If you're not back in an hour, I'm coming for you."

I nodded, unable to form words, and scrubbed my head. Jace had cut my hair so short I probably looked like a boy. He'd said that was the idea. Two boys wandering the road wouldn't get a second look.

But as I rubbed my hand over my nearly naked scalp, I wasn't so sure. It was like every piece of who I was before my date was getting stripped away bit by bit. And I didn't like what was left underneath one bit.

I balled my hands into a fist as I listened to him slide the grate back into position. The street was deserted and I pulled my hood up, keeping my head down as I jammed my balled fists into my pockets.

I had no particular destination in mind. I just needed to get out of the suffocation of the sewers. To get away from my dreams.

The store we shopped at wasn't open yet, but I looked in the window. Shelves lined with the good stuff were closer to the front, making it look like everything they had was beautiful, delicious, and affordable. But it was all a lie, just like everything else.

"You need something?" a kid about my age asked as he jammed a key into the lock. Nothing fancy here like on the island. Old fashioned all the way for us. No wonder Jace had gotten in so easily.

"Or are you just casing the place? I told the boss we needed better security, but he didn't listen. Then a bunch of stuff turned up missing the other day. Food, blankets, flashlight. Stuff like that." He put a little oomph into pushing the door, and it finally gave for him. "Bet you can guess who got blamed for that."

He held the door open. "Well, you coming in or what?"

I shrugged. Probably couldn't linger there anymore. What did it matter?

Aimlessly, I wandered the aisles, keeping my hands safely in my pockets. Everything reminded me of home. I stopped in front of the chocolate and thought of my mom. Of how she cried the day I gave her that chocolate bar.

I picked up a bar and held it in my hands, wanting to feel that connection with Mom again. Wanting to make her that happy again. But I'd never get that chance. All because of...

Movement in the corner of my eye snapped me back to the present. The candy bar was broken in my hand. I shook while I put it back on the shelf, hoping the clerk wouldn't notice.

I glanced over to see Jace's mother pushing a cart full to the brim of goodies. Not just stuff that wasn't moldy but everything. Produce, a bag of chips that was actually sealed, refrigerated food like sliced ham, and even frozen stuff. When my eyes landed on a gallon of ice cream, I nearly made a scene. Ice cream. And an entire gallon of it. How did she afford all that?

I followed at a safe distance, watching her pick up the chocolate bar I'd just smashed and toss it aside with disgust. "You'd think they could get better quality stuff in here."

Why on earth would she think that? We lived in a working zone. We weren't Withouts. We weren't entitled to anything. We were each given an extremely limited number of credits for working. There was no such thing as overtime. We got what we got, and we made do with it. End of story. So how was she paying for all those treats?

She made her way to the register with her full load. I watched her closely, waiting for the other shoe to drop. Would she make up some story about feeding the guards she'd brought down on my head or what?

But she didn't have to. She pulled a huge amount of credits out of her purse, and my jaw fell straight to the ground. My eyes probably bugged out, too, like one of those old-fashioned cartoons from the time before dates.

The worker who'd let me in seemed unfazed as he counted them out diligently.

"Have a nice day, Mrs. Brown."

She didn't bother to acknowledge him as she made her way out. Why would she waste energy on the likes of him?

I watched her go to her car, load it up, then get inside and drive off. When had they gotten a car? It wasn't a nice one or anything fancy like they had on the island, but a car was a luxury not seen around here.

I thought about Sonny and how Jace's parents had brought our enemy right to our door. Sonny's words came back to me. Suddenly, I knew the answer. *If there's one thing I hate more than traitors, it's parasites.*

They were being paid for information. To watch for us. To turn us in.

Without thinking, I'd walked to Jace's house. I watched his mother take the last load of groceries in the house from across the street. When she went inside, I moved closer. Suddenly caring about my safety seemed insignificant. My desire to see her, to watch this woman who knew in her mind she was so right and we were so wrong, seemed more important.

As she stood at the kitchen sink washing her freshly acquired produce, my fingers twitched. She'd taken everything from me. She and her husband. She wasn't even working anymore? They were paying her enough that she could stay home?

Meanwhile, my parents were gone because of her, and Jace and I were running for our lives. Literally living in the sewer while she ate ice cream. And she thought we were being selfish. She thought we were hiding the key to survival from the world.

I had half a mind to beat some sense into her. She looked out the window over the sink, and I swear she nearly saw me. But even if she did, so what? I was just a boy sitting on a bench. I wasn't doing anything wrong.

Regardless, she didn't see me. I still had the advantage. Feeling bold, I got up from the bench and made my way closer to their house. I leaned brazenly against a tree that was nearly in their yard. Facing the window, I could see her getting lunch ready for herself with fresh vegetables and bread. Actual bread. It wasn't even moldy. Okay, I assumed that part, but why would it be? Nothing but the best for Mrs. Brown. I could almost smell it, and the thought made my mouth water.

It wasn't right. None of it. She was living the life of luxury while we were struggling to stay alive. Seeing her living such a different life from us flipped a switch for me.

I was ready to do it. To end her. I actually was. But then my dream came screaming back to me. My dad's face and that look while his blood dripped off his face—I'd done that to him.

No. I couldn't do it. As much as I wanted to. For me. For Jace. I couldn't. Or maybe wouldn't was the better word. I wouldn't let that last piece of who I was go.

With all that they'd been given, would they ever stop hunting for us? They had almost as much motivation to find us as we did to not be found. Sonny didn't make idle threats. I didn't know her that well, and I knew that. Jace's mom must know it, too.

She glanced up again, almost as if she were nervous.

I swore she looked right at me. I didn't look away or run. I stared her down, letting her know I saw her. Did she recognize me? It was hard to say. She didn't break eye contact with me. Not right away at least. The water ran over the green pepper in her hands, and she stood poised, ready to wash it, but instead she was frozen, staring at me. Maybe she did recognize me. Maybe she'd make the call right then. Maybe I'd get caught.

It was a lot of maybes as the seconds ticked by one after another until she finally looked down again and went back to washing her pepper.

Then I realized I hadn't been as confident as I felt. I let out a breath I'd apparently been holding, and realized I was shaking. When did that start?

As casually as I could, I turned and walked back to the sewer, where Jace would be mad I hadn't come back sooner, I realized Jace was right. He'd been right since the moment we surfaced from that sewer water.

We couldn't stay. Someone would get hurt if we did.

THIRTY-ONE

"Crap on a cracker, Rarity. I was just about to go looking for you." Jace said as he slid the grate back into place.

"Sorry," I said, but I sounded absent. How could I tell him? Crow never tasted good, and I was about to eat a heaping helping of it.

"What's wrong? Were you seen?"

"Yes. But I don't think she recognized me. So well done on the disguise." I forced a smile. He narrowed his eyes as he stood with his back to the ladder.

"By who?"

"Your mom."

"What?" His voice echoed through the sewer. I cringed, hoping no one was walking by above us. It was nearly midday by then.

I held up my hands, "Settle down, Jace."

"How could I settle down? You saw her? How? Did you go to their work or something?"

"Actually, she was at the store. Then I sort of followed her home. Brace yourself for the head cannon I'm about to fire at you," I said, then I explained everything, including that delicious looking ice cream.

"How can they..."

"I think Sonny is paying them to spy on us." No sense beating around the bush.

He looked up at me like I'd just thrown a bucket of icy water on his head. "Really?"

"How else could they afford everything? And why else would Sonny have called your parents parasites? They're mooching off the system, hoping they'll be able to deliver us to Sonny and her gang."

Jace sort of flopped onto the ground, leaning his back against the ladder.

"Well, that's just great."

"I think we should go," I said quietly, nearly choking on my crow.

Completely incredulous, he stared. "What?"

"You were right. They'll never stop hunting us. And I'm afraid the longer we stay here, the more apt we are to do something stupid."

"Like what?"

"Like try to hurt them? Get caught? Who knows?" I threw my hands up and turned around. I wasn't proud of any of this.

"Hurt them?" He eyed me, clearly skeptical of my alarmist perspective.

"I...I'm losing track of who I am, Jace. When I saw her, watched her living so comfortably in that house you hated, I don't know what came over me. I didn't wish I'd let you end her. I wanted to do it myself."

He reached for my hand, pulling me down so I was sitting across from him. "Where do you suggest we go?" he asked without any kind of judgment in his eyes.

"I don't know. Away from here is as far as I've gotten. Maybe we'll get lucky and we'll just be able to hide for the rest of our lives. Maybe we'll find some peace."

He snorted. "In case you haven't noticed, Lady Luck is a bit of a jerk who got up on the wrong side of your bed."

"Fair point."

"So...what now?" Jace asked. I could tell he was treading lightly, trying to make me feel like I was in control. Like he trusted me after I'd made a mistake.

"Hey, I did the hard work. I made the decision. You decide how to execute."

He chuckled. "Fair enough. How about we get a nap in and leave at nightfall?"

"Want to gather more supplies?"

He cringed. "We should. But I'm not sure I want to risk it."

"Let's see how tight the patrol is tonight."

"Fair enough."

We bedded down, but I wasn't sure I'd be able to sleep. We were leaving our home for good this time. I'd done it once before. This time, my parents weren't going to go on living their lives without me. This time, I knew what I was losing. Not only my home, but also another piece of myself.

Before I thought I was leaving to die. This time, I was leaving to live. But, it didn't make things any easier.

I pulled the blanket over me and curled my arm under my head, trying to get comfortable. I could feel exhaustion creeping in after my restless night, but the weight of the path before us kept it at bay.

Until I heard Jace shuffling around. Before, we'd slept on opposite ends of the little cove we found for ourselves. We both laid in the shadows on opposite sides. That way, if a patrol did happen to come back this way, they'd have to look right at us to see where we were. Not the best plan, but it was the best we had.

I felt a slight breeze on my back, then the weight of him leaning against me. Back to back. We were in this together. No matter what. And it was that assurance that gave me exactly what I needed—a deep, dreamless sleep.

WHEN I WOKE UP, no light shone through the grate and Jace wasn't there anymore. So naturally, my heart rate went from chill to freak out mode in point two seconds.

"Hey, Sleeping Beauty," he said from the other side of the cove.

When I sat up, my head ached. Had I moved the entire time I was sleeping? No light streamed in from the grate nearby. How long had we been there? It felt like years.

"You ready to blow this Popsicle stand?" he asked.

No. I absolutely wasn't ready. I was still trying to shake off that sleep. But I stood anyway, trying to fake it.

"Sure."

He laughed. "Oh, okay. There's a granola bar in the backpack if you want it. I went and got a few more supplies a little bit ago."

"You left me here?" How in the world had I slept through that?

"Oh relax, I left you a note." He nodded toward my nest, where he'd slept. Instead of a blanket or any kind of bedding remnants, there was a torn piece of paper.

Went for supplies. BRB.

"Informative," I said flatly.

"I just thought it wouldn't hurt to get some more food if we're leaving. We don't know how long it'll be before we'll have a meal again."

He was right. It was a huge risk since they were onto us, but it was worth it since he hadn't gotten caught. I just didn't like how hard I'd slept. What if the guards had decided to patrol the sewer and found me? I never would've heard them coming. I was a sitting duck. And with us leaving, I'd never have that luxury again. Nowhere was safe.

The overwhelming urge to apologize washed over me. I was the weak link between the two of us. He'd made mistakes too, but mine had been more costly. At least, that was how it felt.

Suddenly, all the peace I felt when he laid down next to me was gone.

"What's wrong?" Jace asked as he zipped the backpack. All that was left to put away was my bedroll and the light. He was ready.

"I let my guard down. I could've gotten caught. I could've ruined everything."

He snorted. "You can't blame yourself for being tired."

"Bet I can," I said under my breath.

"Listen. The longer we stay together, the more times I narrowly escape death. Same for you, I think. We're a team." He let a half smile show before he went on. "I knew you were safe. It was fine."

"Oh, it was fine, huh? The entire world could be burning down around us and you'd say it was fine."

"Hey, if we're not getting burned, it *is* fine."

And in that moment, I laughed. I actually laughed. And the more I did it, the more I lost control of it, until Jace was laughing, too, and our laughter echoed through the sewer until tears were streaming down our faces.

When I finally came up for air, things didn't seem so bleak. I thought of my parents and how we used to laugh together like that, and the weight of their fate threatened to close in on me again. Before it could, Jace rescued me from my mind.

"Come on, pick up your crap and let's get out of here," he said as he plopped the backpack in front of me.

He held out the lantern for me. Once I'd stowed my things, we made our way out, leaving our safe haven behind.

We didn't go topside, not right away at least. In the days we'd stayed there, Jace got a pretty good idea of the layout. He thought if we took the system to the edge of town, we'd have a better chance of slipping out unseen.

Seemed logical to me, so I followed him quietly.

It would be nice to get away from that smell I never really got used to. Or so I told myself as we got to the ladder where Jace wanted to go topside.

He said nothing as he climbed up and peered out of the metal grate. Morning was dawning purple, and it was starting to shine dim light down the shaft.

"We should get going if we don't want to be seen."

It wasn't much of a goodbye to our hometown, but it would have to do. He pushed the grate to the side, then climbed out with me right behind him. I waited while he replaced the grate and we stood, jamming our hands in our hoodie pockets and keeping our heads down as we walked to the woods at the end of the dead-end street where the grate had popped us out.

Just like that, without any kind of fanfare, gunfire, or ceremony, we slipped away from the life that had been forced on us and claimed something new for ourselves.

THIRTY-TWO

When I imagined Killer Creek in my mind, it was a lot more impressive. And beautiful with clear water running over smooth, colorful stones.

This was nearly stagnant, brown like the sewer we'd just escaped, and bigger than I'd imagined. With the water being so dark, it was hard to tell just how deep it was in the middle.

"Well, this is less impressive than I imagined," I said as I kicked a stone into the sludgy water.

"Indeed." Sighing, he looked at the woods past the creek.

"What's wrong?" I asked.

"Nothing. Nothing at all. Let's keep going." We turned and walked for ages along the side of the creek. It never seemed to clear up. Once, Jace tried to fish in it, using some of our precious food as bait, but he didn't catch anything. Nothing even nibbled his bait, but I couldn't blame them. There was nothing appetizing about a soggy piece of energy bar.

That first night, we ended up sleeping in the open. Admittedly not smart, but we didn't know any better. The woods were too thick to see the stars, but we knew they were there. It took some effort to clear the ground and make a smooth place to sleep, but once we picked out all the sticks and left the leaves and pine needles, we made a pretty cozy spot.

Jace slept just as he had the day before, with his back leaning against mine, and it helped, though not as much as it had when I reached my exhaustion point. I couldn't help but listen to the sounds of the woods around us. Owls hooting, creatures stirring in the underbrush, the breeze shaking the leaves above us. I pulled the blanket closer to my chin as if that would hide me from any big bad monster out there.

Of course, the only monsters we needed to be afraid of were Sonny and her guards, but somehow, as I laid there listening to Jace breathing deeply—already asleep, the turd —I feared the unknown more than the woman who'd basically murdered my parents in front of me.

SOMEHOW, I'd dozed off, and Jace woke me up when he rolled off our makeshift mat.

We got going again pretty quickly, since we didn't have much to pack up. We kept on following the creek until Jace put the brakes on.

He stopped dead in his tracks and held out an arm. I paused, straining to see what he saw.

"Do you hear that?"

"No," I whispered.

"It sounds like...people. Movement. Machines. Life."

All I heard was the breeze rattling the leaves around us.

"I think we should turn away from the creek." He frowned, clearly not liking that option.

"Without a map or some kind of landmark to follow, how will we have any idea where we are?"

"I don't think we should get too close to a city. Towns mean people. People mean trouble." He was firm about it, and rightfully so. I just hadn't heard the noise the way he had. I still couldn't.

"Maybe it's not people you're hearing. Maybe it's just the wind or something. Why don't we go a little farther? If I hear it, we'll turn away."

Jace's frown deepened, making his eyebrows come together. "No. I think we should turn away now."

I looked at the creek, as gross as it was, it had anchored us in our wandering. Without it, what if we ended up circling back home by mistake? Right back into the hornet's nest?

But he wouldn't be moved. "Okay. Fine. Let's go." I took the first steps away from the creek, arbitrarily to my left, and he followed me, glancing over his shoulder as he went.

"Thanks," he said, but it was short and felt begrudging.

"Sure?" I asked.

He didn't elaborate, and I didn't ask.

That day, we didn't end up back at home. The woods felt huge, and we were smack in the thick of them. No water near us. No lifeline. But there was plenty of shelter that night, and we found an overhanging rock to sleep under.

The next three nights were the same. But our water supply was getting low. Jace wasn't worried, but I was. We'd have to do something about it soon. We'd changed directions two more times when we'd heard city noises. Even I'd heard it once and gotten jittery, just as he had that first time.

City meant being captured so we avoided it at all costs. It became our mantra as we walked.

Until we came across some kids playing in the woods. We hadn't heard a city anywhere near by, but we must've gotten too close.

"Pshew pshew, you're dead." The little voice stopped me dead in my tracks and Jace bumped into me.

I scrambled to take cover, but the kid popped out of the trees to my right and ended up directly in my path. He was looking back behind him, and he hadn't seen us yet. Maybe if we just stayed still...

Alas. Lady Luck really had gotten up on the wrong side of my bed.

"Who are you?" he asked the second he glanced our way.

"Hey kid," Jace said, putting on his friendliest tone. "Didn't mean to scare you."

But clearly, we had. The kid backed up as three more boys about his age came barreling out of the woods in the same direction he had.

"Justin. What are you—" They stopped dead when they saw us.

"Who are you?" the biggest one asked, putting himself between Justin and us.

"We're just passing through, guys. Don't mean any harm, promise." Jace held up his empty hands, and the big kid narrowed his eyes. They weren't buying our brand of crap for a minute.

"You're old. Why aren't you at work?" the big kid asked.

"We're both on a day off. Last birthday before our dates." Jace faked a grim expression. I wasn't buying it, but would they?

"Bummer," one of the other boys said, but the bigger kid still wasn't convinced.

"Want to play with us?" Justin asked. He wasn't afraid once he knew we wouldn't hurt him.

"No. They're busy. They don't want to spend their last birthday with a bunch of kids," the bigger boy said firmly. "Sure was lucky you found someone with the exact same birthday and dates so close together." He widened his stance, and I wondered what he planned. He was big, but Jace was bigger. By a lot. What exactly did he think he could accomplish? We weren't a threat.

Jace stood firm, not backing down, but he also didn't press the boy. Justin put a hand on the boy's shoulder. "Okay then. Let's leave them be."

The big boy hesitated and relented, walking off into the woods. The other one followed, but Justin lingered.

"Be careful out here," he cautioned. "There've been people in black asking questions. That's why my brother is on edge."

Nothing like the phrase *people in black* to get my blood pumping in the middle of the afternoon.

"What kind of questions?" I asked cautiously.

"You've seen them, haven't you? You must be lucky. They aren't very nice."

"Justin, let's go," the big one urged.

Jace nodded. "It's okay. Hey, thanks for the tip," Jace said.

Justin nodded and gave us a wave as he took off after the two other boys, back the way they'd come.

"That was close," Jace said.

I nodded.

"Where do you think they were from?"

"I don't know. Maybe a more rural town?" There

weren't many of those to be honest. All the zones worked, which meant there were cities, factories, and plenty of noise.

"A more rural town that would have water? Maybe some food?" I suggested. Our supplies were getting low. Scarily so.

"No. We need to move away. We'll find water. Don't worry. This isn't a desert. All these trees are getting it from somewhere."

My tongue begged to differ. We'd been able to catch some rain the day before, but even that was waning. It tasted too good, and we drank it too fast.

We walked in silence away from the boys and their apparently rural town until Jace was proved right. And he knew it, too, by the giant smile that plastered across his face. I wanted to gag.

"Hear that?" he asked. I didn't answer, because I did. It was pretty loud after all.

He picked up the pace to the point where I had trouble keeping up with him, until the woods cleared and a crystal-clear river cut through them.

The water was moving quickly, but not so much to make it treacherous. "Think it's safe to drink?" Jace asked as he approached the bank, leaves turning soggy so they no longer crunched under our feet.

"It's pretty clear. And moving. I don't see why not." I was too thirsty to care. If we got worms, we'd deal with it later.

I didn't even bother to fill my canteen. I bent and slurped the manna from heaven from my hands as quickly as I could.

We made camp there that night, and Jace even caught two fish. I'd never had such a delicious meal. Not even on the island. Even if it was super bony, and we both ended up with bloody gums from getting stabbed by fish bones.

We were reluctant to leave such an oasis, so we spent the next day there, too. Refueling. Our supplies and our minds. It was peaceful there. And as I secured some branches over our makeshift shelter, I wondered if this would be our new life. Out in the wilderness, making everything we had with our own two hands. I found myself smiling at the thought. We might actually be okay.

With full bellies, we bedded down for a second night in our newfound paradise. Neither of us spoke about moving on or staying. It was an unexplored topic we both respected with our silence. If we didn't discuss it, the possibilities remained endless.

The sounds of the woods no longer scared me, and I drifted off quickly that night after working hard all day. But my sleep wasn't nearly as peaceful as it had been.

I found myself back at my house, hiding behind that same bush. My parents were out on the lawn, standing next to Jace's parents. Sonny brought the rifle up, but something wasn't right.

"Run," I shouted.

No one but my dad looked at me. "No, you," he said calmly before Sonny melted the skin off his body with that stupid rifle.

I startled awake with a gasp, sitting up straight. The woods were quiet and still. Too quiet. Where had the animals gone?

"Jace," I whispered, nudging him. Groaning, he moved away from me. "Jace," I hissed more insistently.

I couldn't shake the feeling we weren't alone. We needed to move. To get out of there. Or hide. Something. We weren't safe.

My dad's warning echoed in my head.

Run.

No, you.

I held my breath as Jace groggily sat up. "What's wrong?"

It was then I saw the eyes of another person staring at me through the trees.

THIRTY-THREE

"Don't scream." The voice was low. Given that it was whispered, my inclination was to do just that.

Somehow, I managed not to when four people materialized out of the darkness.

Jace stood, widening his stance. "What do you want?"

"To get you out of here," that same voice said. But I couldn't tell which one of them was speaking. They'd surrounded us, leaving us no room for escape.

"We're not going anywhere," Jace said, balling his hands into fists at his sides.

I stepped out from behind him, holding my arms out. The people were covered in mud, only their eyes shining in the moonlight, and dressed in shorts. They had long spears, and two had bows hung across their chests. Seemed to me they weren't exactly fitting the criteria for Sonny's goons.

"Who are you?" I asked quietly.

"We will tell you all this and more. But you need to come with us. Now. They are coming," the one in the center, a tall, well-built guy who didn't look much older than Jace, said.

"They?" Jace asked, but as soon as the word was out in the open, my blood ran cold.

I had no idea who "They" were, but an enemy was an enemy.

"Jace."

He grabbed my arm and pulled me aside. "Don't tell me you're considering going with them," he accused.

"They're not with Sonny. Look at them. Sonny's coming. If we want to stay ahead of her, we need to get out of here. We'll get away from this lot later."

"How can you be so sure?" He eyed the one who'd spoken to us, who was currently watching the woods behind us. The two with bows had taken them off, arrows in their hands, ready to shoot them at any point.

"I'm not. But I do know we can't stay locked in a standoff with these wild men."

"So you'd just willingly go with them?"

A red light cut through the woods, landing on the chest of one of the men. An arrow shot past my head before I could even blink.

"We're done talking about this," their leader said as he rushed forward and grabbed me. He threw me over his shoulder, running in the opposite direction.

"Hey," Jace said as he was unceremoniously tossed over another man's shoulder, who stayed close to his leader.

The light from stunners lit up the woods, but never enough to see the ones pursuing us. Them.

"I can run. You don't need to—"

But the one carrying me shushed me and kept going. The farther we went, the more I realized these guys were pros. They didn't make a sound as they made their way through the woods. Not a single branch cracked under their feet. They never once disturbed the wildlife. And their speed was almost inhuman as they ran until the lights behind us started to fade.

Still, I wasn't sure if they were still there or if they'd just quit shooting at us. I didn't feel great when our captors, for lack of a better term, slowed their pace and eventually set us down.

"That was a bit unnecessary, don't you think?" Jace demanded as he brushed himself off.

"Just keep moving. They're still out there," the leader said. "This way." In the moonlight, I saw him disappear behind a bush the size of a person. How in the world had he even fit in there? Branches stuck out every which way. It seemed impossible until I watched one of the archers follow him.

"After you," the other archer said. Jace looked at me, begging me not to follow them. But they'd gotten us away from Sonny's gang. If not for them, we'd have gotten caught. We'd be strapped to a hospital bed right now. At a minimum, I felt a need to thank them.

After I shrugged, I tried to push my way through the brush, but couldn't find an opening. I parted the leaves more than once searching for an in, but all I saw was more leaves, branches, and opportunities to get scratched to ribbons. Until a mud-covered hand stuck out from the brush and I jumped back with a yelp.

"Come on. We don't have all night," the leader said.

I glanced back at Jace, who looked like he was about to bite a hole through his own tongue, before taking the stranger's hand and letting him lead me into an entirely new world I hadn't known existed.

THIRTY-FOUR

A cave opened up, but the men we followed didn't bother to light torches or flashlights. They just kept walking, as if it were the most natural thing in the world to go deeper into darkness in the middle of the night.

"Care to—" My voice echoed off the cave walls louder than I'd intended, so I started again, this time in a whisper. "Care to tell us who you are now?"

"My name is Rhett. We're scouts. Our job is to find outliers and bring them in."

The air turned cooler, smelling earthier as we walked deeper into the cave.

"Outliers?" I asked.

"Yes. Those who don't want to be part of the system. That's who you are, right? Don't want to be Withs or Withouts?"

My mouth hung open. What had we stumbled on?

"That's right," Jace jumped in before I could explain who we were. We weren't outliers like they thought. We didn't choose it. We were forced. By a miracle.

We walked in silence for what felt like ages. The darkness stretched on infinitely in all directions. Rhett held onto my hand, leading me forward. I held Jace's, making a human train until light pierced the darkness up ahead.

"The sun is up. We've journeyed all night to rescue you," Rhett said.

"Thanks?" I said, not sure what to say. I knew Jace felt more like we'd been captured than rescued, but I wasn't willing to admit that.

Eventually, the light grew bright enough that I let go of Rhett, whose hand had been coarse but warm. Secure. It was odd. I'd never held anyone's hand besides Jace's or my parents. And it felt more comfortable than I thought it should.

Finally, we reached the end of the tunnel. Light poured in. I stopped dead, blinded by it.

I'd never seen anything like what spread out in front of me. A hole in the ceiling let in more light. Rope bridges ran all over the massive chamber, connecting tunnels on every level. Buckets and pulley systems moved smaller supplies across the space. Despite the early hour, people were moving everywhere. Working. Living.

Not all of them were covered in mud, though. They were normally dressed, if not a bit dirty for their hard labor. Women wore long dresses or light pants and shirts. Men wore shorts, and some wore shirts. Others didn't, and the sweat for their efforts shone in the early morning light.

"Where are we?" I breathed as our new friend walked up to me.

"Welcome to Symphero."

"Symphero," I repeated while I watched men, women, and children working. A sound caught my attention, something I wasn't used to hearing in the workplace, and I glanced toward it. A girl who couldn't have been more than eight was splashing water on an adult. Her blonde curls were dripping, and the woman with matching blonde curls appeared to be her mother.

She was pretending to be stern, but the laughter told a different story. "People are happy here?" I was perplexed. Who were these people?

"We are. There's always one or two who can't get along, but they always move on. Those who like it stay."

"Move on? You're not prisoners?"

Rhett frowned. "No."

"So why take us prisoner?" Jace asked.

"We have not taken you prisoner. We have rescued you from them." He said it like that would explain everything, but it didn't.

Them. Who were these people? Why would the Withouts ever give up what they had? Or maybe this was a radical group of Withouts, living some independent commune-style life. What would they do when the found out I was a With? A With who'd survived their date. Their world seemed so primitive. Would they burn me as some kind of witch?

I struggled to rein my thoughts in as we walked around the beautiful chamber. No matter what, they weren't with the government. Whatever they did or didn't to do to us couldn't be as bad as what Sonny's crew would do. Right?

"Where are you taking us?" I asked, looking at the greenery growing up the side of the cavern walls. There was a waterfall on the far side that led to a river cutting through the rocky floor. That must be where the water came from.

"To our leader," he said.

"Are you aliens?" To be honest, I wondered if it fit. Were they an alien race that settled here, and took interest in the humans that occupied the planet? Frankly, stranger things had happened to me in the last few days.

Rhett snorted. "We are not aliens. We are no different from you and your friend."

"You wanna make a bet?" I said under my breath. He narrowed his eyes with confusion, but let it go as he guided us through the massive chamber.

"This way, please." He moved ahead of us, leading us along a rather green path around the outside of the chamber.

There were people fishing the river with baskets full of fish that we walked by. They waved to the scouts, and the scouts waved back. These men weren't tyrants. They were well liked.

A little further down, there were crops growing, and people tending them. Digging, watering, picking. Everyone was busy. Women were sewing fabrics. Men were repairing bridges and cutting wood. Kids were running supplies back and forth. Everyone worked together.

And all the while, they smiled. It wasn't like our work. Dark. Sweaty. Lots of yelling. The smells of trash burning. This was bright. Happy. The sound of laughter carried easily to us, and we'd only been standing there a few moments. They were happy. They did this work gladly.

And where exactly did we fit into all this? What need would they have for us? Why get involved? Having Jace and I here was dangerous to them. If Sonny discovered us...my imagination ran away with me while I watched the smiling faces turn to ash in my mind.

"Rhett. Listen. You don't have to do this. You seem to have a pretty peaceful life here. Those people hunting us. They'll kill you all. They won't strike a deal with you. I've seen them. They ended my parents in front of me."

A tiny gasp brought my attention down, and a mother grabbed a little girl who couldn't have been more than four. The child's blue eyes looked at me in horror. "Mommy, could that happen to you," she asked.

"No, my love. Shh."

Well, I was just knocking it out of the park, right? Ruining our escape, scaring children. Totally batting a thousand.

"They did what to you?" Rhett asked. He looked back at his guard friend, who was frowning deeply. "We will never do anything like that, I assure you."

"It's not you I'm worried about," I said. I don't know where it came from. I didn't know them from Adam, and they'd kinda ambushed us in the dark. Why would I trust them? Because they looked happy?

But for some reason, I didn't want Sonny and her gang descending on these people. I wanted to protect them. And I would draw Sonny's sights like a moth to a flame.

I glanced over my shoulder at Jace, who was looking around with his mouth hanging open at what we'd stumbled into. Seemed like he might be changing his mind about our so-called captors.

"If you keep us here, and they find us, they'll slaughter you all," I warned. But it only made Rhett's frown deeper.

We came to a narrow stairway that wound up the side of the cavern. "This way. She will explain everything," Rhett said.

He walked in front. I followed, with Jace behind me, and the last guard bringing up the rear.

We'd gone forty-five degrees around the chamber by the time we got to the top of the steps and I knew whatever or whoever was inside the chamber would change our fate forever.

The guard who ran ahead was waiting for us, standing in front of a beautiful curtain hanging in the doorway.

"She is waiting for you." He grinned like a schoolboy. He was excited about this. He had no idea what was coming for him. How Sonny and her gang would delight in watching all this burn.

"Jace," I said desperately, hoping he would have some kind of option. Solution. Something. We couldn't let this happen. We couldn't let them feed us to the wolves. They'd get eaten too.

But he said nothing. Only reached for my hand and squeezed it, letting me know whatever was behind that door, whether it was the rhino, or an entirely new beast that would change our fate forever, we faced it together.

THIRTY-FIVE

The guard pulled the curtain back and Rhett went in first, ducking his head, so I did the same when I followed him. Jace never let go of my hand as we entered the smaller chamber.

I say it was smaller, but only because it was smaller than the tremendous cavern we just left. It wasn't really all that small. It was certainly bigger than my room back home. Maybe even bigger than our entire ground floor.

In the back, on a pile of beautifully colored pillows, sat an older woman with short, salt and pepper hair, and skin as dark as the night. Her midnight eyes smiled as she stood with arms open.

"Welcome." She wore a dress just as colorful as the pillows she'd just left. Purple, green, red, blue, every color I could imagine woven beautifully into the fabric. I couldn't help but gawk at her. She was gorgeous. Wise. Kind.

I was drawn to her. I found myself wanting to fall into those open arms. But I didn't. I held my back straight, not knowing who she was or if I could trust her.

Her arms fell to the side as the last guard shoved us

further into the chamber and she frowned. "You've been through much. Seen much. Please, sit with me. Tell me your tale."

I looked at Jace and he shrugged, but didn't move.

"May I offer you something to drink? We've had the most delicious crop of tea this season." She poured herself a cup and two more, leaving hers on the wooden table that lined the wall, and bringing two mugs to us.

"Thanks," I said quietly.

She was so tall, she looked down into my eyes, and up close, I caught my breath. I'd never been near someone so enchanting. Who was she? Would I be responsible for this beautiful person's downfall? Or did she hide behind her beauty? What would she do when she found out who we were?

"I can see you are at war with yourself. Please, let me explain." She held the cup out to me, and I took it from her.

She looked at the inside of my arm as I did it and smiled. "So, it's true. I almost didn't believe it myself."

"What's true?"

The woman held her own arm out for me. There, in brilliant white ink was her date. 3/13/48. Forty years ago. Forty. That was the only explanation. She was too old to have her date be in 2248. That was sixty years away. She had to be at least seventy already.

My mind whirled, and I suddenly felt the need to sit.

"Rarity?" Jace asked, and the woman held her arm out for him as well.

I didn't see his reaction. I couldn't see anything but the numbers on her arm. 48. Could that be right? Were there others like us?

Suddenly, I felt her soft hand on my shoulder, guiding me. I let her lead me to the pillows and she took my cup from me, setting it on a low table nearby. There were crackers and bread on it as well.

"Help yourself," she said, but I think it was more for Jace than me. I couldn't eat a thing. I couldn't function for heaven's sake. Were there really others like us?

"My name is Pisteuo, Pi for short. I founded this place about forty years ago, when I too survived my date."

"Jace, are you hearing this?"

He just smirked as he popped a grape in his mouth. "I am."

How was he not freaking out? I felt like a computer that was not capable of processing the information it had been given, and I needed a major restart. Just stop everything and start over 'cuz she's toast.

"I am neither With nor Without. Just like you. We're Expired."

"Expired," I repeated. "You could've named yourself anything. And Expired is what you came up with? Not something cooler like Defiers or something?"

She blinked at me. "We are essentially expired, are we not?"

I hesitated, and then realized the question wasn't rhetorical. "I...you...we are." I still wasn't used to being part of a group of people who had this same experience. How many of them were Expired? Where did they come from? Were they all hunted by Sonny's group?

"Well, the name suits us. We aren't freeloaders like the Withouts, and we aren't workhorses like the Withs. Everyone does their part and reaps their own benefits. Because of that, there's plenty of time, and resources, to play when the work is done. There's food to eat, shelter, and no fear of being found by *them*."

"Why?" I asked skeptically. They always knew.

"Because we're well hidden underground. They haven't sniffed us out in forty years. They're not going to start today," she said, just a little too confident for my taste. But then again, maybe that's what forty years of safety did to a person. It taught them to live.

She smiled kindly at me, as if she could see my concerns. "I'm sure you have many questions. Why don't you ask one?"

One question. Which one? Could I narrow it down? She chuckled, a deep, melodic sound that made me want to smile with her.

"Well, I'll give you more than one, child. I was just trying to give you a starting point."

Jace got the ball rolling for me. "How did you find us?" I detected a hint of suspicion in his voice, but I wasn't sure she did. It was so faint, almost like he wanted to trust her. Just like I did.

"When I saw you survive your date, Mr. Brown, I knew you were something special. When they announced you died, I didn't believe it for a second. The evacuation of the island only spurred my suspicions you were alive. All I had to do, was watch for you. I've had scouts searching the woods for days for the two of you."

"Two of us?" I asked. "How did you know I was alive? The media never got a hold of that detail."

"No they didn't, Ms. Delman." A sly smile spread across her face. "Should you both decide to stay here, I will tell you more about how I knew. I will definitely have a place for you both."

She let that settle in before prodding me along. "What other questions do you have?

I glanced at Jace and he shrugged, not any more sure

what to make of any of this than I was. One thing was for sure, he was relaxing more and more by the minute.

I decided this was my chance to get information, and it was something I was hungry for in a way I hadn't realized until that exact moment. "How did you start this place? Where did the people come from? Are they all expired, or is it just you? What happened when you expired, and why hasn't anyone heard of this place?"

She laughed out loud, and it pulled at the corners of my mouth. Jace elbowed me and chuckled along with her.

"I came here with my husband before our dates. He'd found it on an expedition. He was charged with finding suitable places for the Withs and Withouts to live. So we explored a lot. Sometimes he could talk them into letting me go too. This place was magical, and he knew it. He saved it for us. When his date came, he didn't want to go to the island. He wanted to be with me. So, we came here. We built a little hut down by the river. I think they use it for hanging their clothes to dry now," she laughed again. "He died in my arms on his date.

"After that, I wasn't sure what to do with myself. I buried him by the river, like they did in the time before dates. It seemed right. Poetic. Lord knows I couldn't haul him out and bury him topside. Lucky for me, the rock in the main cavern is buried under a bunch of mud. Mud deep enough for a man to rest in anyway.

"When I was done, I couldn't bring myself to leave him. And I stayed. It was rough at first. Planting seeds, waiting for them to grow, foraging for food topside when it didn't.

"My date wasn't too long after Charles' so I wasn't too concerned about longevity. Just get by until I could be with him again. And then, something extraordinary happened."

"Extraordinary. That would've been better than expired too," I grumbled. She smiled and carried on with her story.

"My date came, I went down to the river where I'd buried him. By then I'd explored a great deal of the cave system here. There was so much he didn't see. So much potential for this space." She looked past me, toward the curtain, and I wondered if she was imagining herself alone down by the river, waiting to join her love. It was romantic.

"We'd never had kids of our own. We were scared to death they'd be like you, and we'd outlive them." She wasn't alone. The population boom had been over for decades. Fewer and fewer people were having kids. My parents were the exception. And Jace's, well, I think they just wanted a little clone of themselves. How disappointed they were when he ended up being his own person.

"Anyway," she waved a hand as if she were batting an insect away. "I waited all day by that river. I was scared to death to get up and go to the bathroom, for fear I'd die on the loo."

In spite of everything, I laughed. It was a ridiculous image, and I bet it happened to more than a few Withs, and maybe some Withouts too.

"Yes, well, you see I had cause for concern. Anyway, my fears were never realized, and I always made it back to the river. Back to my spot. Darkness fell, and I still sat there, not lighting a lantern, because I didn't want it to catch fire and burn my paradise to the ground. Well, to the underground. You know what I mean.

"All night long I held vigil by Charles. And when morning dawned, I knew something was wrong."

I remembered the swirl of emotions. Joy that was quickly stolen by panic and fear of the unknown.

"Without anything else to do, I got up and rinsed off in

the river, got something to eat, repaired our shelter, and went about normal tasks, thinking I'd miscounted the days. But when a week went by, I knew I couldn't have been that far off. I'd survived."

"Survivors. That's another good name," I declared.

She looked at me sidelong, and I shrugged. "Just sayin.'"

"I had no idea how to make my existence long term. I never planned to go home, but it seemed I didn't have a choice. I couldn't stay there forever, could I? But the more I thought about it, the more I knew I couldn't go back. What would they do? All the fear I felt would be amplified by every single person I met. How could I leave my safe haven for that?

"But then, what did that mean? I would have to figure out how to live here. Alone. Or die trying." She shrugged and took a sip of her tea. Suddenly, I realized my mouth was dry. Like I'd been sucking wind through it for the last century. So I tried the tea too, and it was remarkable. Sweet and refreshing, it tasted like elixir for my soul.

A tiny sound of indulgence may have escaped me when I swallowed, and Jace leaned over. "Should I leave you alone with your tea?"

"Shut up," I said, nudging him with my shoulder.

"I'm glad you like it. I told you it was a good crop this year." She took another sip and went on with her story. "As it turned out, I didn't have to be alone for all that long. Soon, a family found me, and together we made the place a little more livable. I hadn't realized just how lonely I'd been until they came along. The father was on the run. He'd had a mixed bag of Withs and Withouts among his children, and he didn't want his family split up. By the time he found me, all but one of them had died. She's a Without and helps take care of the animals now. She has a gentle spirit and is good with them. Her father finally passed on his date about ten years ago. He never had to see her die." She smiled to herself as she spoke about her old friend.

She'd gotten wistful again, but brought herself back quickly by clearing her throat. "That man, Ron was his name, had friends back home. Friends he said also wanted refuge. He came from the fishing district, where people rarely live to see thirty. He started a bit of a whisper network among the Withs, and it spread rapidly. More and more people seemed to find me, one way or another. Until we built this place into what it is now.

"And as for why no one knows about us. The whisper network is highly respected. They know if they were to tell our secret, this sanctuary would be ended by them. Those who suffer most would have nowhere to go. But maybe you can be the one to end that suffering."

I swallowed hard. Annabelle had said almost the same thing to me. What was it with these people? Sure I had questions, but didn't everyone? All I wanted was a safe place to live. Something Annabelle never had.

I shook my head, not wanting to go down that particular rabbit hole at the moment. "So, you have all kinds of people here? Withs and Withouts?" The idea perplexed me, since we'd always been told historically the two groups couldn't get along. Here they were, living peacefully, in defiance of hundreds of years of history.

She nodded. "We do. Families who don't want to be torn apart by the system. We even have a few Withouts. Just like Ron, when a child is born Without, and their parents don't want to be separated from them, they find me here."

I felt a pit in my stomach, formed like a snowball growing larger and larger, my anxiety rolled around inside me threatening to pummel me at any moment. Now what?

How did we fit into all this? After everything that happened? What could we offer this place except death and destruction?

"What does all that mean for us? What do you want from us?" Jace asked the hard question I couldn't seem to give life to. If I did, and the answer was less than pleasant, what would we do?

"It can mean anything you want it to mean. You can stay here as long as you like, and I hope you do. But you'll have to earn your keep," she winked at me, as if she knew that wouldn't be a problem. "Or you can go your own way. Go back to the spot we found you at. But I would warn you. They've been patrolling the area. I wouldn't stay there long if I were you." The way Sonny's gang had chased us out of there, I knew she was right. If we left the safety of this haven, they'd be on us like a dog's nose to another dog's butt.

We could do anything? "You won't hold us here?" I asked. "I was ready to talk you out of it." My shoulders slumped. I hadn't seen this option coming in the least. Was it right to stay, and draw the hounds to their doorstep?

"Oh, well what would you have said?" she asked. I waved her off, knowing she wasn't really interested, but she insisted.

"Well," I relented. "I would've told you that we're nothing more than bait. Something that once Sonny and her gang get the scent of, they'll never stop trying to break down your doors. And when they do, they'll wipe out every man, woman, and child in this place, and I didn't want that on my hands. All I can think about is that little kid." I turned to Jace. "The one I scared on the way up here?" He nodded. "I didn't want her to go through what I did. What we did. I don't want to bring them down on your heads."

She sat back, leaning against a bright purple pillow as big as her back that was propped against the wall. "I see."

Fear gripped me. What would she say if she knew what I'd done? Before I could stop myself, more words poured out of me. "Maybe you don't even want us here. I've killed people after all. You wouldn't want to harbor murderers."

She looked steadily at me, completely unfazed. Clearly, she was more impacted by what I'd said before. Murder, she wasn't fazed by.

"I can't clear your conscious, child. Death is a serious thing, and you are wise to treat it thusly."

Thusly. Who says that?

"Rarity. I can tell you are something special. I have a feeling you're going to change the world before we're done. I'm old now. I was old when my date zoomed past while I sat back and watched it happen. But you two. You could *do* something. You could stop the hunt. End this chase once and for all." She smiled warmly at us. "For that, I think I'm willing to risk bringing the hounds to my doorstep."

I'll admit, the thought of ending the chase was appealing. But how? Sonny had the world at her fingertips. I had a sharp tongue and my best friend at my side. Surely that wasn't enough to win.

"You two are going to change the shape of this world into something no one has ever seen. I can tell. Surround yourself with the right people, like Jace here, and see how far you go.

"Now, I will leave you to decide what you want to do."

She stood, and it was so abrupt, I didn't know how to respond. I struggled to stand up and meet her, but she held out her hands. "The scouts will know where to find me when you decide. Please, stay as long as you like. Eat. Rest. Come find me when you're ready."

"Thank you," I said, truly grateful for this kindness I hadn't seen from anyone except my parents and Jace. On the island, they were paid to be nice to me. This...this was true kindness.

She left, and the guards waited outside for us. "What do you think?"

Jace shrugged as he took yet another bite of food. "What's to think about?"

"Well, if we stay here and they find us, everyone dies for one thing. For another, it feels a little too good to be true, don't you think?"

Jace put his hands on my shoulders, weighing me down, anchoring me to that place. "It does seem too good to be true. I was suspicious of it long before you were. But the more we walked with Rhett, the more I watched the people out there working together, laughing, happy, the more I listened to Pi tell her story, the more I think we belong here."

"You want to stay?"

"I want to stay," he repeated.

"You trust them?"

"I trust them."

I couldn't stop the smile forming on my face if I wanted to. What if we left the rhino up above, wandering forever searching for us? What if we lived here in peace for the rest of our days? Yes, people still died here. But they were left to live in freedom. True freedom. With true choices.

Tears sprang to my eyes, and I threw my arms around Jace who hugged me fiercely.

"There's no one else I'd want to live underground with," he said, and I laughed through my tears.

"Me neither." I pulled back and looked in his eyes. The

old light was back. The darkness had been lifted from us. We would be okay.

He leaned in and kissed me, making that promise real. True. We claimed our peace for ourselves in that moment.

We walked out of the room hand in hand, fingers laced together, and found Pi near the river, helping to hang some wet rags on the clothesline.

"Ah, two of my favorite Expireds." She beamed at me when she said it, and I groaned.

"I don't think I'll ever get used to that name. But if you'll have us, we'd like to try."

She threw her hands up, and embraced us warmly. "I'm so glad." And I knew she truly was.

That night, she threw a party for us, and everyone welcomed us to the community. Not all were Withs, like Pi had said. But it didn't matter.

A corner of the huge cavern was decorated with string lights, powered apparently by the waterwheel, giving the whole thing a magical feel. Ivy crawled down the back wall, and wood tables with tree stumps for seats were scattered around. There was a clearing for dancing, and a few people playing instruments and singing nearby. It was an actual party.

A blonde girl with such dark blue eyes they looked like the night itself pushed through the dancers and introduced herself while we stood on the fringe. "Hi. I'm Abby."

"Hey." I raised my glass of spiced something or other. It was warm and burned a little when it went down. But it was a good burn. "It's nice to meet you. How long have you been here?" I asked.

She shrugged. "My whole life. I was born right after my dad brought us here. They'd had another who was a Without.

They didn't want to be separated again." She chuckled and flashed the inside of her arm revealing a date that was four decades away. "Turns out they didn't need to worry. We'd have been together anyway. But I like it here. I'm glad we came."

It was odd to talk to someone who'd had their family torn apart by the system. How could that be good for anyone? "Do you get to talk to your sibling at all?"

"No. My parents didn't before we left either. It was as if she never existed for them, except for the picture Mom keeps in her room. We don't even know if she's still alive."

"I'm sorry." What else could I say? She was haunted by the ghost of someone she never knew, and may not even still exist. What an odd place to be.

"So is it true?" A guy who looked about Jace's age asked as he nudged Abby over. She smiled at him, as if they were friends and bumped him back.

"What?" Jace asked.

"About your dates. You survived? I have a bet going with Jeff over there that it's largely exaggerated."

I followed his gesture and saw some older guys, maybe in their thirties, trying to hide the fact that they were watching us. I waved at them, and they sheepishly smiled and looked away.

"It's true," Jace confirmed and held out his arm for our new friend to see.

"Better go pay up," I said, and the guy stomped off grumbling to himself.

"I keep telling him to quit betting on things. He always loses," Abby said.

"He seems nice. What's his name?" I asked.

"Geo. They came here about three years ago. He's cool. Up until today, he was one of the only others near my age.

Then you guys showed up." She beamed at us, as if we'd been some kind of dream come true.

I smiled awkwardly and sipped the cave's special drink as I wondered who was whose dream come true. I watched people dancing and laughing, eating and having fun as not only Abby, but also a stream of people came and introduced themselves. We weren't servants or burdens. We were welcome.

But more importantly, we weren't alone. And we never would be again.

EPILOGUE

ONE WEEK LATER

A clock on the wall ticked down faster than Cedric would've liked. Its numbers burned red now that there was less than a year left. Three hundred and fifty days to unlock the key. He frowned at that clock, cursing it silently.

A soft knock at the door broke his glare at the machine and he tossed a pen down on the metal desk in front of him. "Come in," he barked.

Sonny crossed the floor quickly. She was nothing if not efficient. He knew she would be the one to capture the Expireds. One was unheard of, but two in a row? Never. He smiled at the possibilities.

"Sonny. Welcome. What's the good word?"

She nodded a greeting at him before cutting right to the chase. "I'm afraid they got away."

He tipped his head, certain he'd misheard her. "I'm sorry. I didn't hear you. It sounded like you said they got away." He paused, staring at her. "But I know you would *never* let a thing like that happen." His tone was low. Deadly.

"I'm sorry, sir."

"Sonny, never apologize. It's weak." She straightened a bit. "That'll be all."

She turned and left the room. After the door clicked shut, he stood and went to that infernal clock, smiling. It was okay. It would all be okay. He knew where they were going. And soon, he'd know how to get there too.

After all, he always got his man. He had a whole hospital wing full of them to prove it. True, he'd had to work fast after that girl had destroyed his state-of-the-art research facility. Transferring all those subjects cost him some time. But money talked and made it so people didn't. He had lost a few weeks in the end, but he hadn't lost any subjects. And if he could grab that Holy Grail, it would be worth it. It would all be worth it.

The numbers on the clock clicked down one by one, but there were still numbers there, not zeros. Yes. There was still time.

FREE READ

Now that you're done reading, download a FREE copy of Right or Wrong, the prequel novella to With or Without here! Find out a little more about Jace and Rarity when they weren't Expireds. They were just regular old Withs.

COMING SOON

Them or Us, book 2 in the Expired Trilogy, is coming May, 2020. While you wait, download The Dead Room FREE on all retailers!

Get it now!

ABOUT THE AUTHOR

SM Erickson is an emerging author of dystopian science fiction. This is SM's fourth book.

She LOVES to connect with readers, so please stalk—I mean find her online! And, sign up for her newsletter here for a free read!